Time and Eternity

Time and Eternity

a novel

E. M. Tippetts

Covenant Communications, Inc.

Published by Covenant Communications, Inc.
American Fork, Utah

Printed in Canada
First Printing: June 2008

14 13 12 11 10 09 08   10 9 8 7 6 5 4 3 2 1

ISBN-13: 978-1-59811-548-2
ISBN-10: 1-59811-548-0

This one's for Mom and Dad,
who raised me to be myself
and who have loved me unconditionally through it all.

Acknowledgments

I don't think it'll ever be possible to thank my friend Char Peery enough. She read multiple versions of this novel and provided honest and useful feedback, often mere hours after getting my e-mails. I do not exaggerate when I say that without her, I could never have written this book.

I'd also like to thank the members of the Critical Mass Writer's Group, both past and present. They are: Daniel Abraham, Yvonne Coates, Ty Franck, Sally Gwylan, George RR Martin, John Jos. Miller, Laura J. Mixon, Melinda Snodgrass, S.M. Stirling, Ian Tregillis, Sage Walker, and Walter Jon Williams. They invited me in as an unpublished science-fiction writer, and they let me stay while I remained unpublished for five years. They even let me stay when I tried my hand at spiritual romance, even though none of them are members of the Church. Two of my Clarion West classmates, Samantha Ling and Benjamin Rosenbaum, also read through the manuscript. Ling sent me a long and helpful e-mail critique. Ben talked to me on the phone for three hours—from his home in Switzerland—and went through the book page by page to offer advice and insights. Thanks also to Stephen Betts, who read the manuscript through several times to check for typos and helped me patch up one of the subplots.

And, of course, I need to thank my husband, Trevor, who has always been patiently supportive of my day job, my personal sanity, and my writing dreams, even when these all seemed mutually exclusive.

1

An Answered Prayer

Alice combed her wet hair back from her face and regarded herself in the mirror. *Well,* she thought, *it's done. You're officially a member of The Church of Jesus Christ of Latter-day Saints.* Her red hair looked brown when wet, and her skin even paler and more freckled in contrast. With quick movements, she gathered her hair and twisted it up into a bun.

She finished toweling herself off and hung her drenched white jumpsuit on a peg to dry. The yellow-tiled bathroom had gray metal stalls, but Alice, with a quick glance in the direction of the door, decided to hazard getting dressed in the open.

It was always difficult to put on nylons when her legs were still damp, but with some tugging she managed to do it and then don her black skirt, yellow blouse, and blazer. Staring in the mirror a moment longer, she debated whether she should apply makeup. She hadn't that morning, knowing it would run when she got dunked. *Leave it. They're waiting for you outside.*

From the hallway, she could hear Elder Dugan—she still had trouble thinking of a nineteen-year-old as an "elder"—giving a talk on the Book of Mormon. *Odd,* thought Alice. *My roommate's the only non-Mormon in there, and she's probably staring at the ceiling about now.*

But when Alice slipped into the room, she found her roommate, Cynthia, looking politely interested in what the missionary had to say. Cynthia sat in the second row, and behind her were roughly a dozen more rows of folding chairs, all full, and then two rows of people standing behind that. About half the ward had shown up for the baptism. The fluorescent lights overhead hummed in their annoying way, and the scent of chlorine from the font still hung in the air. When Elder Dugan paused in his speech, Alice darted to her empty seat on the front row.

"Okay," he said in his usual flat and uninflected tone, "Sister O'Donnell is back with us, and Monica Valdez is going to give her talk on the Holy Ghost. We'll go to that point."

As he moved off to sit beside his companion, Elder White, Alice's friend Monica got to her feet and began to speak. "The gift of the Holy Ghost is important," she began, her words tinged with a slight Mexican accent.

Alice meant to pay attention, but Darren slipped into the room just then. She turned to smile at him. He'd also changed out of his white jumpsuit and was wearing a nicely tailored gray suit with a royal blue tie. He responded with a grin of his own and came over to take his place next to her.

"How do you feel?" he whispered as he put his arm around her shoulders.

"Good, I guess," said Alice.

"You guess?" He raised an eyebrow.

"Definitely good."

"Good." He gave her shoulder a squeeze. "And in church you'll get confirmed—no going back then." He winked. Then his tone took on a serious note. "Look, I really respect you for doing this. I know it's going to be a major life change for you."

"A good one, I think."

He smiled again. "I'm glad you think so."

* * *

"You want to know what I think?" Cynthia said as they pulled out of the church parking lot. They were in her beat-up black Jetta again, its smell of aging plastic only thinly masked by a vanilla air freshener.

"Do I have a choice?" asked Alice.

"Well, since your baptism was today, I'll wait until tomorrow if you like." Cynthia looked over her shoulder before turning out of the lot. They drove across the adjoining Los Angeles Temple parking lot to Santa Monica Boulevard. Alice turned to look out at the temple, a large, fawn-colored blocky structure with a tall, straight spire. At its pinnacle stood a traditional angel Moroni, blowing his golden horn, and the afternoon sunlight cast sharp shadows, making the temple look even more imposing than usual. "Just say it," Alice said. She didn't turn around.

"Are you sure about all this?" Cynthia flipped on the turn signal and turned right, merging deftly into the traffic.

Alice gripped the handle above her door more firmly than necessary and turned to watch her roommate maneuver the car into the next lane over.

"Thanks for believing in me," she said dryly.

Cynthia looked at her out of the corner of her eye, shrugged, and said, "It all seems so sudden." She sped through a left turn, making it just as the light turned red. Alice kept her grip on the handle. "And," Cynthia went on, "with all that's happened lately . . ."

"Specifically my family falling apart," offered Alice.

"Right."

"You think I did this so I can marry my Mormon boyfriend and live happily ever after?"

Cynthia bit her lip. They turned onto a side street and then into the driveway of their apartment complex. "Um . . ." she began, reaching up to press the garage door opener. She finished, "Is that part of it? I mean . . . Mormons don't get divorced that often. That must appeal to you. If you marry Darren, he probably won't do what your dad just did."

Alice considered her answer carefully while Cynthia pulled the car into its space next to Alice's white Camry. Cynthia put the car into park, shut off the ignition, and extracted the key, but Alice didn't move to get out. The garage was cool, dim, and quiet. The only sound for several seconds was the ticking of the engine cooling off and the jangle of Cynthia's car keys.

Cynthia reached over to open her door, but when she saw that Alice hadn't moved, she paused, dropped her keys into her lap, and stared down at her hands. "I don't mean to be . . . unsupportive," she said.

"I didn't get baptized for Darren," said Alice. "You know I wouldn't do that."

Cynthia nodded but didn't look at her.

"And I've read the Book of Mormon, prayed about it, and really tried to find the truth."

"I know," said Cynthia.

"But does the low divorce rate and the prospect of marrying for life appeal to me? Of course it does."

Cynthia did look at her then. "Sooo . . . you think Darren's the one?"

Alice shrugged. "I hope so, but we've only been together three months."

"But you're Mormon now, so three months for you is, like, three years for normal people, right?"

"Yeah, very funny."

"And you're twenty-six, which, I think, in Mormon-speak makes you an old maid. A spinster."

"Just be quiet, okay?"

Cynthia stared straight out the windshield at the concrete wall in front of them. "Alice," she said, "do you think that's what Darren's thinking? I mean, do you think he's expecting you to marry him now that you've been baptized?"

"You mean he might think I did it for him?"

Cynthia didn't answer.

"Well . . . I guess that's part of why I did it now," said Alice. "He's off to San Francisco in three weeks, and then we'll have the whole summer apart, and—"

"That's plenty of time for him to figure out that you're not waiting desperately for a proposal." She smiled.

Alice tugged on her door handle and popped her door open. "I'm getting cold," she said.

Cynthia nodded, unfastened her seat belt, and opened her own door.

* * *

Alice's mother called that evening, in tears as usual. Alice took her cell phone into her room, shut the door, and perched on the edge of her bed. She rested her feet on one of the several packing boxes that still littered the floor. The place smelled like fresh paint; Cynthia had insisted on painting Alice's walls a sunny yellow to coordinate with her comforter and new wall hangings—also picked out by Cynthia.

"What's the matter, Mom?" Alice said. She tried to convey the sympathy she felt, but her words always sounded flat in her ears.

"Oh." Her mother sobbed. "It's just . . . I'm overwhelmed, you know?"

"Yeah, I know."

"Your father called just a few minutes ago."

"Uh-huh."

"He doesn't want me to get my own lawyer now. It's the opposite of what he said a week ago."

"Well, I still think you should, Mom."

"Honey, I think he's got a new girlfriend."

Alice took a deep breath and slowly let it out. "I'm sorry to hear that," she said. *But I've known this for a month,* she added in her mind. *Dad was ever so kind to let me in on his secret.*

"And if he does, that means he's really not interested in trying to make our marriage work."

Yeah, pretty much, Alice thought. But what she said was, "Did you ever use that gift certificate to the spa that I sent?"

"Hmm? Oh yes. That was lovely."

"Well, I'm going to send you another one, okay? No arguing."

"Oh, but—"

"I said no arguing." *And please,* she thought, *stop crying.* The sound of her mother crying always unnerved Alice. She felt like she ought to be able to fix matters, and it distressed her that she couldn't.

"You've done so much for me," said her mother.

Alice began to fidget. "I love you, Mom," she said. "Look, I need to go, but I'll call you back later, okay?"

Her mother choked out a tearful good-bye. Alice signed off as politely as she could, then felt bad immediately afterwards. Eager for a distraction, she called out, "Cynth, you still need help?"

"Yeah."

Alice went back to the front room and found that Cynthia had begun unpacking the kitchen. The white cupboard doors stood wide open, and the beige Formica countertop was covered with boxes. Cynthia was stacking glasses into one of the cupboards, but at the sound of Alice approaching, she turned and raised an eyebrow. "Everything okay?" she asked.

"I guess so."

"Is she . . . was she crying?"

Alice nodded. She picked up a knife and sliced at the tape on one of the cardboard boxes on the counter. "I never know what to say to her. I feel like we're strangers, but I sympathize, you know? It's not like I can take my dad's side in all this."

Cynthia put the last of the glasses away and shut the cupboard with a bang. "You really shouldn't have to take anyone's side in all this."

"Yes, that would be great, but—" Alice hefted a stack of plates out of the box and began unwrapping them—"I already tried that. Both of them think that my silence means I side with Dad. Which cabinet do these go in?" she asked, holding up one of their blue dinner plates.

"They need to go in the dishwasher first," Cynthia noted. "But let me unload it real quick." She opened the dishwasher and pulled out one of the racks with a soft clattering sound.

Alice began stacking the plates on the counter.

"So, your mom knows about your baptism, right?" asked Cynthia.

"I told her last week. She probably doesn't remember that it was today, and I'll have to tell her three more times before she remembers, but the short answer is yes."

"Was she okay with it?"

Alice sighed. "I don't think she was listening. Her life just got blown to smithereens. Kind of affects her concentration."

"But she likes Darren."

"Yeah . . . sure."

"Speaking of Darren, he called while you were on your cell. Said you guys were planning on dinner tomorrow and that he was checking to make sure you could meet him at his place at six."

"Uh-huh, his usual double-check call—making sure I haven't secretly made plans with another man since the last time we talked."

"He's going to be a lawyer," Cynthia said. "He's an organized, detail-oriented person."

"Unlike you, Miss Freewheeling Artist who approaches life with reckless abandon."

Cynthia glanced up from the silverware drawer, where she was arranging the forks in a precisely ordered stack. She smiled sheepishly. "They look better like this."

"Fine . . . but I'm going to go unpack my room while you do that, okay?"

Cynthia nodded, and Alice headed back down the hall.

* * *

That night, before Alice went to sleep, she knelt down by her bed and folded her arms to pray. *Father in Heaven,* she began, *I thank Thee for the opportunity to get baptized and to receive the gift of the Holy Ghost. I thank Thee for Darren and Cynthia and Monica. They've all been so supportive of me.*

A drop of moisture landed on her arm, and, with a start, she realized she was crying. She shut her eyes again and shook her head. *Okay,* she thought, *I've got to be honest here.*

Getting baptized was great, but the rest of my life is a disaster. I haven't returned the last three phone calls from my dad, and I haven't I given him my new address, because, to tell the truth, I prefer not having to deal with him. Which is sad. He used to be my best friend.

Darren is leaving in three weeks, and even though he's said he wants to stay together, I worry. I don't want to lose him. He's the most amazing guy I've ever met, but I've never had a long-distance relationship work out.

Then there's the fact that my company is getting bought out. Gretchen says I'll probably be offered a comparable job in Phoenix or Atlanta sometime in the next six or seven months, but the merger is taking time, and the office building in Phoenix needs to be built, and . . .

I hate uncertainty! I wish my life would just settle itself for once and that I could look to the future and have some idea of what to expect.

Alice took a deep breath.

To be completely *honest,* she thought, *I wish I could look forward to a future with Darren. I realize six or seven months is quite a while off, but I still worry. I worry that I'll have to make the decision to move just as Darren's starting to think about marriage but before he's ready to commit, and then I'll leave, and that'll be that.* She bit her lip.

Lord . . . will I be engaged before I have to make a final decision about my job? And will I know that he's the right man for me?

Her nose was starting to run, so she reached over to grab a tissue from the box on her vanity. It was while in the act of reaching that it happened—a sensation like liquid warmth poured directly into her spirit. The intensity increased until she felt almost as if she was glowing, as if her heart would burst with joy, as if her room and the world had fallen away and she was suspended in space.

Then, as quickly as it had begun, it was over. She tumbled forward and had to grab the corner of her vanity.

O-okay, she thought. *I guess that means yes?*

2

Darren

Three Months Later

Alice's cell phone rang right in her ear. She woke, grabbed the phone off her pillow before it could ring again, and flipped it open. "Hello?" she croaked.

"I'm in," came Darren's voice.

"Home? All the way?"

"Yup. I'm going to bed now, but I'll see you at church tomorrow . . . or later today, I guess."

"Great, yeah." Alice sat up and squinted in the direction of her alarm clock, which read 2:33. Light from the streetlight outside shone on her yellow comforter, giving it an orange cast. Her window was open a crack, and a draft of cool air, scented with roses from the vines next door, brushed across the skin of her bare arms.

"What time does the ward meet?" he asked.

"Nine."

Darren groaned. "Oh, yeah . . . that's right."

"But there's the student ward at one. We could go to that one this week."

"Right . . . no, let's just go to our ward. If we go to the student one, you'll have to miss part of it for choir practice."

"True."

"Okay, so if I start snoring in sacrament meeting, just prop me up against the wall or something."

Alice laughed. "All right."

"I missed you."

"I missed you too."

"How are things with your parents?"

Alice let out a deep, frustrated sigh. "Well . . . I was on the phone with my mom until almost midnight. Neither of us knows what my dad's up to, but no one's filed for divorce yet."

"Man . . . I'm sorry. You haven't said anything about it for so long—"

"Oh, I don't want to be a broken record, you know? It's the same old same old week after week with Mom. I signed her up for a feng shui class."

"Um . . . okay."

Alice laughed. "It was Cynthia's idea. Mom's impressed with my Zen-friendly apartment. And, you know, home decorating is something you can spend all your free time on. Leaves Mom less time to stew."

"You're good to her. All right, I gotta sleep. See you in . . . six hours."

"Yeah, see you then."

"Love you."

"Love you too. Bye." Alice snapped her phone shut and lay back down.

* * *

The chapel was packed full of people. Alice stepped just inside the doors, then stopped and stared. The aisle was jammed to capacity— Alice could not take another step—and the babble of voices was so loud that it was almost deafening. Given how large the room was and how high the ceiling, that was quite a feat. At the front of the room, the bishop and his counselors sat on the stand, staring out at the crowd in amazement. Alice's friend Monica stood at the edge of the nearest row of pews. Upon spotting Alice, she wormed her way over.

"Can you believe this?" Monica almost had to shout. "I guess everyone's back for school or whatever this week."

"This is insane," said Alice. "What's the university ward going to be like?"

Monica shrugged. "Maybe all the singles want to be here." She glanced at something over Alice's shoulder and raised an eyebrow.

Alice turned. A tall man with white-blond hair and tanned skin stood in the doorway. He looked the room over in bewilderment. "*He's* good-looking," Alice noted.

"Spencer," Monica answered.

"Hmm?"

"That's Spencer Sharp." As Monica said this, Spencer took a hesitant step forward, then began finding his way through the crowd.

"You know him?" Alice asked.

"Yeah, he's been in the ward before. He's Leslie's older brother, and—" Monica leaned in closer "—very good-looking. I can't believe he isn't married yet."

Alice watched him make his way to his sister's pew, where he greeted everyone and took a seat. He glanced in Alice's direction and flashed her a friendly smile. Alice smiled back and turned her gaze away. A scream of laughter, loud enough to be heard over the crowd, caused both Alice and Monica to turn around. Sarah Nagel's voice rang out in the hallway outside. "You'll love the singles ward," she was saying. "It's just the best. Way better than the student ward, *way* better. I mean, you want a singles ward, don't you?"

Alice and Monica exchanged a look. "She's on the prowl again," said Monica.

"What happened to Kent?"

"Escaped. Last week, I guess he moved to the university ward to get away from her."

"What? He was my home teacher." Alice shook her head and peered out the chapel door to get a better look. Sarah was sashaying down the hall toward them with her hand on the arm of a young man Alice didn't recognize. He had olive skin, green eyes, and close-cropped hair that screamed *recently returned missionary.* "He doesn't look as scared as they usually do," she remarked to Monica.

"Maybe they're dating already, then."

"Brandon!" Sarah's companion interrupted her to get a friend's attention. Alice watched as he let go of Sarah's arm and punched the shoulder of one of the other young men in the hallway. Much to Sarah's horror, the two began shoving each other good-naturedly.

"Hey," she squeaked.

Brandon, also someone Alice didn't know, put Sarah's prospect in a headlock, and the two started wrestling.

Alice exchanged another amused look with Monica and turned to look around the chapel for a seat. The rows of pews were filling fast.

"I'd go upstairs," she said, "but I'd like Darren to be able to find me when he gets here."

"Oh, right!" said Monica. "He's back."

"Yup."

"And?"

"And what?" Alice turned to face her again. From her quick survey of the room, she noted that there were a *lot* of new faces. *Are there still people here that I know?* she wondered. She looked around again, but Monica, Sarah Nagel, and Leslie Sharp were the only people she recognized.

"How're things going with him, silly?" prompted Monica. "Have you seen him since he got back?"

Alice blinked and turned back to her friend. "Not yet," she said, "and things are fine."

"Just *fine?*"

Alice changed the subject. "How's Sean?"

"Still wants me to go to his ward. But I told him no. I like it here. He thinks I want to play the field." She smirked. "Seriously though, you're not going to be here much longer. You and Darren have been together how long?"

"Almost seven months."

"That's *ages.*"

Alice rolled her eyes. "Only in Mormon time."

"I'll bet he has a ring."

Against her will, Alice smiled, but she tried to hide it by rubbing her nose with the back of her hand. "Whatever," she said, trying to sound nonchalant.

"He wouldn't stay with you for the whole summer if that wasn't what he wanted."

"If you say so."

Just then the bishop stood, and everyone in the congregation who hadn't found a seat scrambled for one. Darren breezed in the door at the same moment, and his gaze fell on Alice right away. Alice's mouth went dry. She'd had dozens of pictures of him to look at over the summer, but having him actually *here,* in her presence, was something entirely different. His eyes seemed bluer, and his smile was more enchanting. He beamed at her, then turned to scan the room. "There?" he mouthed, pointing to a few empty seats on the end of a row.

Alice nodded.

"I'm going to sit with Wendy," said Monica, slipping away. The aisle was emptying rapidly around them.

Darren put his arm around Alice's shoulders as they darted over to the seats he had indicated. He let her sit down first, then sat next to her. Alice turned to put her scriptures down and accidentally elbowed the person on the other side of her. "Sorry," she whispered.

"No problem."

Alice looked up. It was the boy Sarah had been hitting on. He smiled back at her eagerly, which Alice found odd.

"Alice, this is Gabe," Darren whispered, "my new roommate. Gabe, this is Alice. Gabe's an undergrad at UCLA."

"Oh, hi," said Alice. They were too pressed in to shake hands, so she just nodded at him. His clothing had that fresh detergent smell, and his trousers were neatly pressed, but his shirt was wrinkled and his hair stuck out in tufts, thanks to his friend's antics in the hallway.

"Hi," he whispered back. "So you're the famous Alice?"

"He's just back from his mission in Paraguay," said Darren.

Again, Alice nodded, smiling politely.

"Morning, brothers and sisters," said Bishop Baker into the microphone. Alice focused her attention on him, and around her all chatter ceased.

* * *

Once sacrament meeting was over, Darren walked with Alice to Sunday School. Alice was pleased. She'd hoped he would come with her to her class—the one for new converts—rather than the regular Sunday School for everyone else. She hadn't specifically asked him to, though. They sat in the back with their arms around each other. Darren traced patterns on her shoulder and kept catching her eye to exchange a smile as the teacher lectured.

After Sunday School finished, Alice kissed Darren's cheek and got up to head over to Relief Society for the third hour. He grabbed her arm as she stood. She turned to look at him. "Meet me at my place afterwards?" he asked.

"Okay."

"Great." He stood up and gave her a kiss on the lips. "See you in an hour."

* * *

Darren's apartment was in a run-down quad in Culver City. The parking area was on the ground floor. There was no garage door or gate, just a concrete pad under the building. To get to the apartment, one had to climb the staircase on the left side of the parking area.

Alice and Darren managed to do this in somewhere between one and three seconds, and then they were inside the front door of his apartment, kissing. It felt so good to actually be with him again. Phone calls, no matter how long, just weren't the same. Alice wrapped her arms around his waist and held him close, savoring the feel of him.

Pulling away slightly, Alice asked, "Where's the roommate?"

"Home teaching."

"What? His first week in the ward?"

"He's subbing for someone. Suffice it to say, he's *gone* right now." Darren took her by the hand and led her over to the couch. His apartment was cluttered, as usual. He had to shift a pile of clothes out of the way to make room for both of them, and Alice picked up a jacket that was draped over the back of the couch and dumped it on a chair. The couch itself was lumpy and smelled like mildew and pizza grease. Still, when Darren put his arms around her, she stopped noticing at once. They resumed kissing. *I can't believe how much I missed you,* Alice thought.

After a few moments, she realized Darren had never been this physical with her before, and he showed no signs of slowing down or stopping as he pressed her back, inviting her to lie down with him.

"All right, all right," she said with a laugh. She gently pushed him off and sat up straighter. Her skirt had begun to ride up, and she tugged it down again.

Before she could settle herself, though, Darren was kissing her neck, and his hand gripped the back of her blouse.

"Darren," she warned, trying to keep her voice light.

"Yeah," he murmured. With his other hand, he undid the top button of her shirt.

"Wait, what are you doing?" Alice nudged him away more firmly and angled herself so that she could make eye contact with him.

He met her gaze for a moment, then looked down. "I really missed you."

"I missed you too. But this isn't exactly kosher, you know?"

"What? Wait, you don't think I was going to . . . you know." Darren looked at her uneasily.

"Well, no," said Alice. "You took me by surprise, that's all." She finished adjusting her clothes and rebuttoned her shirt.

Darren gazed at her a moment longer, then looked down. "I . . . well, it's just, you and I have been together too long to just be holding hands and having good-night kisses and whatever else is 'appropriate.' And if we do get married, it won't be for eight more months if we're shooting for the temple. So we're just supposed to sit around and hold hands the whole time?"

"Get married?" asked Alice. Her hands faltered as she tugged her skirt straight again.

"Well . . . yeah. I've been thinking about it. Haven't you?"

"Um . . ." Alice held out her left hand and glanced at it casually. "No."

Darren laughed. "All right. But anyway, I really wasn't looking to have a gospel discussion with you right now. I'm not going to—you know—compromise your virtue." He put his arm around her and pulled her close to kiss her again.

This time Alice tried to relax, but she just didn't feel comfortable. *Come on,* she thought to herself. *It's not like you've never made out with a guy before. This is Darren, the guy you're madly in love with, and he's kissing you. Pay attention!* She took a deep breath.

Darren pulled back. "What's the matter?"

"Nothing. I'd just rather not go too far with this."

"You don't want to be that close to me."

"No, Darren, it's not that."

"You've *slept* with other men, but with me—"

"Okay, stop. Darren, I thought my past wasn't an issue."

Darren got up from the couch and went into the kitchen, where he put both hands flat on the counter and stared off into space. The muscles along his jaw clenched and unclenched.

"Darren," said Alice.

"It's not an issue. I'm fine with it."

"Well . . . I kind of like the idea of taking it slow for a change."

"How slow is slow?"

"You're the one talking about another eight months."

"Alice, all I want to do is make out."

"Look," she said, "making out usually leads to other things. Unbuttoning clothing and whatever else you wanted to do—I just don't feel comfortable with that."

Darren, she realized, was standing stock still, a horrified look on his face.

She looked over her shoulder and heard the front door click shut. Gabe stood in front of it with a stack of books in his arms. He seemed frozen in place as well. "Hi," Alice said to him.

Gabe glanced from her to Darren, then put his head down and darted past them into one of the bedrooms.

For a moment, Darren looked after him as Gabe shut the door, then he turned to Alice.

"Way too much information," Darren said.

Gabe's radio came on with a blare of static and the opening strains of a hymn. She realized that he was playing a CD by the Mormon Tabernacle Choir.

Alice's face felt hot. "Well, sorry," she said. "You were the one who brought it up."

3
Mother

"Oh, you're overreacting, not to mention being weird," said Cynthia that evening. She was cooking as she spoke, tossing pasta in a frying pan with an egg and one of her herb concoctions. The smell of warm oil, frying egg, and spices wafted throughout the room. Dusk was falling outside, turning the light that shone through the window a gray-blue shade.

Alice sat on one of the bar stools, resting her elbows on the beige countertop.

"So his roommate's the prudish kind of Mormon boy," Cynthia went on. "Big deal."

"I'm still embarrassed, Cynth."

Cynthia looked back at Alice over her shoulder. "Why?" She looked sincerely confused. "If I'd walked in on you making out with your shirt unbuttoned a few months ago, you and I would've laughed about it. Walking in on you talking about it isn't exactly shocking."

"I barely know Gabe, and I feel like I crossed the line somehow."

Cynthia turned off the burner and dumped the pasta onto two plates, one of which she passed to Alice. "You've changed. You know that? This isn't a big deal, okay?"

"But maybe . . ." Alice shut her eyes. Cynthia wasn't going to understand, she realized. She shook her head and waved her hands as if to clear the air. "Okay, never mind. Forget about it. New subject."

"Sure. What?" Cynthia came around the counter and took a seat on the other bar stool.

"I'm taking Mom out to dinner Tuesday night. I promised I would. Where should I take her?"

* * *

Cynthia had suggested a trendy restaurant in West Hollywood, and Alice liked it the moment she set foot in the door. The dining room had frosted glass partitions between the seating areas, dim lighting, and black tables adorned with tropical flowers that gave off a light, perfumed scent. Her mother was fifteen minutes late, so Alice sat at their table and drummed her fingers against the cool, smooth surface of the tabletop until her mother did show up with red and puffy eyes. Her graying red hair was combed straight and limp, and she wore little makeup.

"Oh, Mom." Alice sighed, giving her mother an awkward hug. "You okay?" she asked, noting how thin and bony her mother felt.

"Yes," her mother said. She sat down across from Alice. "You should probably order for me, though." She tried to laugh but failed.

"You promise to eat?"

"Promise."

A waiter in a white shirt and gray slacks came over to take their order. Alice looked up at him and, with a start, realized that it was Darren's roommate. "Gabe," she said, "I didn't know you worked here."

"Hey, Alice. Yeah, I do." He smiled at her.

Alice began to feel flustered. *Great,* she thought. *Mom'll probably start crying any minute, and I'll tell her to knock it off, and she'll flee from the restaurant, and I'll look like a terrible daughter as well as a hussy, and—*She stopped herself to take a deep breath. *Get a grip. Think of what Dad would do if he were here . . . For starters, he'd be nice and charming to the waiter.*

"So, wait," she blurted out, "I thought you were in school full time." The hymn he'd played the other day surfaced in her mind. She drummed her fingers to a different beat in order to clear it from her thoughts.

"Yeah, I am." Gabe turned his entire attention to her. *He's not uncomfortable,* she told herself. Meanwhile, her mother was looking away and trying to make herself as small and unnoticeable as possible.

"But you work here?"

"Uh-huh, whenever they need an extra person or a sub. My family used to own this restaurant." His manner remained open and reassuring.

Alice let herself relax a notch. "Well, I think we're ready to order," she said.

"Right." He pulled a pad and pen out of his pocket. "What can I get for you?"

Alice ordered a salad for herself and baked ziti for her mother. Once she'd passed the menus to Gabe and he'd taken them away, her mother said, "You know that boy?"

"From church, yeah."

"Church . . . right. How is that?" She did her best to sit up straight and look interested.

"Fine," she said. "He's also my boyfriend's roommate."

"Oh? Darren's roommate?"

"Right."

"And how is Darren?"

"He's good, Mom. Things are going well."

"You like him?" Her mother narrowed her eyes.

"*Yes*, Mother."

"Well, just be careful. Your dad and I got married when I was nineteen."

"Which I'm not, Mom. I'm twenty-six, remember?"

"And I thought everything was great."

"Which it was for almost thirty years."

"But then . . ." Her mother started to cry.

"Oh, Mom." Alice tried not to fidget. *I'm so bad at this,* she thought. *Mom, I love you, and I want you to be happy. How can I make you understand that?* Telepathy wasn't working either, so Alice fished out a pack of tissues from her purse, tugged one loose, and passed it across the table. Her mother dabbed at her eyes and sniffled.

"Sorry," her mother whispered.

"Don't be sorry, Mom. I brought you here to help you get *away* from all that."

Her mother nodded but still looked miserable. "Have you talked to your dad lately?" she asked.

Alice shook her head. "I haven't talked to him at all in the last . . . four months?" She felt a twinge of guilt as she said that. Her father, she knew, would never have a meltdown in public. Dinner with him would have been fun; he'd have her laughing by now. *Remember,* she told herself, *he's the reason Mom is like this. He left. He's the one who said he didn't feel like being married anymore.*

"Oh . . ." her mother went on, "I just wondered if maybe he said anything to you about his girlfriend." More tears.

Alice passed her mother another tissue, then reached over to hold her hand. "Mom," she said, "tell me about your feng shui class."

"Oh, I quit, honey."

"You didn't like it?"

"It was fine, but I decided to take yoga instead."

"And how's that going?"

"Oh . . . I don't know."

* * *

Ten minutes later their food arrived. Gabe served it silently and efficiently and disappeared before Alice could even thank him. She had run out of things to say to her mother, and the two of them sat and ate in silence.

When Alice finished her meal, she laid her fork down and said, "I'll be right back, okay?"

She slid out of the booth and picked her way across the dining room toward the women's restroom. As she turned the corner, though, she nearly ran into Gabe. Fortunately, he wasn't carrying any trays of food, only a water pitcher.

"Oh—uh—hi. Sorry."

"Hey, Alice," he replied, steadying the water pitcher so that it wouldn't slosh. "Is that your mother you're with?"

"Yeah."

He nodded, his green eyes fixed intently on her face.

Alice looked sideways at the wall. "Um . . . yeah. She and my dad are going through a rough divorce."

"Oh, no, you don't need to . . . I mean . . . I wasn't trying to pry."

"It's not exactly a secret."

"Well, it's real nice of you to bring her here. I highly recommend this place." He grinned boyishly. "Do you come here a lot? I . . . that sounds like a pickup line."

Alice laughed and shook her head. "My roommate recommended it. She's an interior decorator. I guess her firm did the dining room here."

"Oh, uh-huh."

Gabe seemed genuinely interested, so, with a glance toward the dining room, she continued.

"And she was a waitress before that and cooks gourmet, so I pretty much trust her when she says a restaurant is good."

"A waitress–interior designer, huh? That's impressive."

Alice nodded. "A waitress with a bossy roommate telling her how to save her money and where to invest it and how to pay for school and how many loans to take out and for how much. I made her follow her dreams."

"You do that a lot?"

"What? Tell other people what to do? Yes, but they usually ignore me."

He smiled and nodded with enthusiasm.

"Um . . . how about you?" Alice asked. "You been working here long?"

"I . . . yeah. Since I was a kid. But I got a scholarship for school, so I just work when I can and give most of the money to my sister."

"Older or younger?"

"Younger." He smiled again, and there was a light in his eyes. He clearly liked this sister of his.

"Is she your only sibling?"

"My only family, practically. Our dad passed away ten years ago, and our uncle, who owned this place after my dad, passed away last year. My mom and I are . . . we don't talk."

"Uh-huh." At the word *mom,* Alice felt a pang of guilt. *I really shouldn't leave mine alone for so long.* She cast about for a way to exit the conversation gracefully. "Well, I'm sorry to hear it. I . . . should probably get to the restroom—" she gave him her best attempt at an apologetic smile "—and get back before my mother wonders what happened to me."

"Right. Sorry." Gabe stepped aside. "Nice talking to you."

"Yeah, good to see you," Alice responded. She slipped past him and made her getaway.

4

Plenty of Time

"Hi, Alice?" Darren's voice played on her voice mail. "It's me. Look, I'm sorry I haven't called you back for so long. Life is hectic. But . . . we should do something soon, okay? Call me."

Alice was sitting in her office listening as the time and date of the message played. She hung up and looked at her clock. Darren got out of his next class in a few minutes, so she'd call him back then.

She went back to reviewing the trust agreement spread out on her desk. The background noise of people talking in low voices, the hum of the copier in the next room over, and the ringing of office phones filled her head. Alice massaged her temples and tried to focus.

"Alice?" came the receptionist's voice over the intercom.

"Yeah?"

"Your dad was just here. He left you a note."

Alice sighed. "I'll be right out."

"Actually, the mail cart is here. Charlotte will take it back to you."

"Thank you."

"No problem." The connection clicked off.

A few minutes later, the mail cart came by and the elderly woman who ran it brought the small sheet of folded paper in to Alice. Alice thanked her and looked at the note. It was written on plain, cream stationery.

She unfolded it and read,

> *Dear Allie, I miss you. What can I do so that we can be friends again? Love, Dad.*

Alice tried to fold the paper neatly again but ended up crushing it into a wad, which she tossed into the garbage. *You don't want a friend, Dad,* she thought. *You want another supporter in your war against Mom.*

She looked at the trust agreement again. *Funding provision,* she reminded herself, *find it.*

A few minutes later, her office phone rang, and the display read, *G. Kinny.* Alice grabbed the receiver. "Hi, Gretchen."

"Hi, Alice," replied her boss. "Have you got a moment?"

"I do, yes."

"Great. Come by my office; I want to talk to you about the merger."

"All right. See you in a minute."

"Thanks."

Alice pushed back from her desk and headed for the stairs. Gretchen's office was two stories up, and when Alice arrived, her boss was seated at her desk, frowning at a stack of documents. Alice knocked on the half-open door, and Gretchen looked up.

"Hi, Alice," she said. "Come in and close the door."

Alice stepped in, pushed the door shut, and took a seat in one of the plush chairs. Gretchen had one of the largest offices on the floor. Its furniture was all dark wood, and there was a little ornamental fountain by the door that splashed soothingly, as well as a window that looked out in the direction of Wilshire Boulevard and Westwood Village. From Alice's vantage point, though, all she could see was a patch of gray, smog-tinted sky.

Gretchen herself was in her mid-fifties and had blue eyes and light brown hair, which she usually wore up. Today was no exception. "We have so many decisions to make," she said. "It's been nuts, I tell you." She capped her pen with a click and set it aside.

Alice nodded.

"For you, the decision is this," said Gretchen. "I'm going to head up the auditing department in the new Phoenix office, and I'd like you to come with me. The job that's open there would be a step up from your current position and would mean a raise of almost twenty thousand, so the new directors want you to apply for it. Or they can offer you a job like the one you've got now in their headquarters in Atlanta."

"I'd prefer Phoenix," said Alice, "but if I apply and they refuse, I assume Atlanta's out?"

"No." Gretchen shook her head. "I specifically asked about that. If they say no to Phoenix, you definitely get offered the transfer to Atlanta."

"So I can't lose," said Alice, "which means, of course, I'll apply. But I'll be honest. I'm not a hundred percent sure I want to move to either Phoenix or Atlanta."

"That's understandable. The application is . . ." Gretchen glanced at her flat-screen monitor and waved her hand in disgust. "You'll have to find it. It's on the corporate Web site, I gather. You'll be interviewed by Hank Wingate, who was the head of the auditing department in Houston. I don't really know him all that well, but I'll write the recommendation. I specifically asked for you because I'd love to keep working together. If you do find a better offer from another company though, let me know, all right?"

"Okay," said Alice. "So if I do get the job in Phoenix, when do I need to think about moving?"

"Well, that's the other thing. The general contractor the company was working with for the Phoenix office pulled out, and I gather that's causing problems. I don't know details, but I hear that lawyers have been called." She chuckled. "It probably won't be up and running at the end of March, like we hoped. May or June is the best guess I can give you."

"But if I go to Atlanta?"

"We don't know. That keeps getting shifted around."

"So . . . it's not New Year's?"

"Definitely not. No. All of that has been pushed back."

Alice nodded. *That's good,* she thought, *really good. Gives me and Darren plenty of time to figure everything out.*

"If you can't find the application, call Rodney," suggested Gretchen, "but it should be on the Web site. Can you have it in by the end of the month?"

"That shouldn't be a problem."

"Great."

Gretchen dismissed her, and Alice felt a certain lightness in her step as she returned to her office. Once there, she shut the door and called Darren from her cell phone.

He picked up at once. "Hi, Alice."

"Hi."

"Sorry I haven't called."

"It's all right," said Alice. "You been busy?"

"Yeah. The usual. But since I've already got my job lined up for after graduation, it's kind of hard to care."

"Well, sure."

"Anyway, look, I was wondering if you wanted to come over Friday night. We can rent a movie and order in dinner."

"Sounds great."

"Okay, good. So, Gabe said he saw you at his work."

"Uh-huh. He's a nice kid."

"Yeah, he is. When I see him. He's been working almost every night this week."

"That's gotta be rough, doing that on top of school."

"Well, I don't know the details, but I guess his family's got serious money problems."

"Oh," said Alice.

"Anyway. I'll see you Friday?"

"Yep, see you then."

"Love you."

"Love you too, bye."

* * *

Friday evening, when Alice arrived at Darren's apartment, the lights were low and Gabe was nowhere to be seen. She lingered in the doorway, letting the cool evening air sweep in.

"Something wrong?" asked Darren. He went over to the counter and picked up the phone. "Dinner from Taj Mahal okay with you?"

Alice raised an eyebrow, reached over to the light switch, and pushed the fader all the way up. Brightness flooded the room, making Darren squint. He shook his head. "Fine," he said. "About the food?"

"That'd be great." Alice stepped inside and closed the door. The apartment was much tidier than usual, and the counter was wiped clean. *I bet that's Gabe's doing,* thought Alice, knowing it couldn't be Darren's. She pictured Gabe bussing the kitchen the way he bussed tables at the restaurant. Two movies were stacked on the coffee table, and she went to look at them.

"Darren," she said, turning each one over in her hands, "these are both rated R."

"Hang on," said Darren. "Hi," he said into the phone, "delivery to Culver City?"

Alice put the movies down and frowned. Darren finished ordering, hung up the phone, and came to flop down on the couch. "Sorry, what were you saying?" he asked.

"I stopped watching R-rated movies after I got baptized." Alice gestured apologetically at the DVDs Darren had chosen.

"You did?"

"Yeah."

"Why?"

Alice looked at him. "What do you mean, why? Because the prophet said to."

"Yeah, but that's just advice, not a rule."

"Right," said Alice, "but . . . I chose to follow that advice." She tried to remember if they'd gone to R-rated movies before she'd been baptized. They'd never had a discussion about it. *And here I've been all summer, assuming that he followed this advice too.*

Darren ran his fingers through his hair and shook his head. "You've really changed, you know that?"

"So people keep telling me."

"You're kind of turning into a Molly."

"What's a Molly?"

"Never mind. Just what are your new rules? No making out, no R-rated movies—"

"Darren—"

"I just want us to be clear. Kisses that last for more than ten seconds—yes or no?"

"I don't want to make up a set of rules," said Alice.

Darren rolled his eyes. "Then how's this going to work?"

"You should know the 'rules'—" Alice made air quotes—"better than I do. All I want is for us to be able to get married in the temple if that's what we decide."

"Well . . ." Darren looked up at the ceiling. "It's not like you're the first girlfriend I've ever had. You could *trust* me."

"I do trust you. That's not the issue, believe me."

Darren shook his head and muttered something.

"What did you say?" Alice asked.

"I just wonder what's next. You want to start having a chaperone along on dates?"

"Darren—"

"What? You know, all I did last Sunday was try to show you how much I love you. Now you're getting all uptight and making rules and—"

"I love you too. And if we go back to doing the kind of stuff we did last Sunday, it'll be hard for me."

"Which brings up the trust issue again."

"It's *not* a matter of trusting you," Alice shot back. "Okay? It's not. This is about me. I don't want to push things because . . . Darren, you're really attractive."

Darren rolled his eyes again.

"What?" demanded Alice. "It's the truth."

"Fine," he said. "I think Gabe's got some Disney movies under the TV. Let's watch one of those and then have dinner, and I promise I'll be a good little Mormon boy."

"Darren—"

"Under the TV. Pick one."

* * *

Two hours later, Gabe walked in wearing his uniform from the restaurant. Alice and Darren were eating dinner, and the entire apartment smelled like saffron and cream.

"Hey," Darren said to his roommate without looking up. "You want some?"

"Nah." Gabe shut and locked the front door. "I ate at work. Hi, Alice."

"Hi."

Darren got up and went into the bathroom while Alice continued to pick at her food. "How was work?" she asked Gabe.

"Fine. How have you been?"

Alice looked up at him. "Good," she said.

"Is everything . . . all right?" He glanced in the direction of the bathroom door. "I'm sorry if I interrupted—"

"No," said Alice. Her cheeks began to feel warm. "We were just eating dinner."

"Oh," said Gabe. "I didn't mean to imply—"

"It's all right."

He nodded. "Well, nice to see you again." Much to Alice's relief, he went into his room and shut the door behind him.

* * *

That night, Alice knelt by her bed for a long time. *Darren's fed up with me,* she thought. *I can tell.* They'd fought more since he'd gotten back than they ever had before. She folded her arms. *Um, okay,* she thought, *I'm a little lost here, Lord. I know you told me I'd be engaged to Darren soon. How's that going to work? Should I just not worry about it? Will this all sort itself out?*

She closed her prayer, kept her arms folded, and waited. Nothing. Alice remained where she was a moment longer. *Okay,* she reasoned, *clear answers aren't all that common . . . right? So . . . what do I do now?* She hadn't even had a hint of a response to any of her prayers since the night of her baptism. Alice waited until her knees were sore and her head began to nod. Nothing. Finally, she got up and got into bed.

5

Misunderstandings

Over the next two months, Darren's phone calls became less and less frequent. He blamed it on all the homework he had, but Alice couldn't quite bring herself to believe that. *I know he's in law school,* she thought, *but he was in law school last spring, too, and we went out at least once a week.* What did her father always say about law school? *First year they scare you to death, second year they work you to death, and third year they bore you to death. He's a third year.*

But things weren't bad enough for her to pull him aside for a talk, at least she didn't think so. They were still talking once a week and going out every ten days or so. If she tried to make an issue out of it, they'd probably just get into another fight. *He's changed,* Alice thought. *Five months ago, I could talk to him about anything.* She remembered her prayer the night of her baptism and the answer she'd gotten. *If we're going to get married, there has to be a way through this that doesn't entail more conflict.*

One Sunday, when Alice felt especially low, she turned to Monica. They were walking to Relief Society together, and Alice filled her friend in on all that had happened. On their way down the hall, they passed Spencer Sharp, who waved at the both of them and smiled at Alice. Alice waved back.

After he'd passed, Alice recounted to Monica the awkward movie date when Darren had asked her to lay down "rules."

As she and Monica made their way to some empty seats at the back of the Relief Society room, Monica replied, "Oh, you probably just had a misunderstanding. It's not a big deal."

The other sisters in the ward were still trickling in, filling up a seat here and there as small clusters of friends formed. No one encroached on their conversation, so Alice tried again. "It's not just that. Things have been different this term. He's been distant. We barely even talk anymore."

"He still had his arm around you in sacrament meeting today."

"Yeah, but—"

Monica shook her head. "He loves you. Everyone can tell. You're getting all worked up over nothing. I'll bet you he proposes by the end of the term."

"I don't think so," said Alice.

"Maybe that's why he's been distant. Maybe he's plotting the perfect way to ask."

"Mon—"

"It's possible."

Alice shook her head. "No . . . but that's all right. I don't have to decide about my job until spring." *Heavenly Father must have known we'd need a little extra time.*

"Okay, everyone," the Relief Society president called out from the front of the room. "I have some materials that the bishop wanted us to have. I'm going to pass them around." She held up a stack of papers and a pamphlet. "People keep asking for the proclamation on the family, so that's here, and 'The Living Christ.' Just take one of each."

* * *

After church got out, Alice went to visit her mother. There was no answer when she rang the doorbell, so she unlocked the front door and stepped into the entryway. "Mom?" she called.

She heard a sniffle from the direction of the living room. Alice stepped all the way in, shut the door behind her, and crossed the entryway. "Mom?" she repeated.

Her mother was curled up on the couch. The room was dingier than usual. A layer of dust covered the coffee table, the end tables on either side of the couch, and the shades of the table lamps set there.

"What's wrong, Mom?" Alice asked.

Her mother sat up slowly and pointed to a stack of papers on the coffee table. Alice went over to pick them up. *Summons* read the heading on the first one. Underneath was a paragraph of legalese that Alice skimmed. "Is this from Dad?" she asked.

"Yes," her mother said in a small voice, "he's filed for divorce."

Alice sighed and dropped the papers back onto the coffee table. "When did this happen?"

"Friday."

"*Friday?* Mom, why didn't you tell me?"

"I'm still reeling. The man who came with those papers was so rude. And then I started reading the complaint. Your father claims I don't need any spousal support and that he gets everything his parents gave us when we first got married, and—"

"Hang on," said Alice. "What does your lawyer say?"

"I haven't got one."

Alice bit back the impulse to yell, took a deep breath, and said, "Why not?"

"You remember! Your father told me that we should both use the same one."

"All right," said Alice. She went around to the kitchen and got the phone book from off the top of the fridge. "You're getting your own lawyer," she called back to her mother. "Dad can't just take everything from you. You know that, right?" She stepped back into the living room and found her mother still seated on the couch, staring listlessly into space. "Mom?" Alice prompted.

"I don't want to do this."

You don't have a choice, Alice thought, but she held her tongue. She put the phone book on the coffee table and sat down on the couch next to her mother. "I'll help you, okay? I'll make all the phone calls if you want."

"I don't have any money, Alice."

"You do. Unless Dad drained the checking account."

"No."

"Well, half that money's yours, Mom. It's a community property state."

"But if I spend it all on a lawyer—"

"Mom! You're being sued. You need a lawyer. End of discussion."

Her mother began to cry. Alice hugged her awkwardly. "It'll be all right," she kept saying, even though she could hear how silly it sounded. *Such a lie,* she thought. *This will probably be a complete nightmare.*

* * *

That evening she stopped by Darren's, but Gabe answered the door. "He's asleep," Gabe told her. "He's been asleep all afternoon. I can knock on his door or—"

"No," said Alice, "definitely a bad idea to wake a sleeping Darren. He'll be cranky."

"Yeah."

"Can you tell him I stopped by?"

"Sure."

"Thanks." Alice turned and headed back down the stairs to her car.

When she got home, she realized she still had her stack of papers from Relief Society tucked into her *Gospel Principles* book. She went back to her room, sat down cross-legged on her bed, and began going through them. There were two proclamations by the First Presidency and the Quorum of the Twelve, a card with the Relief Society motto printed on it, and a pamphlet entitled *For the Strength of Youth.* Seeing as how the Relief Society weren't youth, she wondered why the bishop had given it to them.

As she stared at the pamphlet's glossy white pages, she was dimly aware that the apartment phone was ringing. She heard Cynthia answer it, and a second later she heard a knock at the door. "Boyfriend," Cynthia announced, handing her the phone.

"Thanks," she said, putting the pamphlet aside. She went back to sit on her bed while Cynthia went to open the door. "Hi, Darren."

"Hi. Sorry I missed you."

"Oh, no problem. You must've been real tired."

"Yeah. And I've got a cite check this next week. I hope I'm not interrupting dinner."

"No. I was just reading some Church stuff. Actually, I was just looking at the *For the Strength of Youth* pamphlet."

"You're kidding, right?"

Alice looked down at the pamphlet. "No," she said, "the bishop gave it to us today. But does—"

"Alice, we are not having this conversation."

"What conversation?" She reached over to pick up the pamphlet and flipped it open to a random page. On it was advice about modest dress standards. "Does this even apply to us?" She skimmed the page.

"Depends on who you ask." His voice still sounded guarded.

"Okay." She flipped to another page that described appropriate music. "So who would say that it does apply to us?"

"Probably the bishop. Some of the Apostles. Elder Monson gave a fireside talk on that kind of thing a while back."

"And he's our prophet now."

"Yeah. But he's old, Alice. His views are a little out of date."

Alice put the pamphlet down. She couldn't see what was out of date about music standards, but she also knew that asking more questions right now would just make Darren angrier. For what felt like the millionth time, she wondered what had happened to her kind, attentive, deeply spiritual boyfriend from last fall. *I keep waiting for this mood of his to pass, but it doesn't.*

"You really are turning into a Molly, you know that?" he said.

"Darren, what is a 'Molly'? That's the second time you've called me that."

"Let's just drop the whole pamphlet thing."

"Fine."

"Just . . ." He sighed with exasperation.

"Okay," said Alice, "new subject. Your birthday's next Saturday. Can I take you out?"

"Sure."

"What do you want? Movie and dinner?"

"I guess so."

"All right, your choice."

"Okay."

Silence. Alice didn't know what to say next. "Um . . . so I've got an interview for the job in Phoenix."

"Oh, yeah? Is that the one you definitely want?"

"I don't know, but I want to keep my options open."

"Right, yeah."

More silence. Alice chewed her lip. "How're things otherwise?" she asked.

"Fine. Going to be a stressful week."

"Yeah, I can imagine."

"Uh-huh."

After a few more seconds of excruciating silence, Alice made up an excuse to get off the phone and went out to the front room to hang it up. *This is not good.* She went back to her room and picked up the offending pamphlet again. She turned to its table of contents.

Oh . . . a section on sexual purity. Alice flipped to the correct page and began to read. The more she read, the more she understood Darren's reaction. *Even just making out isn't okay,* she realized. They'd broken that rule a bunch of times. *So this is what Darren thinks is old-fashioned.*

6

"*I've Made a Decision*"

The following Saturday Alice drove to the Century City Mall to meet Darren for a movie. As she rode the elevator up from the parking garage, she tried to be optimistic. *We've just been overworked and tired lately,* she thought. *Today should be fun.*

The elevator doors opened to reveal a line of glass-fronted mall shops. Overhead the sky was pale blue, and a jet was sliding its way toward the horizon, leaving a misty white trail in its wake. Alice stepped out, paused to orient herself, then struck out in the direction of the movie theater.

The temperature was perfect—seventy degrees with just the slightest breeze. Alice's tulip skirt fluttered as she strode along, and her hair brushed her cheeks and the side of her neck. She rounded the corner, and the theater towered over her. At the base of the stairs leading up to it stood Darren, and beside Darren stood Sarah Nagel and Gabe. Gabe was wearing a black motorcycle jacket and jeans, while Sarah was dressed in a skirt and blouse. Alice paused, surprised. This was a double date—with Gabe?

Sarah looked somewhat melancholy, even though Gabe seemed to have his entire attention focused on her. When Alice walked up, they both glanced over at her, said hello, and went back to talking to each other.

Alice slipped her arm through Darren's and said, "Are they with us?"

Darren chuckled. "Not really," he said. "Gabe asked me what movie we were planning to see, and I told him. I didn't expect to see him here at the same showing, but I guess he and Sarah have gotten back together."

"Back, huh?" said Alice. They began to ascend the stairs, and Alice could hear Gabe and Sarah following several steps behind.

"Yeah," said Darren, "I guess they dated before his mission."

"Well, good for her."

* * *

After the movie was over, both Darren and Sarah had to use the restroom, so Alice found herself standing with Gabe by the concession stand, the aroma of popcorn saturating the air around them. He was his usual amiable self.

"So," he said. "How are you?"

"Fine," Alice replied. "You?"

"Good."

"You and Sarah are an item now?"

"Nah." He shook his head.

"No?" Alice looked at him.

"No. She asked me out, and I told her I'd go out with her as friends." He slipped his hands into his pockets and leaned against the wall.

"And you think that's the way she sees it?"

"I made it real clear to her. Don't get me wrong—I like her a lot, but we're not getting back together."

That explained Sarah's subdued air. *Poor girl.* "So you guys dated before your mission?" Alice asked.

"Yeah." He nodded. "And she wrote to me for a while during my mission, but she got involved with this other guy and broke it off." He shrugged. "She's a great person, though."

Alice had a hard time picturing any sane person dating Sarah Nagel, but she immediately felt guilty for those thoughts. *I'm being judgmental,* she realized, *and Gabe's just a kid. She likes to gossip about everyone, and he likes to wrestle with his friends at church.*

"So . . ." he began, "I don't mean to be nosy, but . . . how are things with Darren?"

Alice shrugged. "I wish I could say."

"I'm sorry."

"But I think they'll be all right. We're just in a rough patch."

He nodded.

"He keeps saying I'm a 'Molly.'"

"I'm sure he means it in a nice way."

"I don't know what the word means."

"Well . . ." Gabe squinted for a moment. "It's kind of like saying 'goody-two-shoes.' 'Molly Mormon' or 'Peter Priesthood' means someone who does everything right and is perfect all the time."

"Which is an insult?"

"Can be. It can mean you think someone's extreme. The stereotype of a Molly is an eighteen-year-old girl who wears frumpy clothes and goes to college in Utah in order to find a good husband. She won't kiss anyone until she's engaged, and she's a failure if that hasn't happened by the third date with a guy . . . that kind of thing."

"Oh."

"But I don't think—"

Darren emerged from the bathroom.

"Never mind," said Gabe.

"Shall we?" Darren said. He strode over to Alice and held his hand out to her.

She put her hand in his and said, "See you, Gabe."

"Yeah, see ya." He waved.

* * *

That night, over dinner at a small café in Westwood, Darren couldn't seem to focus. Before the food arrived he fidgeted with his silverware, moving it around the table. Every now and then he'd take a hasty sip of water. Then, once the food did arrive, all he did was pick at it.

He was driving Alice crazy. "Darren?" she asked. "Is there something you want to tell me?"

"Um . . . yeah." Darren put his fork down and wiped his hands on his cloth napkin. "Yeah," he repeated.

"Okay . . ."

"Alice." He didn't look at her as he spoke. "I've made a decision."

"Yes?"

"I'm going . . . I'm going to spend the next semester in Washington, DC."

Alice blinked. "You are?"

"Yes. I'm going to do an internship with the Department of Justice."

"Oh." Alice laid her own fork down and rested both hands on the table. She had barely been able to taste her food as it was, she was so distracted.

"And . . . I don't want a long-distance relationship again," he went on.

"Which means that you're either breaking up with me, or you're going to ask me to move across the country." The answer to her prayer came to her mind then. *We're not supposed to break up,* she thought. *We're supposed to get engaged, right?* She tried to imagine Darren whipping out a diamond ring just then but couldn't.

Darren looked very uncomfortable. He shifted in his seat and said, "I wouldn't ask you to move." He was silent for a moment, then he lifted his gaze to meet hers. "Alice, I'm sorry. If there's still a chance for us when I get back, then great."

"You'll graduate when you get back, and then you'll go to San Francisco for your job."

"Well . . . that's true."

"So . . . that's it, then?" Alice stared down at her hands, unable to look him in the eye. *This isn't right,* she thought. *This is definitely not what's supposed to happen.*

"I guess so. I'm sorry, Alice, but ever since I've gotten back, you've been different."

"I got baptized, Darren. I'm supposed to be different."

"Well, you've been very different."

Alice looked up at him. "You preferred how I was before? You think the old Alice would have gone further with you physically?"

Darren glanced around the dining room and said in a low but firm voice, "Alice—"

"I can't believe you're dumping me over this. Darren, all I did was join your church and start living what is *supposed* to be your lifestyle. Pardon me, but I thought you were devout."

"Okay . . . ouch." He looked down at his food.

"You just dumped me. Don't expect me to be nice about it." Alice got up, gathered her sweater and purse, and marched toward the exit. People at the other tables turned to watch her leave, but she kept her chin up. The tears didn't start until she was out of the restaurant and partway down the street. *Just keep walking,* she told herself. *Your car's just around the corner. Keep walking.*

* * *

When Alice got home, Cynthia was sitting at the table going through a stack of catalogs. She looked up at the sound of the door opening. "What happened?" she asked.

Alice shut the door and leaned back against it. Her eyes still stung from the salt of her tears.

"Did Darren—" Cynthia began.

"Yeah, over dinner."

"Oh . . . okay, getting the ice cream." Cynthia got up from the table and went into the kitchen.

Alice stayed where she was. "It wasn't supposed to happen like this," she said.

"Alice, face it." Cynthia got bowls down from the cupboard and the ice-cream scoop from the drawer. "Things have been rocky ever since he got back."

"I tried to do the right thing. That's what the Lord expects of me, right?"

Cynthia paused in the middle of getting the ice cream out of the freezer and looked over at her. "Huh?"

"Nothing." Alice shook her head. She pushed away from the door and went to sit on one of the bar stools.

"You want chocolate or vanilla?" Cynthia asked.

"I don't care."

"Then you get both." Cynthia scooped out a generous portion and put it in front of Alice. "Spoon," she said, handing Alice one from the drawer.

Alice took the spoon in one hand and rested her chin on the other. She stared listlessly at the bowl of ice cream.

"You all right?" asked Cynthia.

"No, I just got dumped." Alice scraped her spoon along the edge of her ice cream.

"I know, but you seem, I don't know . . ."

"Totally depressed."

"Yeah."

Alice frowned, ate a bite of ice cream, then said, "My parents are getting a divorce. My boyfriend dumped me. My job's up in the air. I have *no* idea where I'll be five months from now—"

"Okay, point taken."

"And Cynth, I barely know anyone in my ward. They all come and go so fast. I'm going to church with a bunch of strangers tomorrow. And Darren."

"So skip church. One week won't matter."

Alice shook her head. "I can't."

Cynthia raised an eyebrow but didn't say anything.

* * *

That night, Alice took her journal out and read over the entry she'd made the night of her baptism. *I don't understand,* she thought. *Am I just losing my mind?*

Well, she allowed, *maybe I am. Talking to God and getting answers isn't exactly . . . normal.* She looked at her journal again and flipped back to the beginning. "My boyfriend wants me to read the Book of Mormon," it read, "and pray about it. He knows I'm agnostic and don't need religion. I'm happy where I am."

But then I started reading and praying. What started out feeling like a silly exercise became a transformation for her. The process hadn't even felt like a conversion; rather, it had seemed as though the gospel was something she'd known once and forgotten long ago. Baptism had felt like coming home.

7

Back on the Market

The next morning, Alice woke up determined. She ate her breakfast, showered, and got ready for church. On the drive over to the meeting-house, she felt her spirits begin to lift. *This will be okay*, she decided. *I shouldn't be embarrassed about what happened, and I can face Darren.*

When she arrived at the chapel, Darren was sitting at the front with three girls, all of them much younger than Alice. Alice stopped in the doorway. Sarah, who sat on Darren's left, laughed at something he said and turned to look back up the aisle. For a moment, her gaze locked with Alice's, then Sarah turned back around and elbowed Darren. Darren turned and looked Alice in the eye. Alice held her ground. Darren smirked and turned back around, saying something that made all three girls burst into laughter.

Alice let out a breath she hadn't realized she'd been holding. *Okay. Balcony,* she thought, *I can see better from up there anyway.* As she pivoted, her gaze fell on Darren's roommate, Gabe. He was sitting on the back row of the chapel, watching her. Alice quickly looked away and went to climb the stairs.

"Hey," someone called from behind her. Alice reached the top and turned to see that Monica was standing at the foot of the stairs. "You all right?" Monica called up.

Alice shook her head. Monica jogged up the stairs and gave her a hug. "What happened?" she whispered.

"Darren broke things off."

"Seriously?"

Alice nodded.

"I'm so sorry. Here. Sit here." She pointed to a couple of empty seats, and Alice sat down. Monica sat next to her and kept her arm around her. "How did it happen?" she asked.

"He's leaving next term for an internship, and he doesn't want to do the long-distance thing again."

Monica lowered her brows. "When did he decide—"

"No idea," said Alice. "He never mentioned the possibility that he'd be gone next term."

"Oh . . ."

"Yeah," said Alice. "I wish we could work things out, but in what—three weeks? Four? I don't even remember when the law school breaks for the holidays." She shook her head. *It would take a miracle for us to work things out in such a short time.*

"There are other guys in the ward," Monica reminded her. She reached over with her left hand and took Alice's right. "You won't be single for long."

"Hi, Alice," came a male voice.

Alice looked up and saw that Spencer Sharp had paused near the end of their pew. "Hi," she answered, flashing him a smile as he took a seat a few rows away.

Monica glanced at him and then turned back to Alice with a smirk.

Alice gave Monica's hand a squeeze and felt metal. She looked down and opened Monica's hand to get a better look. Sure enough, Monica was wearing a ring—a beautiful diamond solitaire.

"Yeah," said Monica. "I was going to tell you about that, but now didn't seem like the best time."

"You're engaged?"

"Uh-huh. Sean proposed last night on the temple grounds. We're getting married around Christmastime, provided he can get a cancellation or permission by then."

"A what?"

"Cancellation. A temple divorce from his first wife. Or permission to get sealed again. I guess he started the process last summer, but it can take a long time."

"So you're leaving the ward?"

Monica nodded. "Yeah, I'm sorry. But you won't be alone for long. I can feel it."

* * *

Relief Society was the hardest part of the day. Sunday School had been a nice break as there were only four people in the class, two of them the missionaries. Relief Society meant facing the other sisters in the ward. When Alice walked into the Relief Society room, Monica grinned and patted the empty chair beside her. Alice squared her shoulders and went to sit down.

On the other side of Monica sat Leslie, Sarah Nagel's best friend, who was busy admiring Monica's ring and exclaiming things like, "You're sooo lucky!" and "It's beautiful!" Her white-blond hair was up in pigtails, and she looked like a little girl in her enthusiasm.

Alice took a deep breath. "Congratulations," she said to her friend. "I think I forgot to tell you that."

Monica smiled and shook her head. "It's all right. I really am sorry about what happened with Darren."

"So did you guys really break up?" Leslie asked, her eyes twinkling with excitement.

Alice looked from her to Monica and back again. "Um . . ." she said.

From behind her, Alice heard someone whisper, "He is so cute."

Alice looked back over her shoulder and frowned.

"Ignore it," said Monica.

"I know," the other girl whispered back. "He asked Mandy to go out with him next Friday."

Okay, that really *hurts,* Alice thought. *He's already asking other people out? Here in the ward?* "How am I supposed to ignore it?" Alice asked.

"They're just excited that there's someone else to date," said Monica. "They don't mean any disrespect."

Oh, of course, thought Alice. *They mean to rejoice over my breakup in the nicest possible way.* She did her best to ignore the whispers.

* * *

As soon as Relief Society was over, Alice bolted for the parking lot. Her car was parked at the far end, but she reached it before anyone else emerged from the meetinghouse. Throughout the course of Relief Society, she'd learned Darren's social calendar for the next three weeks, and none of it involved her.

With clumsy hands, she pulled her keys out of her purse and tried to jam the right one into its slot in the door. She was vaguely aware of the sound of a motorcycle buzzing its way toward her, but she didn't look up until it pulled up behind her car and stopped.

She stood up straighter to see who it was. It was Gabe. He'd pulled his helmet off and was looking at her with concern. "You all right?" he asked.

"Fine," she said. "Just need to get home."

Gabe moved his bike a few feet closer, then shut off the motor and propped it on its kickstand.

"I heard about last night," he said.

"Yeah, well." Alice shrugged. She looked back at the meetinghouse. People were beginning to stream out of it. Leslie and Sarah stepped out the door, laughing about something.

"So what just happened?" asked Gabe.

She turned her attention back to him. "Nothing." She kept her voice calm and level.

"But you came running out here. I thought maybe Darren said something to you or—"

"No," Alice cut him off. "I'm just . . . I'm escaping from some girls in Relief Society who can't keep quiet about how happy they are that he's back on the market." She resumed fumbling with her keys and ended up dropping them on the pavement. *Get a grip.* She stooped to pick them up, but Gabe beat her to it and handed them back to her.

"That's awful," he said. "I'm sorry."

"It's all right." Alice took her car key between her thumb and forefinger and shook it loose from the other keys. This time she took a deep breath to steady herself before inserting it in the car door. It slid home, and she twisted it, popping open the lock.

"For what it's worth," said Gabe, "I think he made a big mistake."

She paused and looked up at him. "Well . . . thanks," she said. She tugged open the door and ducked inside.

Gabe went back to stand by his bike and watched her pull out and drive off. He waved as she drove past. Alice waved back.

* * *

Alice got home and shut the door firmly behind her. "Cynth?" she called out.

There was no answer.

Just as well. She went to the refrigerator, took out some leftovers, and put them in the microwave. Then she sat down on the couch and rested her forehead in her hands.

What do I do now? After a moment's pondering she got down on her knees and folded her arms. "Lord," she began. Then she stopped herself. *How do I put this? I can't just say, Lord why did you lie to me, can I? How about, Lord, are you real or am I going insane? That makes absolutely no sense in a prayer. Do I even want to be praying right now? How else can I figure out what I'm supposed to do? Lord, I need help. Please.*

The microwave beeped, but before she could get up, her cell phone rang. She fished it out of her purse and looked at the display. The number wasn't one she recognized. She flipped the phone open with her thumb and said, "Hello?"

"Hello." It was a woman's voice on the other end, an older woman's, and she had an accent of some kind. Spanish? Italian? Alice couldn't tell. "I . . . is this . . . Alice O'Donnell?" she asked.

"Yes."

"Hi. My name is Lorraine Spinelli. You are a-a money manager?"

It irked Alice when people called her at home. She did her best to keep her tone polite. "I'm an accountant. I'm sorry, I don't believe I know you."

"I'm . . . my son is Gabriel? Gabe? You call him Gabe?"

"Oh," Alice started.

"I . . . please, I need help."

"Did Gabe give you my number?"

"No. He does not know that I'm calling you. Please don't say anything to him." The woman sniffled. "I am wondering if you can help me. I know you don't know me, but I don't know who else to call." She started to cry in earnest.

Um . . . right. Alice knew the logical thing to do was hang up. She never could understand why people thought that just because she was friendly and cared about people, she deserved to have to work for free. Besides that, Darren had already warned her that the Spinelli family had money problems. Getting involved was not a good idea.

"S-Sister Spinelli?" she said.

"Oh no, don't call me that. I haven't been to church in ten years. I should not be bothering you, but you see . . . I have just inherited some money from my brother-in-law, and I am very, very bad with money. I have lost a lot of money. I . . . if I put this check in my bank account, it will disappear. But I have a daughter to support and no husband. My husband is dead. Never mind. I should not have called you." She continued to cry.

There it was, a request for free work, and Alice knew she ought to turn it down on principle. People rarely took her free advice anyway. Except for once, years ago, when Alice had gotten tired of waiting in a restaurant. She'd gone to look for the waitress and found her sitting in the back alley, sobbing, a piece of paper clutched in one hand. The piece of paper, it had turned out, was an acceptance letter to an interior design program. The tears were because the waitress didn't think she could afford the tuition. Alice had given her a ten-minute lecture on education loans, which then led to many free dinners at the restaurant and a friendship. Now Cynthia was an interior designer and Alice's roommate.

"What do you need, exactly?" Alice asked the woman on the phone.

"To know what to do! I don't understand money."

Alice chewed the inside of her cheek. "Do you know how to balance a checkbook?" she said.

"I . . . no. What does that mean?"

"How well do you read English?"

"I read. But it is not my first language."

"And when your husband was alive, he kept all the accounts?"

"Yes."

"And you never learned."

"It's true."

"And . . . you can't go talk to your bishop?"

"I'm not a member of the Church anymore. They took me off the rolls."

Alice winced. *So much more than I ever wanted to know about Gabe's mother,* she thought. "I'm not sure what I can do," she admitted. "I mean . . . do you need help setting up a budget or . . . or what?"

"Maybe. I just don't want this money to be gone in a few months. Gabriel, he keeps the accounts usually, but he has school. I don't want to take up more of his time."

"How much money are you talking about here?"

"The inheritance? Seventy thousand dollars."

"Well . . . that's a lot."

"I had more. When Gabriel's father died he left us more. But that is gone now. Gabriel . . . he is still mad."

"Never mind that." Alice took a deep breath. This was no small project, but already the woman had stopped crying. "If you want to talk about your monthly expenses and income," said Alice, "it shouldn't be too hard to work out a budget. Just a simple one."

"Yes? Would you help me do that?"

"I . . . sure . . . but I need to tell you again, this is not what I do for a living, okay? I can tell you my opinion, and that's all."

"It would help."

"All right." Alice got up and went to her room to fetch a notebook. "First question, are you in debt? Do you carry credit card balances?"

8

Lorraine

Cynthia walked in a couple of hours later. Alice was still in her room talking to Lorraine. The battery had run low on her phone, so she'd had to plug it in. "Right," Alice said, "so your telephone company can analyze your phone calls and name a better long-distance plan for you. The one you have sounds too expensive."

"How do I do that?"

"Read me the top of your bill."

Lorraine did, and Alice went to boot up her laptop. Cynthia came to stand in Alice's doorway. "Who are you talking to?" she asked.

Alice put her hand over the mouthpiece. "Long story," she mouthed. "Okay, what was that, Lorraine? Right. I'm going to their Web site. Let's see here . . ."

Out of the corner of her eye, Alice saw Cynthia walk over to her bed, sit down, then lean forward to look over Alice's shoulder.

"Yes," said Alice, when the Web site popped up. "They've got a flat-rate long-distance plan, and that would be better for you. Unlimited calls for twenty dollars a month."

Lorraine paused, then said, "Yes?"

"Yes, so you need to call them and switch your plan. Now, let's go back to your landlord charging you to fix your window. You shouldn't pay for things like that. That's the landlord's job."

"Alice," Cynthia cut in, "it's two, and it doesn't look like you've eaten lunch. Aren't you starving?"

Alice looked at the clock. To Lorraine she said, "Sorry, that was my roommate. I'm afraid I have to go, but do you think you can finish balancing your checkbook?"

"I think, yes," said Lorraine.

"Okay, so . . . you've got my number. Call if you need more help."

"Yes, okay. *Thank* you. You're so kind!"

"No, seriously, it's . . . it's all right." They said their good-byes and hung up.

Cynthia still stood in the doorway and was giving Alice a quizzical look. "And that was?"

Alice sighed. "Gabe's mother."

"Who's Gabe?"

"Darren's roommate."

"Who?"

"Darren's roommate. The kid that walked in on me in that totally embarrassing situation? Him."

"And she called you, why?"

"Good question," said Alice. "Because she has financial problems."

"And Gabe—"

"Nope," said Alice, "he didn't give her my number. I don't know how she got it."

"That's *weird*."

"Yes, it is, but what am I supposed to do? Tell her to get lost?"

"No. I might, but you never would." Cynthia smiled. "You want lunch?"

* * *

The next day felt empty. Work dragged on, and when Alice got home, the evening ahead seemed interminable. Cynthia made an elaborate dinner that Alice barely tasted. Then, at seven, Lorraine called. Alice found herself all too eager to talk to her about new ways to cut her expenses. There was nothing quite like someone else's problems to get her mind off her own.

Two nights after that, Lorraine called again, and Alice found herself drawing up a spreadsheet of her spending habits and accounts. Over the rest of the week, Alice elaborated on it, putting in all kinds of detail. It took care of her free time. Each night she read her scriptures, and each night and morning she prayed, but her prayers felt hollow. It was hard for Alice to pour her heart into them.

The next week in church, Gabe was as friendly as ever. "Hey, Alice," he said when she walked into the foyer. "How've you been?" He'd been sitting in one of the chairs with his scriptures open, but when he saw her he flipped them shut and stood.

Alice gave him a rueful smile.

He frowned. "I'm sorry."

"How's your family?" she asked.

"My sister's good, I think. I haven't seen her in a while."

Alice took a good look at his reaction. He didn't seem the slightest bit uncomfortable or uneasy. *So he really doesn't know about his mother's phone calls,* she thought. *Weird.*

A laugh rang out in the hallway. Sarah's. Then Alice heard Darren's voice. "Okay, so dating Alice wasn't the best idea. I admit that." They were still around the corner, so Alice couldn't see them. She turned and dashed up the stairs to the balcony, desperate to escape before they found her.

* * *

That afternoon Alice skipped choir again. Cynthia was out when Alice arrived back at their apartment. Alice wasn't sure if she appreciated the opportunity to be alone or not. *The problem with Sunday,* she thought as she flopped down on the couch, *is that it gives me way too much time to think.*

Did I do something wrong when I was dating Darren? Is it my fault it didn't work out? That thought made her stomach turn. *Come on,* she chided herself, *you were yourself, you told him you loved him, you followed the commandments. The Lord should be pleased with that, right?*

She folded her arms and bowed her head.

Maybe, she thought, *I don't have to make a final decision about my job, so I don't need to worry about getting engaged. No, that doesn't make any sense. The company's sold, the documents signed, and my job in LA won't exist in a few months. Okay, come on, Alice, focus and pray.*

Maybe I misinterpreted that prompting? How though?—I'm not dating anyone else. I'm angry at Darren. He's been a total jerk for quite a while. If he wanted to get back together he'd have to make the first move—but wait, am I supposed to be thinking stuff like that after having a revelation like I did? Alice . . . focus.

It was no use. Even after she'd quieted these thoughts, no prayer came to her mind. It was like swimming through molasses. She got up and went to get some leftovers out of the fridge.

Lorraine called just as Alice was sitting down to lunch.

"Hello, Alice?" she said. "Do you have a moment?"

"Sure." *Talk as long as you want,* Alice thought. She headed back to her room to get her laptop.

"The budget we did?" said Lorraine. "I forgot an expense. Gina's dance lessons. I would like to be able to pay for them, or at least part of them. They are very expensive."

"Gina?" Alice hefted her computer, brought it back into the front room, and began to set it up on the table.

"My daughter. Gabriel's sister."

"She's a dancer?"

"She's only fourteen, but she wants to be a dancer, yes. Her brother is paying for her dance lessons now, and that isn't right. He needs money for himself."

"Oh, okay." *So that's where his money from the restaurant is going.*

Cynthia breezed in the front door just then, letting it slam shut behind her. "You're here," she said. "Okay, color-test time!" She went to the kitchen, got a newspaper, and came over to spread it across the rest of the table.

Lorraine said, "I keep telling her how expensive it is, but she doesn't want to stop dancing. She thinks this will be her job."

"Well, if that's what she wants," said Alice, "she should give it a try."

Cynthia went back to her room and reemerged with two small cans of paint, which she set down on the newspaper. Each can made a metallic thud.

"It is not a good job, though," said Lorraine.

"Well," Alice replied, flashing Cynthia a smile, "my roommate is an interior designer. Not an easy job to get either."

Cynthia gave her a quizzical look as she began prying the lids off the paint cans.

"A professional designer?" asked Lorraine.

"Yeah, with a good job."

"But her family probably had more money."

"Nope." Alice shook her head. "She financed the schooling and everything on her own."

"With lots of help from my roommate," said Cynthia, loud enough for Lorraine to hear. Then she lowered her voice and said, "Who is that?"

Alice put her hand over the phone. "Lorraine. Turns out her daughter's a dancer."

"Gina is a good dancer," Lorraine admitted. "I just worry about her."

"Well, let's factor the cost of lessons into your budget," said Alice. "Give me some numbers. And then let's talk investments for the inheritance money like we said we would, all right? I'm thinking you may want to put it into real estate or equity. You may even consider a 529 for Gina."

"I'm confused already."

"It's all right. Let me explain."

While she spoke, Cynthia painted a large patch of dark red on the wall and stepped back to frown at it. Then she fetched another brush and painted another patch of slightly different red on the wall next to the first patch. The smell of wet paint mingled with the spicy scent of Alice's lunch, which still sat untouched on the table. Alice watched with interest as Cynthia squinted at each patch of color, then went to get a third can of paint. They both looked fine to Alice, but Cynthia was particular about these things.

Once Cynthia had spread three different colors on the wall, she packed the paints away and went to rinse out the brushes. Alice looked at the three blobs of color and noted that they all went very nicely with the beige carpet and the honey-colored wood of the dining room table.

"So," she said to Lorraine, "did any of that make sense?"

"Yes. I am taking notes here. A moment." Lorraine muttered to herself in another language.

"Do you speak Italian?" Alice ventured.

"No, I am Argentinian, from Buenos Aires. I was speaking Spanish."

"Oh yeah?"

"But I am also Italian. My family came from Italy to South America. Gabriel's father was Italian too, from New York. So my children are one hundred percent Italian, but they don't speak it, I don't speak it, and their father didn't speak it." She laughed.

"Uh-huh."

"Did you see Gabriel at church this week?"

"Yes."

"How is he?"

"Seems fine. I don't really know him all that well."

"Is he dating anyone?"

"Um . . . I don't think so. I don't know."

"Silly boy. He is very picky, you know?"

An image of Gabe and Sarah together flashed in Alice's mind, but she immediately felt ashamed. She scratched the side of her nose and picked at her food with her fork. After a few seconds, she realized that Lorraine had gone silent. "Lorraine?" said Alice.

"About Gabriel," said Lorraine.

"Yes?"

"He watches all of the accounts. He gets the statements from the bank and gives me money once a week. He leaves it with his sister."

"I see."

"Even when he went on his mission, he handled all of the money. He gave his sister a check card and told her how much to give me. If I put this money in the bank, he—"

"You haven't deposited the check yet?" said Alice.

Lorraine paused. "No," she said. "I would have to give it to Gabriel to do that, and I don't want him to know I have this money."

"Whose name is the account in? His?" She forcibly pulled her thoughts away from the tax implications.

"He—I don't know."

"Can you read to me off a statement—"

"I don't get statements."

"Not even copies?"

"No. Only Gabriel gets these."

Alice heaved a sigh. "Well . . . there's nothing stopping you from opening your own account at another bank."

"I don't know how."

"It isn't hard. But if Gabe's been helping you, maybe you should tell him—"

"Please." There was desperation in Lorraine's voice.

"It's your money," said Alice. "Let's get it into an account in your own name."

9

And That's That

Darren managed to date most of the rest of the Relief Society in the weeks that followed, or so it seemed. Every Sunday he sat next to someone new, and about half a dozen hangers-on sat around them. What was even worse was that he acted as if breaking up with Alice hadn't affected him much. He'd smile at her in the hallways but wouldn't stop to talk. She never caught him looking at her. He seemed perfectly happy to move on.

She tried to talk to him, to say hello in passing or ask him how he was, but he always responded with a slightly amused look, as if he found her attempts at conversation pathetic. Alice soon learned that her self-esteem fared better if she just stayed away. So she began to avoid him at church—only to go home and worry herself to shreds. *Time's passing,* she thought. *In a few weeks, I'll know for sure that the revelation was false. It felt so true, though, so . . . what does that mean?* She'd pace and ponder about it, but then Lorraine would call, or her mother, or Cynthia would come to her with ideas for redoing the front room, and Alice would focus on that instead.

Then, one Sunday, several weeks later, Darren was gone. He hadn't even bothered to say good-bye. He simply wasn't at church one week, and Alice realized that he'd left. She stood in the doorway of the chapel, looked over the congregation, and wondered whether she should feel hurt or relieved. She definitely felt confused.

Gabe slipped past her, and before she could think, she put her hand on his arm.

"Hey, Alice," he said, stopping and turning toward her. When he saw her expression, his grew serious. "He moved out Wednesday."

"Right." She nodded. "So . . . you have a new roommate?"

"Yeah." He pointed across the room at a short, dark-haired boy who looked about Gabe's age. "Ely."

"Ely, huh? Is he from a farm in Nebraska or something?" She realized that she was being rude and shut her mouth.

But Gabe only smiled. "Ely, as in short for Elijah. He's from New Mexico."

"That's a pretty state."

"Yeah." Gabe's expression made it clear he'd never seen New Mexico but was willing to take her word for it. "He's nice. Not as much of a slob as Darren."

"That would be a relief."

Gabe nodded and Alice expected him to leave, but he stayed, seeming concerned. "I tried to call Darren," he said, "about his security deposit, but he's already changed his cell number. You don't happen to know the new one, do you?"

Alice shook her head. *So he really is gone,* she thought, *and that's that.*

"You all right?" Gabe asked her.

"Yes, I'm fine. I'll see you around." She spotted Monica sitting in the back row and went over to sit with her. She was comparing engagement rings with two other girls. *They're probably no older than twenty, and they're already getting married and leaving the ward.* There were now almost a dozen weddings planned for winter break.

"Hi," said Alice.

"Alice!" said Monica, turning toward her. "Guess what?"

"What?"

"The cancellation came through!"

"The what?"

"Sean's temple divorce."

"Oh, well that's good." Alice opened her purse and rummaged around for her chapstick.

"So we're getting sealed next week!"

Alice fumbled and nearly dropped her purse on the floor. "Next week?"

"Yes!" Monica clapped her hands together. "I am so excited!"

"No way," said Alice. "What happened to just before Christmas?"

"Well . . . this'll be just before Christmas."

"But you've only been engaged a month," she protested.

"Four weeks."

"Or in other words, a month."

"It isn't *that* short of an engagement."

"Compared to what?" asked Alice.

Monica laughed. "Well, outside the Church maybe it's short."

"Mon, you can't leave me alone so soon. I'm . . . still a vulnerable new convert." She forced a smile she didn't quite feel.

"You'll be fine."

"You don't know that. How do you know I won't go inactive and start putting anti-Mormon literature on people's cars while they're in church?"

"Oh, don't be ridiculous. Look, I was wondering if you'd help with the reception. We're having it here, in the cultural hall."

"You mean the gym." Alice still had trouble with the term *cultural hall*. The first time she'd heard it, she'd assumed the person was talking about an exhibit hall in the church building, perhaps a place where Latter-day Saints displayed their handicrafts and sang hymns. The fact that the "cultural hall" was an indoor basketball court had come as a shock. Latter-day Saints had strange ideas about what constituted "culture."

Monica gave her a patient smile. "My mother's going to need help setting up," she said.

Alice tugged her datebook out of her purse and flipped it open. "And this is next Saturday?" The day was blank.

"Yes. The sealing is at ten. So the reception will start at ten thirty or so. People can just walk here from the temple."

"All right." Alice penciled in the time. "And how long is the reception? Five minutes? Or is that too long for a Mormon reception."

"*You're* in a mood today," said Monica.

Alice realized that she'd crossed the line. "Sorry." She forced a smile. "It's been a rough week. I am happy for you. And I really do want to help."

Monica slipped her arms around Alice and gave her a hug. "You won't be alone when I leave," she said.

Alice shook her head but said nothing.

* * *

"Cynth," Alice said the following Friday night, "are you free tomorrow?"

Cynthia was up on a stepladder screwing halogen bulbs into one of the kitchen light fixtures. "Hmm? I was going to paint trim."

"So if I help you paint, will you help me at ten in the morning?"

"Do what?"

"Cook."

Cynthia looked down in surprise. "What?"

"Monica asked me to help her mother 'set up' for her wedding reception tomorrow—"

"She's getting married *tomorrow?*"

"Yes, but that's not the scariest part. It turns out that 'setting up' means cooking hors d'oeuvres. I just found out."

"Why'd she ask you?"

"I don't know. I guess it didn't occur to her that I don't know how to cook."

"No way are you going to be set loose in a kitchen on your friend's wedding day, Alice." Cynthia climbed down from the ladder and moved it over to the other light fixture. "No offense," she said, "but you could do property damage and poison everyone."

"See, I knew you'd understand."

"So . . . ten?"

"Please?"

"Sure. Are people going to act all weird around me?" Cynthia climbed up the stepladder, looked around for a moment, then pointed pleadingly at the box of bulbs on the table.

Alice went to fetch it and handed it to her friend. "What do you mean? That they'll try to give you a Book of Mormon?"

"Or ask me how many kids I have or . . . you know, talk about craft projects the whole time."

"I don't know. I just ignore that kind of stuff."

"Which is a talent, really."

"You're a saint, Cynth."

"No, by definition *you're* a saint. I'm most definitely not."

* * *

Monica's mother was only too happy to have another helper show up the next morning. Alice and Cynthia walked into the church kitchen at 9:45, and Sister Valdez looked ready to pull her hair out. Fortunately, Cynthia took the recipe Sister Valdez was holding, glanced at it, and managed to grab exactly the right kitchen utensil, brandishing it in a way that bespoke competence. Sister Valdez calmed down at once.

"I need to get over to the temple," she said. "Other people were supposed to come . . . but I guess they'll come later. Sister Boone is supposed to be here to cook!"

"We'll be fine," said Cynthia as she started rummaging in the cupboards. Alice did her best to look like she wasn't just standing around, but she knew better than to try to help Cynthia cook.

"All right, see you in forty-five minutes." Sister Valdez darted out.

"Okay," said Alice. "So we have forty-five minutes to do all the hors d'oeuvres and set everything up and . . . this is crazy."

"Go set up tables or something," said Cynthia. She walked over to the refrigerator and peered inside. "This isn't hard." She pulled some phyllo dough out of the freezer. Alice took one look at it and headed for the gym.

The gym had a beautiful wood floor and was large enough for a full basketball court, complete with baskets. According to Monica, there was supposed to be a dance floor at one end, tables and chairs at the other, and a buffet table along one wall. *And I get to decide where.* Alice frowned.

Just as she located the folding tables, Gabe walked in, followed by his roommate, Ely. "You'd better be here to help," Alice said.

"What can we do?" Ely asked.

Alice heaved a sigh of relief and began giving them directions. As she set out the chairs, Gabe and Ely traded quips and hauled the tables into place. As Alice counted out the number of seats, Gabe said to Ely, "Hit me in the stomach."

"Why?" said Ely.

Alice shut her eyes a moment, then resumed counting.

"Just do it. I want to see if it hurts."

"You haven't been working out that long."

"Come on, try it."

Alice sized up the dance floor, wondering if they could make it smaller to leave room for more tables.

"Ooof," said Gabe.

"Ha."

"It didn't hurt."

"Liar. Ouch!"

"Ha! Look who hasn't been working out at all."

The two began to wrestle, then Ely took off across the room, Gabe hot on his heels. Alice tried to ignore the sound of their horseplay as she finished her calculations. The young men ran out one of the doors, in another, then back out into the hallway. "Okay," she called. The footsteps stopped, and Gabe and Ely stuck their heads around the doorframe. "I need four more tables—two there, one there, and one there." She pointed.

"Okay," said Ely, punching Gabe in the stomach.

Gabe doubled over and said something under his breath that sounded like a curse.

Cynthia stepped in with a cookie sheet of little puffed pastry hors d'oeuvres in each hand. "Someone who wants me to call her Sister Boone is here," she said. "She's got cookies and temple mints. What are temple mints?"

Alice shrugged.

"Mints shaped like the temple," Gabe supplied. Another boy walked in, and Gabe greeted him with a punch in the arm. "S'up?"

"Right," said Alice, "of course."

Cynthia put her hors d'oeuvres down on the buffet table and left. Alice began spreading tablecloths on the rest of the tables, and a moment later, Cynthia returned with a tray of mints that she showed to Alice. They were pressed into the shape of the Salt Lake Temple.

Which is weird, considering they're getting married just across the parking lot in the LA Temple, thought Alice. *Maybe the temple mint mold-makers only do Salt Lake.*

Ely began to set up the sound system at one end of the cultural hall while Gabe and the other boy began hanging decorations at the other end. Alice approached the buffet table, where Cynthia was arranging the puffed pastries on plates, and was immediately warned back.

"Away from the food!" said Cynthia.

"But it's already cooked."

"I said back. Let *me* arrange it."

"Cynth, you're embarrassing me in front of all my church friends. If the guys hear you, they'll tell the rest of the ward, and I'll never get a date."

Alice had whispered, but a bark of laughter from Ely proved she'd still been too loud. He'd come over by Cynthia and was doing something with the wiring along the wall. "Whatever," he said. "My sister can't cook, and I think half of Snow College has proposed to her."

"Oh, that's reassuring. So if I get desperate, I can always go to Snow College."

"Yeah, really desperate," said Ely. "It's a junior college in Ephraim, Utah. I don't think there are many professional money manager people there."

"I'd rather stay single," said Cynthia. She and Ely exchanged amused smiles. "Okay," she said. "I'm going home to start painting. You stay away from the food." She pointed at Alice with mock severity, then left.

Commotion from the hallway let Alice know that the wedding party had arrived. She smoothed her skirt and ran her hand over her hair, hoping she looked calm and composed.

Monica swept in, wearing a formfitting white dress and a veil that nearly touched the floor. Alice immediately felt disappointed for her friend. *She just got married in the temple,* she thought, *and now she comes to a reception in a gym with crepe-paper decorations and plastic tablecloths.*

But if Monica minded in the least, she didn't show it. She came right over to Alice and gave her a hug. "Oh, thank you!" she said. "Mom said you saved the day!"

"My roommate did," said Alice. "She did all the cooking. She saved your life."

Monica gave her a baffled look, then turned as the rest of the wedding party came in. Sean looked attractive in his tux, and his young daughter and son were dressed in their Sunday best. Three other girls walked in wearing bridesmaid dresses, accompanied by three men in tuxes. Family streamed in behind them. Alice didn't know any of them.

Soon the room was crowded with people hugging and laughing and socializing. Ely put on some atmosphere music, then went to join everyone else.

Alice found herself standing alone. She folded her arms across her chest and tried not to look awkward.

10

Dancing

Half an hour later, Ely put on some dance music, and everyone paired up. Alice sat by herself, holding a little plate with a half-eaten temple mint on it.

Well, she thought, *I guess I should get used to this. Monica's out of the ward now, so I'll do a lot of sitting by myself, surrounded by people I barely know.*

Someone's shadow fell across her, and she looked up. Gabe was standing by her chair.

"Hi," she said.

"Hi. You want to dance?"

Alice realized then that a slow song had just started to play. "Um . . . sure," she said.

As they made their way out onto the dance floor, Gabe put one hand on her waist and with the other held her hand. His skin was smooth and cool to the touch.

"So, how have you been?" he asked.

"Fine. You?"

"Been good. I'm kinda glad Darren's gone. But maybe I shouldn't say that."

"You can say it to me," said Alice. "I'm supposed to be the bitter ex-girlfriend, right?"

Gabe smiled. "Think he'd be jealous right now?"

"No," said Alice. The image of Gabe and Ely horsing around flashed in her mind. "No offense, but you're twenty-one."

Gabe laughed. "So . . . how old are you, exactly?"

"Twenty-six."

"And you have a . . . master's degree?"

"I'm a CPA," she said. "And you? What are you studying?"

"Chemical engineering."

"Oh, taking all the easy classes, I see."

This time his eyes twinkled when he smiled. "I want to go to med school," he said.

"That's a lot of school."

Gabe shrugged. "Well . . . yeah, and it'll be hard. It's what I want, though."

"Well, you obviously know how to manage a full schedule. I don't know how you find time to do everything you do."

"What, school and work?"

"School, work, your calling, coming to help out today, not to mention dating all the girls that must come beating down your door."

Gabe actually seemed to blush at that. He looked away. "Whatever," he muttered.

Alice realized then that they were dancing rather close, and she missed a step. He met her gaze again, and she was suddenly very aware of how green his eyes were. How his mouth quirked just so, hinting at a smile.

The final notes of the song were playing. Alice let go of him as soon as the music died out, thanked him for the dance, and returned to her seat. *Alice,* she thought, *you have problems. He's just a kid. You're going to traumatize him.*

Gabe, for his part, disappeared out the door, and after about five minutes, Alice realized he'd left. *Oh, that was smooth,* she thought to herself. *Drive away the only friend you have left in the ward.*

* * *

When she got back to the apartment, the door was open. Alice thought that was odd. As she drew nearer, she could hear voices.

"I told you, she isn't here," came Cynthia's voice.

"When do you expect her back?"

Alice froze.

"What makes you think she lives here, Mr. O'Donnell?"

"I don't know what I ever did to make her hate me this much." Alice's father sounded hurt. "I know she lives here. I recognize her things."

Alice shut her eyes and took a deep breath. "Hi, Dad," she said, stepping through the doorway.

Her father and Cynthia stood in the middle of the room. At the sound of Alice's voice, her father turned. Cynthia backed away, then headed for her room.

Alice shut the front door behind her, leaning back on it to make sure it latched. Her father was considerably thinner than he'd been the last time she'd seen him. His left hand was sans wedding ring. Alice glanced at this, then looked him in the eye.

"Allie," he began.

She folded her arms across her chest.

"Did you get my notes I left at your work?" he asked.

"Yes, I did."

"You're going to tell me to leave, aren't you? You're going to say you don't want me in your life anymore."

"No," said Alice, "but if you've come to complain about Mom, you've come to the wrong place."

Her father nodded. "So, that's what this has all been about."

"Just like I've told you so many times."

"Well," he stood up straighter, "I haven't come to complain about your mother."

"Good."

"I've come because I have news."

Alice shook her head. "I don't want to hear it."

"I've met someone, Allie."

"I thought you'd already met someone. You're on your second girlfriend already?"

"Well, actually—"

"You're still married."

"Only technically."

"What's that supposed to mean?"

"That the marriage is over, Allie. I gave it thirty years. If I'd been smart, I might have walked out after one, but I didn't. Just because I worked on it for thirty years doesn't mean I have to go on like that."

"It's not over in Mom's mind."

"I know." He looked down.

"When you decided to walk out, she fell apart."

"I can imagine."

"And you left me to pick up the pieces."

"No, Allie, that's not your job, and if you try to make it your job, your mother will never learn how to do it herself. Now you're getting a taste of what *I* lived with all of those years. It's exhausting, Allie. I just . . . I couldn't do it anymore."

"I thought you said you weren't here to complain about Mom."

"You're the one asking questions. I'm just giving you straight answers."

"*Look*. You never said stuff like this before. For the past twenty years—"

"I know. I kept my peace. That's how it was, though, the entire time, and now that you're all grown up, I don't see why I should pretend any longer."

Alice rolled her eyes and shook her head. "This is exactly why I didn't give you my new number."

"I just wanted to see you. Your number's finally been listed. Or . . . Cynthia's. I assumed it was the same. I miss you, kiddo. This divorce— I don't want it to drive a wedge between us."

"Too late."

His shoulders sagged. "I'd like to invite you to dinner at our place," he said.

"*Our* place?" She folded her arms across her chest again.

"Yes. Her name's Suzie, and we moved in together last week."

"No thanks, Dad. Leave me out of this . . . whatever it is you're doing with your life, okay?"

"Well . . . my offer stays open." His voice was tentative. "Give me a call if you want to reconsider."

The silence stretched between them.

Her father looked away, nodded as if to himself, then said, "If you'll excuse me?" He gestured toward the door.

Alice stepped aside and opened it for him, then shut it once he'd left. *Great,* she thought. *Just what I need—another source of stress.*

* * *

The next day at church, Alice realized she had no one to sit next to. Monica was gone. Gabe met her gaze for a split second, then looked away. Alice took one look around the chapel and decided to go upstairs.

The balcony was still fairly empty. She took a seat on the front row, all the way to one side. No one came to sit next to her.

11

Counsel

No one noticed her again until after New Year's. She was in the hallway outside the chapel and already slightly late for Sunday School when the bishop found her. He was a heavyset man with salt-and-pepper hair and a very round face. "Alice," he said, "could I meet with you for a moment?"

"Sure," she replied. She followed him down the hall and around the corner. His office was on the left—a very square, boxy room, with generic, pressed-wood furniture. Midmorning sunlight streamed in through the window, illuminating the dust mites that floated in the air. A picture of Christ was on one wall next to a picture of the prophet in his suit.

Bishop Baker sat behind the desk and gestured for her to take a seat in one of the chairs. "And go ahead and close the door," he said.

Alice obeyed, and once she was seated, he said, "So, how was your Christmas?"

"Fine," said Alice.

"Did you spend time with family?"

"My mom, yeah."

"That must've been nice."

"Uh-huh," said Alice. *No, not really.* After Christmas, she'd gone online and found her mother a cheap vacation package to Cancun. Anything to get a break from the hours of moping.

"Well," said the bishop, "I called you in here because I figured we should change your calling. You've been a substitute Relief Society teacher for how long?"

"Nine months."

His eyebrows shot up. "Nine months?"

"Yes. Since my baptism, pretty much."

"I didn't realize it had been that long. And you haven't taught once?"

"No. They always called Cathy or Rachel. And now I guess it's Stephanie? Is that her name?"

"Mmm, yes. All right, I was wondering if you'd be willing to serve as a greeter instead."

"Sure," said Alice. "What's a greeter do?"

"They greet everyone as they come in for sacrament meeting and pass out the programs—what?" He stopped when he saw her expression. "What's wrong? You don't want that calling?"

Alice quickly schooled her features. "Um," she said, "is that really a calling? I mean, don't get me wrong . . . it sounds like a great way for me to meet everyone, but . . ."

The bishop laughed. "It's a real calling, I assure you."

"All right."

"Great. We'll release you from your current calling next week and sustain you for this one. And then you can come by here after the meetings and we'll set you apart."

"To be a greeter?"

"Right. We'll set you apart and give you a blessing of counsel at the same time."

Alice stared at him. "Greeters need to be set apart and to have special blessings?"

"Well," said the bishop, "I realize it may sound like a silly calling to you, but everyone who has a calling gets set apart. When I was in a singles ward in Utah, my calling was to fold the programs, and I got set apart for that."

"All right," said Alice. "Is that all?"

"No, actually, there's one other thing."

Alice waited for him to say more, but he just looked at her for a moment.

When he did speak, it was to say, "How have you been lately?"

"It's been a rough few months."

The bishop waited again.

Alice looked away for a moment and tried to guess what he wanted her to say. She drew a blank and turned back to meet his gaze again.

"Anything you'd care to talk about?" he asked. "Is it your parents?"

"Yes, that's been rough."

"Anything besides your parents? Monica leaving? Your breakup with Darren?"

"Well," said Alice, "yes, there is that."

"That still bothers you? Even now?"

"Sure. I really cared about him."

"I see. Well . . . I'm sorry to hear that. I mean, not that you cared about him, but that he hurt you so much."

She shrugged. "That's life."

"It is. Now, what is it you're not telling me?"

Alice raised an eyebrow. "What?"

"You're holding something back. I can tell."

Alice looked away. "Well . . ."

"Up until a month or so ago, you were very outgoing and confident. Now you're reserved. Maybe I'm reading too much into all this. Maybe it's just you not being very close to anyone in the ward, but my guess, Sister O'Donnell, is that you're struggling spiritually."

"Struggling?"

"Maybe that's too strong a word."

She considered that. She hadn't really prayed for a while, not sincerely and with real intent. She'd tried, but it was so hard. Facing God meant facing questions about the revelation, or whatever it was. "Well," she said, "yeah. Maybe it is the right word."

"Care to tell me about it? Has something happened?"

"Uh . . ."

"Or, more to the point, *what* has happened?"

Alice looked up at him again.

He stared steadily back at her.

Alice steeled herself, took a deep breath, and said, "I . . . the day I got baptized, something . . . happened."

The bishop cocked his head and waited for her to go on. When she didn't, he asked, "Did someone say or do something to you? Someone in the ward?"

"No, nothing like that. It was more of a . . . supernatural experience." She shook her head.

Much to her surprise, the bishop didn't bat an eye. "Elaborate."

"I think I had a revelation."

"What about?"

"Does this happen a lot?" Alice asked.

He shrugged. "Things like this do. Revelations do happen—let's be clear about that. But I often see young people who can't let go of dreams or wishful thoughts. That's common too."

"Oh. Well . . . I've wondered if that was what happened to me. I mean, I did pray about something I really wanted, but what happened was . . . intense—burning in the bosom and all that."

"So you've studied Doctrine and Covenants section nine on revelation?"

"Of course."

"Well, that's good. May I ask what this experience was about, or is that too personal?"

Alice shrugged. "It was . . . about Darren."

"I see. Marriage to Darren?"

"Pretty much. Engagement. Before I have to decide what to do about my job." But her interview for the Phoenix job was the next week. She'd have to make a decision sometime in the next few months.

"And the revelation was specifically about Darren? The Spirit used his name?"

"Yes—wait . . ." Alice considered that. She'd read her journal entry so many times she knew the words by heart. "I asked if I would be engaged to the right man for me," she said. "That's all. I didn't use his name. But I was thinking about Darren, so I assumed—you mean it doesn't necessarily have to be him?"

The bishop shook his head. "No. It probably isn't, given what's happened. And I need to reiterate, it might have all been wishful thinking."

Alice shook her head. "I've considered that a lot. I really don't think it was."

"All right. Fair enough. Has talking about it with me made you feel any better?"

Alice nodded and sat up straighter. It seemed a huge weight had been lifted off her shoulders. "It does, thanks," she said. *I was really dumb not to have come here first,* she thought.

"Good," said the bishop. "Now I have another question for you. Have you thought about going to the temple?"

She shook her head.

"You'll be eligible to receive your endowment in four months. That means you could join the temple prep class in eight weeks or so . . . depends on their lesson schedule. I don't *normally* recommend that singles who aren't going on a mission or getting married do this, but I'd recommend you if you'd like."

Alice shrugged. "I don't know much about the temple."

"There is a group doing baptisms at the temple a week from Tuesday. You don't need a full recommend to do baptisms. Perhaps you should go with them and see what you think."

"Sure, okay."

"Great. Then let's do a recommend interview. I think you could really benefit from setting your endowment as a goal for yourself."

* * *

That afternoon, Alice sat on her bed with her scriptures. According to the Bible Dictionary, the temple was "literally the house of the Lord . . . a holy sanctuary in which sacred ceremonies and ordinances of the gospel are performed . . . A place where the Lord may come . . . the most holy of any place of worship on the earth."

Alice pondered that. *Okay,* she thought, *so the purpose of the temple is to bring us closer to God. Closer how?* She looked at her recommend, a sheet of white paper the bishop had folded in four. *This gets me in,* she thought, *to what is literally the house of the Lord. Do I want to go there?* The answer came to her at once. *Yes,* she thought, *of course I do. I need to. To get more counsel, I'll go to Him.*

The apartment phone rang. Alice heard Cynthia answer it, then say, "Hang on." Cynthia padded down the hall and stuck her head in the door. "Spencer?" she said.

"Who?"

Cynthia shrugged and held the phone out to her. Alice got up to take it.

"Hello?" she said.

"Hi, Alice. It's Spencer Sharp."

"Hi." Alice was confused.

"I'm the ward temple coordinator."

"Oh!" said Alice. "Hi."

"I'm not sure if we've met. I'm the guy—"

"With the really light blond hair who usually passes the sacrament." *And who Monica calls the best catch in the ward.*

"Yeah, that's me. And you're—"

"A redhead. Um . . ."

"Darren Jarmer's girlfriend?"

"Former."

"Oh, really?" His tone became more interested. "Since when?"

"Well, last fall sometime."

"Really? I didn't know. So you're coming to the temple with us on Tuesday?"

"Yes. First time."

"First time?"

"I'm a convert."

"*Really?* That is so great. We'll all meet in front of the temple at seven in the evening."

"Okay."

"So, yeah . . . um . . . see you then. Or I guess I'll see you Sunday *and* then."

"Okay, see you."

She clicked the handset off and took it back out into the front room to hang it up. Cynthia was sitting on the couch, reading.

"Who was that?" she asked.

"A guy from church."

"A cute guy?"

Alice looked over at her. "*Yes,* but don't—"

"Does he have a girlfriend?"

"I don't know."

"Make sure to check."

"Whatever." Alice went back down the hall to her room. She could hear Cynthia chuckling.

12

Spencer

The following Wednesday, Alice was having a slow day at work. *This is what happens when I choose to come into the office during the holidays,* she thought. She'd actually gotten to the bottom of her in-box. It was just before noon, and her job interview wasn't until one that afternoon.

The intercom crackled on. "Alice?"

"Yes?"

"Um—"

"Allie," came her father's voice, "it's Dad. Let me take you to lunch?"

"Oh, hi, Dad. I'm going to have to work through lunch."

"Sir," came the receptionist's voice, "you shouldn't just go—" The intercom switched off.

Alice shook her head and picked up the first document she could lay her hands on. She pretended to be reading it intently when her father walked up and stopped in her doorway, one arm resting casually on the frame. "Too busy for your father?" he asked.

"Hello to you too." Alice put the document down.

"Allie, your mother is in Mexico."

"Yeah, I know."

"Where'd she get the money to do that?"

"I arranged it. It was a Christmas present."

"You did *what?*" He stood up straighter. "We've got a hearing calendared for tomorrow morning!"

"I didn't know that."

"You know your mother. If you're going keep acting as her babysitter, you need to look out for these things. Or is this some petty game you're playing to sabotage our divorce?"

Alice got up from her desk and went to put her hand on the doorknob. "Dad," she said firmly, "do *not* make a scene here. You come in and lower your voice or leave. Is that clear?"

Her father straightened up and strode in. Alice shut the door behind him.

"I'm not trying to cause a scene," he said.

"Do you have anything else to say?"

"Only that I'm angry. You should have known better."

Alice leaned back against the door and folded her arms across her chest. "I don't keep her calendar."

"Well, you ought to check it before you fly her out of the country."

"Please."

Her father sighed with exasperation. "Allie, I'm going to propose to Suzie."

"What?" Alice pushed off from the door. "You're still married."

"But I will be divorced in time to get married this summer. I've indulged your mother's nonsense long enough."

"And you'd define 'nonsense' as what? Trying to get a settlement that she can live off of until she can go back to school or find a job? Trying to put her life back together after her husband walks out on her?"

"Allie, that's enough." He stepped forward and put his face near hers. "I am tired of your attitude," he said in low, forceful voice. "I am *tired* of having you accuse me. I didn't make your mother the person she is."

Alice didn't flinch. "If you don't like my attitude, don't talk to me."

He stepped back, looked at her for a moment, then began to pace. "I spoke to Cynthia this Sunday. I came by to see you. Did you know that?"

Alice shook her head. Cynthia hadn't told her.

"She said you were at church. What's that all about?"

"I was at church."

"*Which* church? I never took you to any church when you were a kid."

Alice set her jaw.

"Allie?"

"The Church of Jesus Christ of Latter-day Saints." She walked quickly to the other side of the room so that the desk was between herself and her father.

"Which church?" Her father looked confused.

"The Mormon Church. I got baptized last year."

"Oh, great. You've joined a cult. Well, that's a positive development."

"Thanks, Dad."

"Allie, I know you better than you know yourself, and I think you've carried this way too far. Blaming me for your mother's problems is one thing, but running off to join a fringe group that happens to be big on marriage and children is quite another. Get out while you still can."

"This is not about you."

"No, it's about you. You affiliating yourself with a bunch of self-righteous, conservative types who don't believe in divorce."

"Yeah, well, they're really into working *through* problems and *honoring* covenants and—"

"Well, doesn't that sound nice? So you can someday have a husband who stays with you even though you make him miserable."

"Thanks, Dad." Alice's patience was wearing thin.

Her father gave her a disgusted look. "I expected better of you."

Alice didn't bother to answer that. She just looked her father in the eye and waited until he looked away.

"Anyhow," he said, "I wondered if you have a number where your mother can be reached."

"I'll give it to her lawyer."

"All right. Do it soon, please."

"I will. Is that all?"

"I suppose."

Alice nodded. "Well, good-bye then." She sat down, picked up the document she'd been holding before, and did her best to look interested in it.

Her father sighed in exasperation and left, leaving the door open.

She squeezed her eyes shut. *Don't cry,* she commanded herself.

After a few minutes, she got up and closed the door again. *Get control, get control,* she thought. *You've got a job interview in an hour.*

* * *

The interview was very straightforward. Alice went to Hank's corner office, sat down across the desk from him, and answered questions about her work, her skills, and her education. Hank was a slim, middle-aged man with thinning hair and a strange habit of nodding the entire time she spoke. Partway through the interview she had to look away in order to avoid getting seasick.

She still hadn't applied for any other jobs in the LA area, so she felt like she'd better act like she cared about this one. At the end of the interview, Hank smiled, shook her hand, and told her, "Well, we'll let you know our decision in the next couple of weeks."

"All right, thank you," replied Alice. "I don't mean to get ahead of myself, but if I am offered a place in Phoenix, how long would I have to decide?"

He nodded enthusiastically. "A while. The office will probably not be ready until July. The construction is on hold right now. Assuming we can get that office open in July, we'd need a response from you by May."

May—four months off.

* * *

The next Sunday, Alice stood at the door of the chapel handing out programs. She hadn't been officially sustained yet, but no one in the bishopric seemed concerned that she'd mess it up too badly.

People slowly trickled in. Leslie came to take a program, but she was by herself. She went into the chapel and sat with Sarah and some other girls her age. Gabe came over to get a program and flashed Alice a smile. She smiled back and couldn't help but wonder when she'd hear from Lorraine again. The woman's last phone call had been nearly a month ago.

A tall blond man appeared at the other end of the hallway. It was Spencer. Alice tried not to stare. *He's not with anyone,* she noticed

He caught sight of her and picked up the pace. "Hey, you're Alice, right?" he said.

She nodded and held out a program to him, which he took, glanced at, then folded in half.

"So," Spencer said, "you're definitely coming Tuesday?"

"Yes."

A couple other people came by and had to reach around him for programs. He didn't seem to notice.

"That really is great. Um . . . yeah." He looked flustered. In all the months they'd been in the ward, Alice had never seen him look the slightest bit ruffled.

"I look forward to it," she said.

"When were you baptized?"

"April."

"Here?"

Again, she nodded.

"Uh-huh." He began to fidget. "So . . . uh . . . yeah. I'll see you Tuesday, I guess." He darted into the chapel.

Alice looked after him. *Okay,* she thought, *I take it he's not involved with anyone.*

* * *

In Relief Society, Alice found a seat at the back of the room. A few seconds later, Leslie came and plunked down in the seat next to her.

"Hi," said Alice, somewhat surprised.

"So, okay, I'm supposed to ask you if you're seeing anyone." Leslie stared up at the ceiling.

"Says who?"

"My *brother*. I think he expects me to be all artful about it." She waved her hands as she spoke. "But I'm not in the mood. Are you seeing anyone? If my brother asks you out, will you go with him? Just say yes or no."

Alice looked at her. "What do you think I should say?"

"I think you should say, 'Yes, Spencer, but don't make your sister do this ever again.'"

"Does he do this a lot?"

"No. He's being all weird right now."

"Okay. Yes. And give him a break, okay?"

"Whatever." Leslie got up and darted out of the room.

Alice looked after her, confused. The meeting would start any minute.

A few seconds later, Leslie returned. "I told him to call you and to leave me alone."

"Fair enough."

"He is such a *dork!*" Leslie went over to sit with her friends in the far corner of the room. Alice shook her head and smiled. *Well, this is a nice development.*

* * *

Two days later, Alice stood with a group outside the LA Temple. Sarah and Leslie sat off by themselves on a bench, whispering and giggling. About half a dozen other ward members milled around on the sidewalk. The lawn had just been watered, so the air was slightly humid, and it was after sunset, so the temple's high-powered floodlights were on. They illuminated the smooth stucco front of the building. Alice stared up at it, tilting her head farther and farther back until she could see the angel Moroni at the top.

"Hi," came a voice from behind her. She looked around and saw that Spencer was standing a few feet away.

"Hi yourself."

"So, I tried calling you yesterday."

"You did?" said Alice.

"In the evening. But no one picked up."

Alice nodded. "If you called the landline, no one was home. I had dinner with a client, and my roommate had to work late"

"Oh, well I was just wondering . . . uh . . . if you want to do something Friday night." He looked her in the eye for a split second then looked away. His eyes were dark brown and very expressive.

"Sure," said Alice.

Gabe suddenly jogged up from the direction of the parking lot. He wore his motorcycle jacket and backpack over his suit. Sarah broke off her whispering in Leslie's ear and leaned forward to look at him.

"All right," said Spencer, "that's everyone. Let's go in."

Alice couldn't help but feel a bit nervous as she headed toward the door.

Still, she followed the others and showed her recommend at the desk. An elderly man dressed in white looked at it and handed her a round, red sticker. "Put this on your clothes," he said.

"It means you're not endowed," explained Gabe. He'd taken a place in line directly behind her.

"Gee, thanks," she replied.

His face flushed. "I don't mean like—just wear the dot."

Alice stuck it to the front of her blouse and followed the group down the stairs.

13

The Temple

After the baptisms, Alice sat on one of the pews in the baptistry and stared down at her hands. Her hair was still wet and was beginning to soak the collar of her blouse. She hadn't wanted to take the time to blow it dry, though.

This gave her more time to sit and reflect. The ordinances were simple enough. She'd been baptized and confirmed for and in behalf of deceased people who hadn't had the opportunity to receive the ordinances while they'd lived. *Proxy work. Kind of like shareholder voting proxies. Or . . . not quite.*

Around her, the rest of the group was whispering among themselves, talking about their day, their plans for afterward, and the like. Alice was surprised that they would talk about worldly matters here. She reached forward and grabbed a set of scriptures from the back of the pew in front of her. Glancing at the spine, she saw that it was a Bible.

She flipped to 1 Corinthians 15:29. "Else what shall they do which are baptized for the dead, if the dead rise not at all? Why are they then baptized for the dead?"

She reread the verse, then shifted her gaze to the rest of the chapter and skimmed it. *What does this have to do with growing closer to God?* she wondered.

I guess acting on my faith in God requires stronger faith. More like a real conviction rather than just a wish. I don't feel like I've got the strongest testimony these days, but I don't feel like I wasted my time here. It all feels right.

Gabe joined her on the pew. He sat at the far end and looked over at her. Alice glanced at him and smiled, and he smiled back. Spencer sat down on the other side of her and said, "About Friday. Are you free at six thirty? Can I pick you up then?"

"Sure," said Alice, "sounds great." She went back to reading the Bible. Spencer lingered a moment longer, then left her alone to think.

Sarah sat down on the other side of Gabe and tried to get a conversation going. His answers were quiet and patient. *Sarah,* Alice thought, *get a clue.* She shook her head.

After a few minutes, Sarah moved to another pew and began talking to another guy. *On the prowl again—which is something else I'm pretty sure we're not supposed to be doing in the temple.*

"So . . ." Gabe, who'd moved toward Alice, whispered, "is this your first time coming?"

Alice looked up at him and nodded.

"It's so great that you're here." His hair was wet but neatly combed, and his clothes showed creases where he'd folded them.

"Thanks," she told him. "Do you come to the temple a lot?"

"Yeah. I try to come every week."

"Every week?"

"Mmm-hmm."

"That's a lot." *There's no way Darren went once a week,* she thought. *I don't know that he went at all while we were going out, except that one time his cousin got married.* "Am I supposed to be coming every week?" she asked.

"No. I mean, you could. But that's for people who have their endowment, really. Are you planning to receive your endowment?"

"I don't know." Alice glanced back down at the Bible in her lap, closed it, and turned her attention to Gabe. "I want to, I think, but I don't know anything about it."

"Have you read *The Holy Temple?*"

Alice shook her head.

"It's by Elder Packer. And there's this little pamphlet that's got excerpts from the book in it and pictures."

"Pictures?" asked Alice. "Of what?"

"Some of the rooms in the temple and—"

"Rooms *in* the temple?"

"Uh-huh." Gabe paused and looked at her for a moment. "If you go to the visitors' center next door, they've got a picture of the garden room of this temple," he said. He pointed in the direction of the visitors' center.

"I didn't know that was allowed."

"Well, I think the pictures were taken before the temple was dedicated. I mean, the public can tour a temple before it's dedicated and see what it looks like."

"True," conceded Alice.

"I have a copy of *The Holy Temple*, if you want to borrow it."

Alice shrugged. "I'd like that. Thanks."

"I'll bring it to church on Sunday."

Alice smiled at him again. *I guess we're back to being friends. That's a relief.*

* * *

That evening when Alice got home, Cynthia stuck her head out of her room and said, "There's a letter for you from your work. I put it on your bed."

"Thanks," Alice replied. She went back to her room and found the envelope, surprised to have gotten a response so soon. She tore it open. The letter read:

> *Dear Ms. O'Donnell,*
> *It is my pleasure to offer you a position with the Phoenix branch office . . .*

She skimmed down to the bottom.

> *Please inform us of your decision by May 15. The anticipated start date is July 17 . . .*

Cynthia padded up behind her. "Good news?" she asked.

Alice nodded but didn't turn around. "I think so. They're offering me a place in Phoenix and a twenty-thousand-dollar raise."

"Wow."

"Yeah." Alice refolded the letter and put it in its envelope.

"So you're going?"

Alice looked back over her shoulder at her roommate. "I don't know. I have to think about it." *Five and a half months isn't very long for me to meet a guy and get engaged,* she thought. *How strong is my faith now?*

* * *

Two evenings later, Lorraine called. "Hi!" said Alice. "I haven't heard from you in ages. How are things?" She flopped down on her bed and propped her chin on her hand.

"Things are good," said Lorraine. "And I have decided something."

"Yes?"

"Yes. I think I would like to buy a condo. Do you think that's a good idea?"

"It isn't a bad one," said Alice. "It's the ultimate rent control."

"Yes. And I can deduct the interest from my taxes. But . . . so . . . what do I do now? I talked to one realtor and . . . I don't know . . ."

"Oh, that's no problem. My friend Monica Valdez—I mean, Sanders—is a realtor, and she's easy to work with. Would you like to talk to her?"

"Yes. That would be nice."

"Okay. Can I give her your number?" Alice reached out and grabbed her datebook to see if she'd scribbled Monica's number down in it.

"Yes, of course."

"Great! How is everything else going?"

"Good. I have quit smoking."

"Congratulations." Alice hadn't been aware that Lorraine smoked.

"You know how I did it?"

"How?"

"I added up how much money I would save if I stopped." Lorraine laughed. "For years I tried to stop for my health and for my daughter, but it never worked. What does this say about me?"

"Hey, whatever gets the job done."

"Very kind of you. So, can I ask you something else?"

"Sure."

"Would you . . . I shouldn't ask but . . ."

"Name it."

"Would you come look at condos with me?"

"Sure."

"It isn't too much?"

"No. It sounds fun."

"I would like that. I am always afraid, you know? Even if your friend Monica is nice, I don't trust people who want to tell me to spend my money."

"That's wise." Alice sat up and closed her datebook. She couldn't find Monica's phone number, and she didn't want to interrupt the call to dig it out of her cell phone directory.

"And this realtor? You know her from church?"

"Yes." Belatedly, Alice made the connection. "I—is that all right?"

"Oh, yes. That's fine."

"Because if you're not comfortable—"

"No, no. I still have many friends in the Church. I *like* the Church. I just . . . I cannot be a member."

"I'm sorry." Alice was careful not to say any more, feeling it was none of her business.

"It was my choice. I . . . when I lost my husband and then all my money, I called one of my home teachers."

"Uh-huh."

"And he wasn't very nice to me. He yelled at me and called me lazy and said that I shouldn't ask him for money."

"Did you do that?"

"No. But he told me that the Church didn't need people like me and that the bishop would tell me the same thing."

"Now hang on," said Alice, "did you talk to the bishop?"

"No. I couldn't. I was too embarrassed. I stopped going to church—"

"He could have helped you. Your home teacher was wrong. You could've gotten new home teachers."

"Yes, probably." Lorraine sounded tired. "But it wasn't just him. None of my friends would help me. People were very rude to me about my husband's death. They expected me to just pick up and move on and . . . it was hard." She was silent for several seconds. "I guess it isn't a good reason to leave a religion, though, is it?"

"I don't know," Alice said honestly. "I'm not you. So I can't say."

Lorraine chuckled. "You are always kind. So how is my son?"

"I haven't seen him much."

"Is he dating anyone?"

"Uh . . . not that I know of."

"What's the matter with him?"

Alice laughed. "I could be wrong—he might be dating. I honestly don't know. He doesn't lack for options."

"No, he never does. He's good-looking, don't you think?"

"Yes. He is."

"But he is very picky."

"Do you . . . um . . . do you ever talk to him? At all?"

"No. Not anymore. Not since he went to college."

Alice pursed her lips. *I shouldn't have asked that,* she thought. *This is none of my business either.*

"He has been angry with me since his father died."

"I see . . ."

"And he is like that. Once he decides how he feels about something, he doesn't change."

"I'm sorry to hear that."

"We all have flaws. That is his, but I have been telling you too much. You didn't want to know these things." Lorraine chuckled.

"No, really—"

"You are always so nice. Tell me, how are you?"

The two chatted for a few more minutes, and then Lorraine had to go. Alice pulled up the contacts menu on her cell phone and called Monica.

The line rang twice, then she heard Monica's "Hello?"

"Hi, Monica. It's Alice. I've got a prospective client for you. You're still doing real estate, right? Part-time?"

"Yes," said Monica. "What's the name?"

Alice gave her Lorraine's name and number, then said, "She may be considered low income. I don't know how that works or whatever . . ."

"Okay, well, if she is, it's actually perfect, because there are some great new complexes being built in the Valley. I was looking at the brochures just today."

"You don't mind?"

"Of course not. Don't be dumb. Spinelli . . . why do I know that name?"

Alice felt her face grow warm. "Well," she said, "it's Gabe's mom, but he doesn't really talk to her. They're estranged. She and I are friends, though, and I'd like to come along when you take her to see the properties, if I could."

"Of course. Should I call her now?"

"I know she's home."

"Okay. Well, why don't I do that?"

When Monica ended the call, Alice closed her phone and went to see what Cynthia was cooking for dinner. It smelled wonderful, whatever it was. She found her roommate tossing vegetables into the wok.

"Five minutes," said Cynthia without looking up.

"You don't *have* to feed me," said Alice.

"Shut up. We've had this conversation before. Five minutes, okay?"

"Okay. Um, Cynth? Has my dad been by since that one Sunday you didn't tell me about?"

Cynthia looked up. "No," she said. "I kind of threatened to call the police."

"Really?"

"Yeah. Has he come to your work?"

Alice nodded.

"What?" Cynthia took the wok off the stove and turned off the gas. She turned and put one hand on her hip. "Alice, you didn't tell me."

"You didn't tell *me*."

"I was trying to protect you from all that. You said you didn't want to talk to him so—"

"Cynth, be honest; is this getting to be too much for you? I can help you find a new place if it is."

"Nope. Don't even, Alice. I am not leaving you to live on your own."

"But these aren't your problems."

"They aren't your problems, either."

"But this is *my* family. And you know that you don't owe me anything."

"I owe you everything, but this isn't about that. You're my friend, and I'm not leaving you alone. All right? Besides, it isn't that big a deal. It's not like your dad gets violent or anything, just pushy."

Alice opened her mouth to reply, but her cell phone rang again. "Hello?" she answered.

"Hey, it's Monica. You free a week from Saturday, in the afternoon?"

"I think so."

"Okay, then meet me at my office at one."

"Okay, great. See you then!"

"Yep, see you then."

14

Dating Again

The following evening, Spencer picked Alice up at six thirty. He drove a silver BMW, which surprised Alice. She'd never noticed it in the church parking lot, and Spencer had always struck her as frugal, with his stylish but not designer clothing. Even though his car was a bottom-of-the-line BMW, it was still quite a car. The interior was black leather and smelled expensive.

As soon as they'd both gotten in and strapped on their seat belts, Spencer said, "I made reservations at this sort of Italian-American fusion place, but I didn't ask you if you like that kind of thing. Do you? Because we could go somewhere else if you prefer." He tapped his fingers on the steering wheel as he spoke.

"Actually, that sounds perfect." Alice made sure to smile at him.

"Cool." He twisted the ignition key, and the engine started with a purr. "Italian food is my favorite," he stated.

"Oh yeah?"

"Yeah. Followed by Mexican, I guess."

"Have you been to Mexico?"

He nodded. "For my mission."

"Oh yeah? Where?" Alice realized this was probably a typical first-date conversation for a couple of Latter-day Saints.

"Mexico City." He launched into a description of what it had been like to serve there, how much he liked the people, and how many baptisms he'd had. He drove up the freeway on-ramp, and they headed east.

After a few miles, Spencer seemed to run out of things to say about his mission, so Alice asked him about his job, and he began a long description of the schooling he'd had in order to become a physician's assistant and why he'd chosen his field. All the while, they sped along the 10. The sun was setting, and the streetlights were lit, casting pale halos onto the asphalt freeway.

"After I did some work up in Anchorage, I moved back here to be near my family. Family's really important to me."

Alice only nodded in reply.

"My six siblings and I—" he began, then said, "Oh wait . . . I need to be in this lane."

Alice watched as he maneuvered into the exit lane and took his foot off the gas. They coasted down toward the surface streets below.

"Anyway, as I was saying, my siblings and I are pretty close, usually. My sister has been wrapped up in her own stuff lately."

"That's nice you've got a strong relationship, though," Alice remarked.

"It is." Spencer swung the car around in a U-turn. "I saw a parking space back there," he said, "but that's the restaurant." He pointed.

Alice turned to look. She almost laughed aloud. The restaurant had an all-too-familiar weathered brick facade and bright orange door. Alice wondered if Gabe was working tonight.

* * *

Their waiter was a nice young man who wasn't Gabe. Alice took a surreptitious look around the room but didn't see any familiar faces. *Probably his night off,* she figured.

Dinner was a surprisingly relaxed affair. Alice usually worried about dumping half her dinner down her front and having things stuck in her teeth afterward, but with Spencer, she simply asked a question now and then, and he filled in the rest. He met her gaze and hazarded the occasional smile.

"I've only been back to Mexico once since I got off my mission," he finished one story. "It's been eight years, and I live in Southern California. Isn't that sad?"

"I haven't traveled much myself," tried Alice. "I've been offered a job in Phoenix, but I've never been there."

"Oh yeah? When does the job start?"

"July. But I need to decide by May."

"Oh . . . and do you think you'll go?" His smile faded.

Alice shrugged. "Depends on whether or not it seems like a good idea then."

He nodded.

Hmm. Halfway into our first date and he's already thinking about July. If this guy is the answer to my prayer, I guess he would have to act fast. Am I ready to move that fast?

Someone reached across the table to take her water glass and fill it. Alice looked up to say thank you and saw that it was Gabe.

"Hey, Alice," he said. He didn't sound as upbeat as usual.

"Hey. How are you, Gabe?"

He nodded and shrugged.

"In a talkative mood, I see," teased Alice.

He paused, looked at her, and smiled, but it was a halfhearted smile. Before she could ask him if he was all right, he moved on to the next table. Alice turned her attention back to Spencer, but out of the corner of her eye, she watched Gabe make a slow circuit of the room with his pitcher. He glanced back at her, then looked away quickly.

Oh no, thought Alice. *Was that jealousy?* She glanced over at Gabe again and found him staring at her. He turned away at once. Alice focused her attention more intently on Spencer. *Best just to ignore that*, she thought.

* * *

In church that Sunday, Spencer winked at Alice when she handed him a program. Alice smiled in return and was surprised at how easily the smile came to her. It seemed almost foreign to smile. *Wow*, she thought, *I didn't realize how down I was before.*

Leslie and Sarah came by, whispering to each other. They each took a program without looking up. Three other people also brushed by without giving Alice a second glance, even though she said hello to each one.

Then Gabe emerged from one of the side hallways, carrying a book in his hand. His expression was sour. He wouldn't look Alice in the eye, so when she handed him a program, she held onto it until he looked up. "Hi," she said to him.

"Hi. Oh, here's the book I said I'd loan you." He held it out to her. It was a white hardcover.

"Thanks," she said. She let go of his program and took the book from him. "So how are you?"

"Tired. Worked late."

"I'm sorry to hear that."

"Oh well." He shrugged and walked into the chapel.

Alice glanced up at the clock, put the rest of the programs on the table, and went into the chapel herself. Spencer waved at her from the middle of the room. He'd saved a seat for her. She smiled at him as she took it, and he smiled shyly in return. They didn't talk during the meeting, but it was nice to have someone who wanted her around.

* * *

The following Saturday, Alice drove out to Monica's office in Century City. The building's waiting area was very swank—granite tile with modern paintings and sculptures for decorations. Alice walked in at five minutes to one and found Monica just emerging from the back.

"We're meeting Lorraine out in the Valley," she said. "She's really nice, by the way. I like her."

"So you've already met with her?"

"Yeah, she came in this week to give me all her financial info and tell me what she wants and all that. I don't think she likes this place, though." Monica gestured around at the expensive decorations and leather couches. "I think we kind of made her uncomfortable." It was then that Alice noticed that Monica was dressed in khakis and a denim blouse rather than her usual suit.

"Look, I'm sorry if I sent you someone who is . . . not in your usual market."

"Don't be silly, Alice. The money here is nice, but it's not the only reason I got into real estate." Monica gestured for Alice to precede her out the door.

"Oh yeah?" said Alice.

Monica laughed. "My family are immigrants, and we didn't start out with much either. My parents own a construction company. They've built several low-income housing complexes."

"Really?"

"The last one they built sold out a year ago. I do know the builders of the ones we'll be looking at today, though." Monica hefted her briefcase and grinned as they made their way down the hall to the elevator.

The drive out to the Valley took half an hour and involved a lot of sitting in traffic. When they pulled up to the first complex, a tall, lanky girl and a woman who looked like a shorter, feminine version of Gabe were standing out front waiting. Monica parked along the curb right next to them.

"Lorraine!" she called as she got out of the car. "You know Alice."

"Hi," said Alice. She stepped onto the curb and pushed the car door shut behind her. "We've never actually met in person."

Lorraine looked slightly surprised. "You are Alice?"

"Yes, hi." Alice stepped over and shook her hand. Lorraine smiled warmly.

"This is Gina, Gabriel's sister." Lorraine pointed to her daughter.

"Hi," said Alice.

Gina smiled shyly at her. *She definitely has the build of a ballerina,* Alice thought, *and the graceful presence of one.* She didn't look much like her brother. His eyes were green while hers were brown. His skin was olive, hers fair. But her hair had the same medium-brown tint and slight wave to it, and she had that same attentive look whenever anyone spoke.

Lorraine looked up at the condominiums that towered over them. "I . . . are you sure . . ." she began. "I don't want to spend too much and—"

"Positive," said Monica. "Come see."

Alice could see why Lorraine was nervous. The complex was nice. It was brand-new and had nice landscaping, a swimming pool, and a security station in the lobby. Alice could only guess at what Lorraine's current apartment looked like. Probably nothing like this.

"These have a seller's agent attached to them," Monica explained as they walked through the lobby. "I spoke to him about an hour ago. He should be here." She peered into the inner courtyard and frowned.

Lorraine began to fidget. Her face was so expressive that Alice could practically read her thoughts: *I don't belong here. These girls are nice, but young, and they don't know what they're doing.* Gina kept her gaze fixed on Alice, which after a minute began to make Alice feel uncomfortable.

A man in a suit emerged from one of the side doors and flashed them one of the fakest smiles Alice had ever seen. "Ms. Sanders," he said to Monica. "I'm Mark Huffington." His voice was smarmy, and his entire demeanor bespoke arrogance and condescension. From the way he looked Monica over, Alice could see that he was already prepared to underestimate her.

Well, thought Alice, *that explains Monica's smirk in the elevator. This should be fun to watch.* To Lorraine she whispered, "Don't worry. Monica knows what she's doing. Honest."

15

Gina

The condo unit Mr. Huffington showed them was beautiful. It had a spacious front room, an open-design kitchen, lots of windows to let in natural light, one bedroom, and a loft that would be perfect for a teenager like Gina. The place still smelled of new carpet, fresh paint, and wood shavings. Lorraine and Gina were both hesitant to go in, but Monica brushed right past them, walked into the living area, turned around to give it a good look, and shook her head.

"This is a ground-floor unit," she said, "which means it's already under contract. You told me you had units left on the upper floors that weren't under contract."

"Yes . . . well . . ." said Mr. Huffington, "the price—"

"We'd like to see one please." Monica marched out of the condo without a backward glance.

Lorraine gave Alice another worried look, but Alice only shook her head. *It's all right,* she wanted to say.

Mr. Huffington took them up four stories in an elevator and unlocked the door of another condo. This condo was like the one they'd first seen, but it also had a view. Alice was surprised. She had always assumed that anything in LA County with a decent view was priced somewhere in the stratosphere. This view wasn't fabulous, but it wasn't bad either. It showed the Hollywood Hills. She went over to the window to get a better look. Gina followed her. The girl was silent, which made her attention to Alice feel even more strange.

"Now this," said Mr. Huffington, "even with the income assistance program, goes for a lot." He quoted a price that made Lorraine blanch.

"As of when?" Monica tugged a packet of papers out of her brief-case and tossed them casually on the kitchen counter. "According to your most recent sales—"

"That was three months ago."

"Mr. Huffington. Real estate doesn't appreciate *that* fast, and the last time I saw Gary, he didn't mention anything about such major price increases."

"Yes . . . well. I'm just passing on what my boss told me. Y-you know Mr. Clovis, then?"

Lorraine frowned and came over to where Alice and Gina stood. "I cannot afford even half of that," she said in a low voice. "I don't need a place this nice."

"Monica's just getting started," Alice assured her. "Do you like the place?"

"It's beautiful."

Alice looked at Gina, who nodded.

"Well," said Alice, "why don't we walk around while Monica works this guy over?"

Lorraine cast another worried look in the direction of Monica and the other realtor but followed Alice and Gina into the unit's bedroom. It was a nice size. Not huge, but big enough to fit a bed and a dresser. The bathroom had a shower, no bathtub, and limited counter space. The closet was nearly the size of the bathroom.

There was also a very small balcony that overlooked the pool. Alice flipped open the lock on the sliding glass door and pushed it to one side. Lorraine peered out and shook her head. "I cannot afford this," she repeated. "It is nice but . . ."

"Let's go look at the loft," said Alice.

They headed back into the front room. The ladder was built into the wall and had smooth wooden rungs. Alice was glad she'd opted to wear jeans that day. In the background, she could hear Monica saying, "But you know people have had problems with this layout. I mean, guests have to go into the master bedroom to use the bathroom."

"That is a point," Alice agreed. She gestured for Gina and Lorraine to precede her up to the loft.

Gina climbed up the ladder. Lorraine paused and asked, "Will that bring the price down?"

"When Monica points it out? Yes."

"But not far enough," said Lorraine. "It is not possible to—"

"Now these aren't oak cabinets," Monica was going on in the background.

"Just wait and see," Alice suggested to Lorraine.

Lorraine nodded and hoisted herself up the ladder. Alice followed her.

When she reached the top, she saw that Gina was sitting over by the railing, looking down at Monica and Mr. Huffington. Alice went over and sat next to her. Monica was tapping her foot impatiently. "No, they're *not* solid oak—they're veneer," she said. "You know that. And yes, the kitchen is nice, but the linoleum is three years at best, and the countertops are just Formica. You know that's the cheapest possible surface."

"But the carpet is an upgrade," Mr. Huffington pointed out.

"From a three year to a five year? Five years, Mr. Huffington. That's not all that long. And the washer and dryer hookups in the bathroom? People have complained about those too."

"Washer and dryer?" asked Lorraine. Alice turned back around to face her. She was sitting in the middle of the floor. "I don't have a washer and dryer," she said.

Lorraine looked around the loft, and Alice tried to follow her gaze. It had a low ceiling but plenty of room for a twin bed and a desk. There was enough room for a person to sit up straight in a desk chair, even stand if they weren't too tall. Gabe would have to stoop. *If he ever comes here,* thought Alice. Gina also looked over the loft with an appraising eye.

"The view is very nice," said Lorraine.

Alice turned to look. It was true. One could see straight out the windows from the loft.

"Mr. Huffington, don't be ridiculous," said Monica. "You know that this complex was finished seven months ago and that you *still* have four of these single-bedroom units. I'm not worried about someone walking in and buying this one while we're talking right now."

"Yes, but this one is only available because the last buyer failed to qualify for financing. We've had a lot of interest."

"Lorraine? Alice?" Monica called out.

"Yes?" Alice called back. She peered through the railing.

"Alice, why don't you take Gina out to look at the pool and the grounds? Lorraine, if you'll come here a second?" Monica said something in Spanish.

"All right," Lorraine replied as she eased herself onto the ladder and climbed down.

"That's our cue to leave so they can really start bargaining, I guess," Alice told Gina. They followed Lorraine down.

"Who are you calling?" Alice heard Mr. Huffington say as she and Gina hopped off the ladder and headed out the front door. A breeze ruffled Alice's hair when she stepped outside, and she had to hold it back from her face with one hand.

"I'm just calling Gary," said Monica. "I'm *sure* he told me the water heater isn't that big, Mr. Huffington."

Alice shut the heavy wooden door and turned to flash a grin at Gina.

The girl smiled back at her; then, without warning, she asked, "Are you dating Spencer Sharp?"

"What? Wait—what?" Alice stopped in her tracks. "Can you repeat that?"

"Gabe said he saw you on a date with Spencer last week."

Oh, and Gabe told his sister this, why? Alice turned to walk toward the elevators. "Well . . . I did go on one date with him. Do you know Spencer?"

"No." Gina followed. "Gabe's been trying to get up the nerve to ask you out, you know," she said.

"Has he now?" She remembered their dance at Monica's wedding and felt her face flush. *I should not have flirted with him,* she chided herself. *But still, is he nuts?*

They reached the elevator, and Alice pushed the DOWN arrow button. "Gina," she said, "does Gabe know I've been talking to your mother?"

The girl shook her head. The elevator door opened, and they both stepped in. "I didn't tell him. I think he might get kind of mad if he hears that Mom inherited money from Uncle Victor."

Alice nodded. The elevator door closed, and they descended slowly.

"So how, exactly," she asked Gina, "did your mom get my number?"

Gina looked down at her feet. "I . . . Gabe told me once that you helped your roommate and lots of other people with money, so when my mom got this inheritance . . . I went and got your phone number from his cell."

Alice nodded. "I see." *He had my number in his cell?* She did some quick calculations. *Wait a minute . . . that was before Monica got married.* Her face grew warmer still. *I can't believe this,* she thought.

The elevator pinged, and the door opened. Alice and Gina stepped out and began walking along the flagstone path that curved in the direction of the pool. The air in the courtyard was warm and smelled like freshly mown grass and lilacs. The sun was almost directly overhead. Alice took her sunglasses out of her purse and put them on.

"I'm sorry," said Gina, "I just wanted—"

"No, no. Don't be sorry. I'm glad I've gotten to know your mom. Really."

"Gabe said you were really, really smart."

Why would he assume that? wondered Alice. They reached the pool, which was small and shaped like a kidney bean. No one was swimming, so the blue water was still. Chaise lounges were set out in a neat row, their white plastic still new and unweathered. Alice stepped up to the decorative iron railing and leaned her elbows on it. A breeze stirred the air, bringing the scent of chlorine with it.

"What else did Gabe tell you?" she asked.

"Everything. He's always talking about you."

"Since when?"

"Since he moved into the ward. You used to date his roommate, right?"

"Yes."

"Gabe was really jealous."

Alice shook her head. "Gina," she said, "you know how old I am, right?"

"Twenty-six," she said promptly.

"Right. So I'm five years older than Gabe."

"Yeah, I know."

"Well . . . five years is a lot."

"So, you don't like him?" Gina looked crestfallen.

"I like him fine, as a friend. He's a really great kid, but I've never considered getting *involved* with him."

"Oh." Gina looked down. "Yeah, that's what Gabe said you might say."

Alice was at a loss for words then. Fortunately, her cell phone rang. "It's Monica," Alice told Gina. "We should probably go back upstairs."

* * *

The first thing Alice heard when she opened the front door was Mr. Huffington saying, "We can't go lower. Mr. Clovis is giving you a steal here. It's the best we can do."

Monica frowned, said something to Lorraine in Spanish, and scribbled a note on a sheet of paper on the counter in front of her, which she then passed to Lorraine. "We'll *think* about it," she said. "We've still got four other units to see."

Lorraine took the paper and turned so that she faced Alice and Gina and had her back to Mr. Huffington. Her eyes went wide, and Alice went over to see the note.

"I . . . I still don't know," said Lorraine.

"I think it'd be manageable," whispered Alice. She calculated the monthly payments in her head. "It'd be tight for the first few years, but hey, it's an option."

Lorraine blinked and shook her head in disbelief.

"All right," Monica was saying. "We can find our own way out, thank you." She came over to Alice and winked as she opened the front door. "First one down," she said. "The others probably won't take this long."

"Is it always this fun?" Alice whispered to her friend.

Monica only smiled.

* * *

At the end of the day, Lorraine had her choices narrowed down to two; one of them was the first unit they'd toured. "The other one has a better floor plan," she acknowledged as they stood by their cars

reviewing the listings. "And it is cheaper." Gina was practicing pirou-
ettes up and down the sidewalk. Her spirits seemed high in spite of
the conversation she'd had with Alice about Gabe. The sun was
setting, and everyone's shadows stretched out long and thin.

"Consider the pool, the landscaping, and the brand-newness of the
other one," said Monica. "It would be a great place to live. And it's a
real opportunity. I don't mean to brag, but no other realtor is ever
going to talk the price on that thing down so low. I just happened to
know that Gary has had a hard time finding qualified buyers, and he's
happy to have someone preapproved. He's wanted that place sold out
for ages."

"I like that one best, Mom," said Gina, pausing mid-pirouette.

"I am tempted. But, Monica, your commission will be so low!"

Monica laughed. "Don't worry about that. Think about which
one you want and call me."

Lorraine nodded, and Alice saw that she was blinking back tears.

"So—" began Alice.

But Lorraine cut her off with a hug. Then she turned to hug Monica.
"*Thank* you," she said. "You two have done so much for us."

16

Disaster Date

The next day at church, Spencer beckoned Alice to sit next to him again once she'd finished passing out programs. "I'm so sorry I haven't called all week," he said as she slid into her seat on the padded bench. "I work long shifts the third week of every month."

Alice only shrugged. "Sounds rough," she replied. She pulled her scriptures out of their case and set her purse down on the floor by her feet.

"It's not so bad," said Spencer. He turned sideways in his seat so he could face her. "But I was wondering if you were free Saturday afternoon?"

"I think so."

"Would you like to go for a walk on the beach?"

Alice looked over at him. *That would be potentially romantic,* she thought.

"Or," said Spencer, "we can do something else?"

"Sorry," she answered, shaking her head as if to ward off a distraction. "The beach sounds nice."

"Yeah? I know this really great beach near where I grew up. It's got these big tide pools. I used to spend hours out there when I was a kid."

Not just a beach walk, thought Alice, *a beach walk with nostalgia. He really isn't wasting time.* "Okay," she said. She felt a bit more upbeat. It was nice to have someone interested, especially the "best catch in the ward."

Spencer smiled. "Okay," he agreed.

The bishop got up then and began to speak. Alice glanced over at Gabe, who was sitting across the chapel from her. He quickly looked away.

How often does he stare at me like that? Alice wondered. Now he was looking down at his hands, and she couldn't see his expression. *Gabe, you are such a nice guy. Just . . . just find a better match than me, all right?*

* * *

That afternoon, Alice ate lunch with Monica in the meetinghouse courtyard before Monica went to her family ward. The weather was warm and still. Alice had brought whole-wheat rolls and chilled lentil soup flavored with lime—leftovers from dinner the previous night. As they ate, Alice filled her friend in on the conversation she'd had with Gina. "So anyway, that's why Lorraine called me," she finished. "She thought I was some kind of specialist who helps people with their money. Meanwhile, Gabe apparently likes me."

"What an odd kid," said Monica.

"Gee, thanks."

"Well, it is odd. You're not his type."

"But guess who I went on a date with," said Alice.

"You went on a date?"

"With Spencer Sharp."

"Are you serious?" Monica paused, her spoon half raised to her mouth. "How was it? What's he doing nowadays?"

Alice shrugged and looked down at her soup. "He's a physician's assistant."

"And?"

"Well . . . he talked about stuff, like his family."

"What about them?"

"That he has six siblings."

"Names? Ages?"

"What is this, a test?"

"Yes," said Monica, "to see if you were listening."

Alice chuckled, shut her eyes, and tried to remember. "Um . . . one older sister, four younger sisters, and one younger brother. Names are Danielle, Megan, Leslie, Natalie, Beth, and Jordan. Leslie's the only other one in the ward."

"Impressive."

"Thank you."

"So are you guys actually dating?"

"We went on one date a couple of weeks ago, and we're going on another next weekend."

"Oh," said Monica, "that's way too long between dates. Remember, this is Spencer we're talking about."

"Pardon?" said Alice.

"You can't waste time. If you're interested, you've got to make that clear. It's not like there are a lot of good-looking, well-off guys our age who are still single. Most of the best ones are married by the time they're twenty-five."

Alice nearly dropped her spoon. "I'm over twenty-five, Mon."

"Oh, it's different for women, you know."

Alice set her soup aside and tried to keep her cool. "He's twenty-nine, and that isn't very old," she pointed out.

"In the Church, it is. For a guy. You know, older unmarried guys in the ward are sure to be a little wacko. And—"

"Okay," said Alice, cutting her friend off. "*That* is wacko. It is *not* old, and I do not believe there's any correlation whatsoever between being wacko and not getting married. I just don't see any evidence. Take a look at the people in *your* ward, for example."

Several other people who sat nearby paused in their conversation and gave Alice amused looks.

Monica, however, did not seem amused. She looked as if she were trying to teach a simple concept to a difficult student. "Marriage helps you better yourself, you know? You have someone else to show you how to improve."

"But marriage isn't always an option for everyone, Mon. If you don't have Mr. Right or Ms. Right banging down your door, you do the best you can. There are a lot of well respected, unmarried people in the Church."

"Name three."

"Sean wasn't married, lucky for you."

"He *was* married. It just didn't work out—and that wasn't his fault. But you know what? I think he's a better person for it."

"All right, well, what about me? And the whole singles ward?"

"But you hope that's temporary."

Alice felt her temper rise. "What if it's *not?*"

"Hey, relax, all right? I don't mean to insult you. I'm sure you'll get married."

"But I'm twenty-six. According to you, I've been wacko for a year."

"You're a convert. That's different."

Alice cast about for a way to change the subject. "Did Lorraine pick a condo?" she asked.

It worked. Monica was distracted at once. "Oh, yeah, the brand-new one," she said. "Which reminds me, she wants us to come over for a housewarming dinner in three weeks."

"Really? She got the new one?"

"Yeah, and I got them to knock two thousand more off the price." Monica smiled.

* * *

The following Saturday, Spencer picked Alice up at three o'clock. He was dressed up slightly in khaki pants and a button-up shirt, which caught Alice off guard. She'd worn a skirt and sandals and was glad the outfit could pass for sort of dressy.

When they walked out to the car, Spencer came around to open the door for her.

She thanked him and sat down in the cushy leather seat.

"So," he said when he'd gotten into the driver's seat and settled himself, "that beach I want to take you to? It's a drive. Like, a forty-minute drive. We don't have to go if—"

"That's fine," interrupted Alice.

"Okay," he said. He glanced over at her and grinned.

Alice smiled back and put on her seat belt.

"So, like I was saying, I love this beach." He started the engine and pulled away from the curb.

"Uh-huh," said Alice. "You used to go there a lot?"

"*All* the time, when I was a kid. We used to catch fish out of the tide pools."

Alice nodded. They merged onto the freeway and were soon speeding along the 405. She leaned against the door and watched the other cars slide past.

Changing the subject abruptly, Spencer said, "I have a nosy question."

"Uh-huh."

"How long did you date Darren?"

"That's not nosy."

"Okay, good."

"Um . . . almost ten months."

"Ten months, huh?" He glanced over at her again. "He the first Mormon you ever dated?"

"Well . . . active Mormon, yeah. Before him, I lived with a guy who was inactive."

Spencer started. He looked away and did his best to hide it, but Alice saw it all the same.

Guess he wasn't ready to know about my scandalous past. Well, I can't change it.

"Lived with . . . like . . ." said Spencer.

"Like I'd never do now. But that was then, before I began reading the Book of Mormon."

He nodded and looked pensive.

Alice didn't quite know how to fill the awkward silence. Fortunately, her cell phone rang. She pulled it out of her pocket and looked at the number. *Mom.* "I'm sorry," she said to Spencer, "might be an emergency." She flipped the phone open. "Hi, Mom."

"Alice! While I was out of town your father and his lawyer tried to have a hearing without me—"

"Yes, I heard about that. I'm so sorry. I didn't know. I wanted to get you away from all this."

Spencer glanced over at her.

"But now they're trying to say I don't need spousal support, because I can afford to go on vacation."

"Well, Dad knows better."

"He does?"

"Yes, of course he does."

"I should never have gone."

"I'm really sorry about what happened."

Spencer glanced at her again.

"Alice!" Her mother burst into tears. "They're going to take everything. The house, the car, my mother's property up in Sacramento, the furniture—" her voice got shriller with each item—"my jewelry. They'll probably try to make *me* pay your *father* spousal support!"

"Mom, you know they can't do that."

"Oh . . . every time I turn around it's gotten worse."

Alice remembered what her father had said about wanting to marry his girlfriend. *You have no idea,* she thought. "Mom," she said, "do you need me to come over for a while tonight?"

"Are you busy now?"

"Well . . . yeah."

Spencer, though, was exiting the freeway.

"I'm on a date," said Alice.

"Oh, dear." Her mother choked back a sob. "Your father's on his way over. He sounded so angry with me."

Spencer pulled the car into a gas station and shut off the engine. "What's going on?" he asked.

Alice put her hand over the phone. "It's my mom. She's having a rough time." To her mother she said, "It's okay, Mom. Everything will be fine."

Spencer frowned.

"Alice," said her mother, "I just can't do this. It's all too much."

"Okay . . . look, what do you want?"

"Oh . . . nothing." She kept crying.

"Right. Hang on." Alice took the phone from her ear and turned to Spencer. "I am so sorry," she said, "but this is kind of a family emergency."

"It's all right." His disappointment was clear.

"Could you . . . could you take me home? I know I'll owe you one."

"No problem."

"Okay, Mom, I'll call you in a few minutes. I love you." She snapped the phone shut. "Spencer, I am *so* sorry."

"What's going on?"

"My parents are divorcing, and it's not going well. Dad's on his way to Mom's house right now. I hope I can beat him there."

Spencer nodded. "Oh . . . I'm sorry." He restarted the engine and turned the car around.

17

Picking up the Pieces

When Alice got to her mother's place, her father was already there, hollering.

"And I *told* you about that hearing. You obviously can't hold it together well enough to keep a simple appointment!"

Alice tried the front door. She found it unlocked but hesitated, not sure she wanted to be in the middle of this.

"Of course I'm having a hard time," her mother shouted back. "My husband just up and left me a year ago!"

A year, thought Alice. *Wow, it's been a year already.*

"Annabeth, you've got to let it go, all right? We're not going to be married anymore. You've got to stop dragging your heels over this."

"Easy for you to say. You're ready to remarry and forget all about me."

"Yes! Yes, I am. You've finally noticed that, have you?"

Alice turned away and sat down on the steps leading up to the front porch.

The front door opened, then shut with a bang.

"Allie?" came her father's surprised voice.

Alice twisted around and looked up at him. "Dad," she said.

"You . . . I didn't know you were here. How are you?"

Alice didn't bother to answer that. She got up, slipped past him, and went inside the house, closing and locking the front door behind her. "Mom?" she called out. "You're getting new locks, okay? I'm going to go call a locksmith. And what's your lawyer's number? You need a restraining order or something for Dad." The house was silent. After a moment, Alice heard her mother sniffle.

Alice crossed the entryway and went into the living room, which was now a disaster area. It hadn't been cleaned for weeks. A thick layer of dust covered everything, the garbage can was overflowing onto the floor, and there were several sets of dirty dishes scattered around on the coffee table, the chairs, and the floor.

Alice's mother cowered in a fetal position on the couch. Alice heaved a sigh. "You want me to call somewhere and order dinner for us?"

"Okay," her mother said. She didn't look up.

"Okay," said Alice. "And . . . I'm hiring you a maid."

* * *

That night, Alice couldn't sleep. She hadn't gotten home until after midnight. Her mother had finally stopped sobbing, had eaten some food, and then had gone to bed.

Alice had called Spencer while her mother picked at her food. "It's no problem," he'd said. "You've gotta be there for your family. I'm just sorry you couldn't come today. I'll be working long shifts again next week so . . ."

"We'll go some other time," said Alice.

"I'm working late this week except for Wednesday. You free that evening?"

"I have a client meeting."

"Oh."

"Saturday?" she suggested.

"I work until one A.M."

Alice laughed. "Well, we'll figure something out."

"Yeah, okay. I don't know my schedule the week after next, though."

"That's fine. When you do, we'll set something up."

"Okay." There was relief in his voice. That made her smile.

Now Alice tried to lie still in bed and relax, but she was still too tense and upset. The sound of her father shouting and her mother crying still echoed in her memory. *Okay,* she thought, sitting up and throwing off her covers. *I've got to find something useful to do.*

Her gaze fell on the book Gabe had loaned her. She picked it up off her vanity and opened it to the first page.

This copy had obviously seen a lot of use. The spine was worn, and the pages had been marked on. Sentences had been underlined, and notes were jotted in the margins.

Alice began to read, and as she read, the tension eased from her shoulders. She remembered sitting in the baptistry, reading her scriptures. The bishop had asked her twice since then whether she wanted to get her endowment, but she hadn't given him an answer yet. Gabe had scrawled in the margin of the book that the endowment "teaches what is necessary to return to God." That concept hit her like lighting. *Well, if you put it that way,* she thought, *that sounds like exactly what I'm looking for.*

Two hours and four chapters later, she put the book down and fell asleep.

* * *

The next morning, Alice found a seat at the very back of the chapel a few seconds before sacrament meeting began. She found it hard to keep from yawning, and she knew she had dark circles under her eyes.

Gabe walked in during the opening hymn and scanned the room for a seat. He paused, staring at her. There was an empty place next to her. He looked uncertain about taking it, though.

Alice shifted over slightly and gestured for him to come over.

He slipped gingerly into the seat. The hymn was just winding up, and Alice folded her arms for the opening prayer. After that, the bishop began making announcements.

"So how are you, Gabriel?" Alice whispered.

Gabe looked at her.

"Or do you prefer Gabe?"

"My mother called me Gabriel," he said.

I know. She still does. I'm having dinner with her in two weeks. But you have absolutely no idea about that, do you? Do you even know she's moving? Alice had elected not to ask Lorraine or Gina whether they had told Gabe anything about their new situation.

"Thanks for the book, by the way," she said.

"Oh yeah? You read much of it yet?"

"Just the first four chapters."

"That's a lot."

"Hardly."

"It's not necessarily an easy read, you know."

"Well, thanks."

"So . . . are you taking temple prep?"

"I want to. I'm still not sure I'm ready."

Gabe shrugged. "I think you are."

"Why?"

"Because I saw how you were during baptisms in the temple."

The organist began playing the opening strains of the sacrament hymn, cutting their conversation short. Alice wanted to ask him what on earth he meant, but he didn't so much as look at her for the rest of the meeting. He kept fidgeting and then got up to leave as soon as the closing prayer was finished.

* * *

Eight days later, just as Alice was getting home from work, Spencer called again.

"Do you like Mexican food?"

"Sure."

"Great, how about I bring Mexican over to your place tonight? Is this too short notice? I know this great takeout place."

"Oh, you don't need to do that," she said. *But it'd be nice to have another date with you, given how awful the last one was.*

"Is your roommate going to be home?"

"Yes," said Alice, "she is."

"Good . . . I just feel that would be more appropriate."

Alice blinked. "All right."

"I'll see you in about half an hour?"

"Right."

They signed off, and Cynthia wandered out from her room. "Who was that?" she asked.

"Spencer. He's bringing dinner, and you're invited."

Cynthia clasped her hands to her chest and batted her eyelashes mockingly. "Really? I get to be third wheel? Lucky, lucky me!"

"All right, sorry. I should have asked first."

"Never mind. At least I get free food out of the deal."

* * *

Spencer showed up half an hour later with a large bag that smelled like ground beef and salsa. Alice answered the door and invited him in. He glanced around the front room at the deep red walls, the spotless beige carpet, and the leather couch framed by two floor lamps. "Nice place," he said as he went to put the bag down on the kitchen counter. "Um, Alice?" His tone was worried, his voice low. "Where's your roommate?"

"In her room. I'll go get her if you want—"

"Oh, no, that's okay. I just wanted to make sure she was here. I don't believe in being alone together on a date, you know?"

"So, do we need to invite someone along when we go to the beach?" she asked.

"Huh? No, that's outside."

"Oh . . . right."

"Can I ask you something?"

"Sure."

He furrowed his brow for a moment and then sat down on one of the bar stools. She sat down on the other one.

After a few moments of hesitation, he finally said, "I've never kissed anyone, and I don't believe in doing so until I'm engaged."

"Okay," Alice said. *Is this normal?* she wondered. It had been so different with Darren.

"I mean, I like you—I really, really like you," said Spencer. "So don't feel bad if I don't kiss you goodnight. It doesn't mean—"

"I understand."

"Okay, different topic."

"Okay."

"How set are you on moving to Phoenix?"

"I'm not set on it. I'm glad I have the opportunity, but I don't know what I'll want in May."

"So you could, hypothetically, stay if you had a good reason?" His smile was hopeful.

Alice nodded.

"Can I ask you if you're planning to go to the temple?" asked Spencer.

"I really want to."

"That is so great." Now there was a light in his eyes.

This guy, Alice realized, *is serious about the gospel. That's . . . very attractive.*

"What about . . ." said Spencer. "What about your career?"

"What about it?" said Alice.

"Do you plan to work the rest of your life? I mean, if you got married and had kids—"

"We're not getting engaged tonight, are we?" she asked, her eyebrow quirked.

Spencer chuckled and shrugged shyly. "Well, no. I am looking to get married, though. I mean . . . I don't want to get involved if marriage isn't a possibility. Does that make sense?"

"Yeah," said Alice. "So it would depend. While I have young kids, I'd like to be home full-time. When they're older, though, I'll see what makes the most sense. Does that answer your question?"

"I guess so."

"I think being a parent is the most important responsibility there is," she added.

Spencer nodded. "Me too. So . . . about your past."

"What about my past?"

"I'm sorry if I seemed uncomfortable about it." He looked down for a moment before lifting his gaze again. "I've never dated a convert before."

"You haven't?"

"No. Was the repentance hard? Before you got baptized?"

"Alice?" Cynthia called from her bedroom. "Can you come help me with something?"

"Sure," she replied. To Spencer, she said, "Be right back."

Cynthia was holding the door to her room open, and the moment Alice stepped over the threshold, her roommate took her by the arm, hauled her all the way in, and shut the door behind her.

"Who *is* that guy?" Cynthia demanded.

"Spencer," said Alice. She pulled away and rubbed her arm. Cynthia's grip was strong. Cynthia's room had been transformed again since the last time Alice had been in it. The walls were the same dark beige, but now they had lighter beige trim. The bed had been moved over to the far wall, and the place smelled like pumpkin-spice scented candles.

"What is he doing here?" Cynthia asked.

"Okay, you remember the conversation we had half an hour ago, right?"

"That's not what I mean." Cynthia paced back and forth for a minute then put her hands to her forehead and said, "I can't believe what he just said to you."

"What, the repentance question?"

"All of it!" Alice could hear that Cynthia was struggling to keep her voice low. "Alice, he just read you the riot act."

"Oh, he did not," replied Alice. She went over to sit on her roommate's bed and leaned back against the padded headboard. "He was just figuring a few things out. And he's nice! I mean—"

"A *few* things? He just told you that you're not allowed to kiss him and that if you're not planning to stay in Los Angeles and stop working when you get married, he's not interested. And this is the second date!" Cynthia planted her hands on her hips.

"I think you're overstating things."

"No, I'm not. That's what he said."

Alice took a deep breath. "My mind's not made up about him," she confessed, "but I want to give him a fair shot."

"You have. Can we kick him out now?"

"Cynth!"

"I'm serious. I'm all for being tolerant of your religion, but this takes it way too far. That guy isn't looking for a date. He's looking for a demure little wife."

"And I wouldn't mind getting married."

"There are *arranged* marriages less confining than what that guy's offering."

"Cynth, stop, okay?" Alice sat forward. "I hear what you're saying, but I don't agree. I . . . this conversation would probably make more sense to you if you knew about our last date."

"Okay." Cynthia nodded. "Tell me what happened on the date."

"Well . . . I kind of mentioned that I used to live with Brian."

"So?"

"So, that freaked him out a little."

"Ditch him."

"I'm not ready to do that yet. I'm not getting married to him or anything. This is just a date. Now, you don't have to eat dinner with us, but please stick around the apartment, okay?"

"So I can chaperone?"

Alice got up. "Please, Cynth."

"Fine, but you and I are going to have a talk after this."

I can hardly wait. Alice went back out to the front room. Cynthia followed.

"Spencer," Alice said, "this is my roommate, Cynthia. Cynthia, Spencer."

Cynthia lifted her chin slightly. Spencer got to his feet.

"I'll get the plates," said Alice. "Would you like to join us, Cynth?"

"No, thanks."

Alice nodded, took a deep breath, and went to set the table. Cynthia retreated to her room.

"So," said Spencer, "she's not a member of the Church?"

Alice shook her head. She got glasses and filled them with water from the pitcher in the fridge.

"Has she read the Book of Mormon?"

"No."

"Why not?"

Alice looked over at him. "I don't think she's interested."

"Have you asked her?"

"Well, no, not exactly."

"Maybe you should."

Alice nodded. *Easier said than done,* she thought as she brought the bag of food over to the table. He pulled her chair out for her. Alice sat down, and they bowed their heads to ask a blessing on the food.

18

Preparing for the Temple

"He sounds like a really great guy," said Monica the following Saturday night. She and Alice had met up in the lobby of Lorraine's building and were walking toward the elevator together. Monica carried a white pastry box, and Alice had a flat, gift-wrapped package. It was dusk, and crickets were chirping. Low lights along the walkway illuminated their path.

"My roommate freaked out," said Alice.

"Well . . . that's overreacting. Are you guys a couple now?"

Alice shrugged. "Pretty much. I mean, it's only been two dates, but he said he wants to be exclusive."

"Wow, good job, Alice." Monica held up her hand for a high five. Alice gave her an odd look.

They took the elevator up to the fourth floor and presented themselves at the door of Lorraine's condo. Lorraine answered and gave each of them a hug. "Here are my girls, my angels!" she sang out. "Come in, come in. Gina! They're here."

"'Coming," came Gina's voice from the loft.

"We brought dessert," said Monica. She held out the box she'd been carrying.

"And this," said Alice. She held out the present. It was a serving platter Cynthia had assured her was the perfect size and in a style that was neutral enough to go with any *décor*.

"Oh, you shouldn't have!" said Lorraine. "You girls. Tonight I want to do something for *you*." She took the boxes and ushered them into the living room, where her worn cloth couch and chair now filled the space nicely. "Sit down, sit down," she said. "Gina! Are you coming?"

"Yes." Gina's voice sounded listless.

Alice sat on the couch and turned to see the girl climb slowly down the ladder. Monica began speaking in Spanish and followed Lorraine to the kitchen.

Gina hopped down the last two rungs.

"Hey," said Alice.

"Hello."

"How are you?"

"I'm good."

"How's your dancing?"

"Fine." Gina went over to the chair and sat down.

"Is something wrong?" Alice asked.

Gina looked toward the kitchen. Monica stood at the end of the counter talking to Lorraine while Lorraine cooked something that smelled wonderful—tomato sauce with some kind of sausage.

"Um," said Gina, "no."

"Liar."

Gina looked down at her hands. "You are dating Spencer, aren't you?"

Alice nodded. "I'm sorry."

Gina shrugged.

"I hope you like gnocchi!" Lorraine called out.

"Sounds great," answered Alice.

"Okay." Lorraine said a few more words in Spanish to Monica, then called out, "Come sit down!"

Alice did her best during the meal to be upbeat and attentive, but Gina was morose. Even her mother cuffed her gently and said, "What is wrong with you? You don't like the food?" Gina hastily shook her head at that but glanced mournfully at Alice.

Please, thought Alice, *don't. Gabe's a nice kid. Emphasis on* kid.

It was going to be an awkward evening.

* * *

"Well," said Bishop Baker a few weeks later, "how is your temple preparation going?" It was evening, and the view out the window of his office was inky blackness. The bishop looked tired and careworn, but his smile was genuine.

"Well . . ." Alice looked down at her feet.

"Oh dear. Care to elaborate on that?"

In spite of her nervousness, she smiled. "Okay, so I've been going to the temple prep class, like you told me to." Alice had been rather unnerved when she'd discovered that Gabe's roommate, Ely, was the teacher.

"Mm-hmm."

"I don't get any of it. I mean, I don't think we talk about anything. It's all so vague."

"Care to give me an example?"

"Well, I asked about how symbols are used in the temple. I'm reading *The Holy Temple* by Elder Packer, and I was curious about that. Ely wouldn't tell me anything. He just said, 'We don't talk about the actual ordinances,' and moved on."

"Which is true. We don't."

"Okay, so *how* am I supposed to prepare? How can I get ready for something when I don't even know what that something is?"

The bishop leaned forward and rested his elbows on his desk. "I can tell you exactly what the endowment is, Alice. It is—"

"The ordinance that teaches us what we need to know to return to God."

Bishop Baker looked surprised. "Yes," he said. "That's right."

"I just have this paranoia that I'm going to get in the temple and find out that the true gospel is . . . totally weird. I mean, how do I know I'm not going to get locked in a room and asked to sacrifice goats or something?"

The bishop chuckled. "Those were the old temple ordinances. Back in Old Testament times."

"And they were bizarre. How are today's ordinances not? I mean . . . returning to live with Heavenly Father . . . does it lay out a road map? Give us secret passwords and a decoder ring? I don't get it."

"It isn't secret—"

"Then why can't we talk about it? And don't just say it's 'sacred.' As far as I can see, that's just code for secret."

The bishop blinked.

Alice realized she was sitting forward, her hands clenched in fists. She took a deep breath and forced her hands to relax.

"Do you still have any close friends who aren't members of the Church?" the bishop asked.

"Yeah. My roommate. She's my best friend."

"All right. Is there anything you don't tell her? About your faith?"

"Yeah. My revelation, or whatever it was. I haven't told her about that."

"Why not? Is it a secret?"

"I just don't think she'd understand."

"Why not?"

"Um . . . because she'll think it's weird?"

The bishop chuckled. "I was trying to get you to say that it was sacred. That it was a personal experience that might easily be misunderstood if you told just anyone about it."

For a moment, Alice just stared down at her hands. "I guess I understand," she said. "But really, it's also because I know it's strange. I wouldn't understand if I were her. I mean . . . I still wonder about it myself sometimes."

"Then perhaps you'll find aspects of the temple strange in that same way," said the bishop. "If you read your scriptures, though, and prayerfully consider what you learn in temple prep, you won't be in for any major surprises. And once you're endowed, you'll see a new dimension to the scriptures and talks by Church officials. I promise that we talk about the temple and refer to its ordinances all the time—you just don't recognize the references right now."

"So, even if the temple seems strange to me, it won't seem any stranger than the average devout Mormon does?"

"Well . . . yes." The bishop laughed.

Alice found herself laughing right along. "Okay," she said. "I should be able to handle that, then."

"Perhaps this would be a better way to put it; the Lord wants you to know certain things, but He can't tell you at just any time, any place. He wants you to come to His house so that He can teach you in His own way. If you decided to tell your roommate about your experience, you'd prepare her, wouldn't you? And you'd choose a time and place that seemed appropriate."

"True."

"So, do you want to go to the temple?"

"Yes. I do."

"Okay, the next step in your preparation is to get your patriarchal blessing."

"What's that?"

The bishop put his head to one side and regarded her. "No one's ever told you about them?"

"No." She shook her head.

"It's a blessing by the stake patriarch—ours is Brother Dmitri. Unlike other priesthood blessings, this one is recorded, typed up, and filed in the Church records. It's where you learn about your lineage, Alice, about which tribe of Israel you belong to."

Alice nodded. "All right."

"And it'll also give you some counsel that will serve you over the course of your life."

"Okay," she said. "And do I need a recommend?"

"You do, and we'll do the interview for that now. You may also bring a friend along to your blessing, if you'd like. Spencer perhaps?"

Alice shook her head. "We've only been going out for a little while. A month or so."

"I see. Well, he's a good man, and I think he's quite serious about you."

"He's definitely goal-oriented."

The bishop gave her a tolerant smile. "By that I assume you mean to say that he's thinking of marriage."

"Well . . . yeah. I mean, he's nice and all but—"

"Alice, be kind to him. He's got a good heart."

Alice nodded. "I will."

* * *

"Me? Witness your patriarchal blessing?" said Monica, her voice so shrill that Alice had to hold the cell phone away from her ear. "Are you serious?"

"Yeah, of course. Who else, Mon? So . . . it's not too much trouble?" Alice sat on her bed, her back to the door. She could hear her roommate coming home, so she lowered her voice. They still hadn't had that "talk" Cynthia had insisted they were going to have.

Alice was dreading it. She had begun working even later than usual to avoid it.

"No trouble," said Monica. "This is a huge honor. Okay, this weekend. I'm penciling it in right now."

"And," said Alice, "I have something else to ask."

"Sure, what?"

"The bishop said that most people fast. I'm a little hypoglycemic. I mean, I don't know if it'll be a problem but . . . can you drive me? Just in case I get dizzy?"

"Of course. That's a good idea. All right! See you in a few days."

* * *

Alice only meant to fast for twenty-four hours, but her alarm clock's battery died that Friday, so she didn't have time to eat breakfast. Then work was so hectic that she didn't eat lunch. She still wasn't ready to face Cynthia that evening, so she didn't venture into the front room for dinner. The next morning she felt more than a little faint. She said her morning prayer, then flipped open Gabe's copy of *The Holy Temple* and tried to read that until Monica came for her at one.

"You look pale," Monica told her.

"I'm fine," Alice fibbed. In truth, she felt exhausted and disoriented. Her stomach boiled with hunger.

Monica drove her out to the patriarch's house in Brentwood. Alice leaned against the window the whole way and kept her eyes closed. The cool glass felt good against her cheek.

"You excited?" Monica asked.

"Yeah," Alice replied. To herself she thought, *I feel like I'm going to pass out. I must have overdone the fasting thing.*

"Okay, we're here."

Alice opened the door, then remembered she was still wearing her seat belt. It took her two tries to get it unfastened. Monica had come around to her side of the car by then. She put her arm around Alice, helped her to the front door of the house, and pushed the doorbell. The patriarch's wife answered. Alice barely caught her name, as she was having to concentrate too hard on putting one foot in front of the other.

"Downstairs," Monica whispered to her. "You sure you're okay?"

Alice nodded and picked her way down the stairway. Monica led her down a narrow hall and into a small office where the patriarch, an elderly man, sat in front of his desk. "Sister O'Donnell," he welcomed her. He gestured for Alice to sit in the remaining empty chair. Monica seated herself on the battered gray-and-white couch that was set against the wall.

"Now," the patriarch began, "why don't you tell me a little about yourself?"

Alice began to talk, hoping she made sense. She told the patriarch her name, about her job, about her baptism, and that Monica was her friend. She was developing a splitting headache, though, and the room was out of focus.

"All right," said the patriarch when Alice had run out of facts. "Let's have a prayer and then we'll do this blessing. Sister Sanders? Would you please?"

Alice folded her arms and bowed her head. Monica's voice droned words Alice had trouble understanding, but at least she heard the word "Amen" and was able to repeat it at the right time.

* * *

Three hours later, Alice sat cross-legged on her bed with her journal open before her. She still felt a little woozy even though Monica had taken her out to lunch, giving her a chance to replenish her blood-sugar levels. She marked down the date and began to write.

> *Had my patriarchal blessing today and was so out of it I barely heard a thing. Except partway through, I suddenly felt okay and could hear just fine. The patriarch told me that I should choose the man I marry very carefully. I should make sure that he appreciates my worth. It's weird, but that's the only part I remember. After that, I nearly passed out.*

> *I'm definitely not fasting for more than twenty-four hours again. That was a big mistake.*

She closed her journal and lay back on the bed. Even after a full meal, she was ready for a nap.

19

The Talk

Six weeks later, Alice and Spencer finally stood on the beach on a narrow strip of sand along the waterline. The rest of the beach was rocky and, just as Spencer had promised, gorgeous.

"Alice," Spencer was saying, "I really, *really* like you. I mean . . . I think I love you."

Alice looked out toward the horizon, where the light blue sky met the darker blue water. The day was windy, and the wind had a chilly bite to it. She was glad she'd braided her hair that morning. Her skirt flapped in the breeze. "I . . . Spence, I'm sorry. This is all going really fast for me."

"I see."

Alice looked down at her hands and began to fidget.

"So you're saying you're not ready to talk about marriage. We've been going out for three months—"

"Which still feels short to me. I guess I'm not used to Mormon time." It was more than that, though, and Alice knew it. Although they'd been on a lot of dates over the past three months, she wasn't feeling a connection. They'd held hands, she'd kissed him on the cheek, and he hugged her sometimes, but Alice couldn't shake the feeling that he was more a good friend than a boyfriend. But she felt like she *ought* to love him. The bishop even vouched for his character.

"When do you decide about your job?" asked Spencer.

"In three weeks." *No pressure there,* thought Alice. "I've applied for jobs in LA, but none of the offers I've gotten is competitive."

"You have?"

Alice looked at him. They were both wearing sunglasses, so it was hard to read his expression. "Yeah."

"But you don't want to talk about—"

"I do like you," said Alice. "I may want to stay in town regardless of what happens with us. I don't know."

"All right." He nodded. "That's fair. To be completely honest with you, though, I'm ready to get engaged. I know you still have to think about it, but I also know that you and I could have a good marriage."

Alice nodded, not quite sure whether she meant to agree with him or just show him she'd heard him. *We're on a beach, he's a gorgeous guy with a good job and good heart, and he wants me to be with him for the rest of his life. Why doesn't this take my breath away?*

"And I know your roommate doesn't want you to marry me."

Alice shrugged. "That's not her decision." What Spencer said was true, though. Cynthia had made it clear on many occasions that she did not like Spencer one bit and kept pressing Alice to have a "talk" with her. Alice continued to avoid her. She'd taken to working late and eating microwave dinners. When she was home, she kept herself busy studying the scriptures in order to prepare to go to the temple.

"Do you think you'd be able to commit to a marriage?" Spencer asked. "After how things worked out for your parents, do you wonder if you can make a marriage last?"

Alice turned and began walking then; the movement helped her hide her irritation. Spencer meant well, she believed that, but he wasn't always very tactful. He kept pace beside her. The sand was still wet, and they left a trail of shallow footprints behind.

"I'm not my parents," she said. "I would never walk out on my spouse."

Spencer nodded. "But are there a lot of divorces in your family?"

"No. Yours?"

"None."

Alice looked up at him. "None?" she said.

"Yep, none."

"Your aunts and uncles—"

"And cousins and parents and grandparents. No divorces. I don't know about my second cousins and people like that." He smiled wryly.

"That's impressive," said Alice.

"It's just a matter of approaching marriage with the right attitude, you know? You have to be really committed, and you have to stay committed even when things get hard."

Alice nodded. "I agree."

"Any two righteous people can get married." He held out his hand to her.

Alice paused, then took it. Holding hands with him always felt awkward. His grip was a little too tight, and he walked faster than she did, so she had to lengthen her steps to keep up.

"The tide pools are this way," he said, heading for the rocky part of the beach. "Come on." He tugged her arm, and Alice had difficulty climbing up onto the rocks one-handed.

Once she did, though, she found herself standing at the edge of a large tide pool, easily ten feet across. The water in it was crystal clear and still as glass. The wind wasn't as bad up on the rocks, since they stood on the lee of several large boulders. Alice dropped Spencer's hand and squatted down to peer into the pool. Two fish, the same color as the rocks, darted away from her shadow. She smiled.

"You like this?" asked Spencer. He squatted beside her.

"I do. Yes."

"There are tons of these around here. Come on." He took her hand again and led her on. The rocks were dotted with pools. Several contained fish and one a jellyfish, its translucent body pulsing ever so slightly. Alice knelt down to get a better look at it, and her shirt slipped off her shoulder. She absentmindedly tugged it back into place.

"Uh, Alice?" said Spencer.

"Yeah?" She looked up from the jellyfish.

"Is that a tank top you're wearing?"

"Under my shirt? Yes."

Spencer looked uncomfortable.

"What?" asked Alice.

"You know, I'd feel better if you didn't wear those. You're preparing to go to the temple in a week, and you know you won't be able to wear tank tops after that."

She raised an eyebrow. "A lot of people in the ward wear tank tops under their shirts in order to be *more* modest."

"Right, but look at how loose your shirt is."

Alice looked down at her offending shoulder and tried a different approach. "If we came here to swim, I'd be wearing a swimsuit."

"Right, but you should be in the habit of dressing modestly whenever you can." He knelt down next to her. "Also . . . about your skirt."

"What about it?" She looked down at her loose-fitting, ankle-length skirt.

"That fabric's kind of sheer."

The fabric was lightweight, and she could see shadows through it, but nothing more. "It's summer weight," she said. "If the fabric were thicker, it'd be very uncomfortable."

"Okay, but . . ." Spencer clasped his hands together and frowned. He seemed to be picking his words carefully. "I just find that obeying the rules leads to great blessings, and bending them is a bad idea. I mean, there's the spirit of the law and the letter of the law, you know?"

"Sure," said Alice. "So, explain to me why we don't need a chaperone when we're outside. I really don't think anyone can see us here."

His eyes widened slightly. "Alice," he said, "you know what I mean."

She shook her head. "I'm afraid I don't. But look, I don't want to start an argument. I know I have to get rid of my tank tops before I go to the temple, so this issue won't come up again."

He nodded.

She looked back down at the water. Over the last three months she had studied her baptism-day journal entry from every angle she could think of. Spencer, she knew, was a good man. He was a loyal and devoted, though sometimes socially clueless, Latter-day Saint. The signs, she thought, all seemed to point one way. So why didn't she feel good about it?

* * *

Alice had two messages on her voice mail when she returned home from the beach. One was from the ward clerk, reminding her that her temple recommend interviews with both the bishop and the stake president were Tuesday night. The other was from Lorraine, inviting her to dinner at six that Saturday evening. "Monica says she will come," said Lorraine.

Alice flipped open her cell phone, called Lorraine back, and got voice mail. "Hi," Alice said after the beep. "Dinner at six on Saturday works for me. Let me know what I need to bring." While she spoke, there was a knock on her bedroom door, and Cynthia slipped in without waiting for her to answer.

Alice slowly closed her phone and turned to face her.

"Hey," said Cynthia.

"Hey."

"Please, Alice, can we talk? I'm sorry about whatever I said or did that made you mad. Really. I just . . . there's a lot about your life right now that I don't understand."

Alice put her phone down on her vanity and sat in her chair. "Okay," she said.

Cynthia went over to the bed, sat down, and pulled her knees up under her chin. "Okay," she said. "Look, about Spencer. He's—I don't understand why you keep dating him."

"He's a nice guy," said Alice.

"Well, no. He isn't."

"Cynth."

"I've gotta be honest with you, Alice. You know me. Not a big fan of lying."

Alice rested her elbows on her vanity and her forehead on her hands. "I know you think he's a domineering Mormon male," she said.

"Stereotype, Alice. Domineering Mormon male *stereotype*, not to mention self-centered. But not all LDS guys are like that. Darren wasn't like that."

"Darren deviated from the stereotype in . . . other ways."

"So is that it? Spencer is more devout? He doesn't break the rules?"

"That's part of it."

"Okaaay, but—"

"Cynth." Alice sat up straight. "My religion is important to me."

"I get that."

"And maybe you think his attitudes about kissing and stuff like that are stupid—"

"No, not stupid."

"Or naive."

"I never said that."

"But they matter to me. I respect him."

Cynthia nodded. "Uh-huh. That I understand. But he doesn't respect you. He never asks you what you think or what you want—"

"That's not true."

"And he tries to push you around and have his way. I don't think he loves you."

"Well, he'd disagree with you there. And besides that, he believes in commitment."

"So? That alone isn't enough to make him attractive, unless . . ." Cynthia's voice trailed off.

"Unless what?" Alice asked.

"Unless your biggest fear is being left by the man in your life."

"Cynth!"

"Is that part of it?"

"Please."

"It's a serious question."

Alice took a deep breath and tried to compose herself. With her right hand, she fidgeted with the knob on the drawer of her vanity. Her journal lay inside, its pages well worn from long nights of reading and writing, searching for answers that refused to come easily. "I just feel that Spencer may be the right person for me," she said. "I need to give him a chance."

"Okay. Why?"

"I can't tell you."

"Why not?"

Alice let go of the drawer knob and put both hands in her lap. "Because you wouldn't understand, and it's personal." *And because it has to do with my religion.*

"Alice, come *on*. You and I have been friends how long? Have I ever disrespected you?"

"You're doing it right now."

"Well, not on purpose. Why won't you talk to me? Give me a chance to understand you? You know how much I care."

"Cynth, it's *personal.*"

"Fine." Cynthia got up. "But if you ever *do* want to talk, you know where to find me." She crossed the room and stepped out the door, closing it behind her.

Alice watched her go. *She's really mad at me now,* she thought. *But she'd have me committed if she knew I was following a revelation from God.*

* * *

Gabe was early to church the next day. Alice handed him his program and the book she'd borrowed. "I finished it," she told him. She'd stayed up late Saturday night reading.

"Already?" he said excitedly.

"What do you mean already? It's been ages."

"Did you like it?"

Leslie and Sarah walked up then. Gabe stepped to one side so that they could get their programs. "Hi," tried Alice.

"Hey," Sarah answered.

Leslie gave Alice a distracted look and turned to go into the chapel. "So I told him 'what*ever*,'" she went on to Sarah.

"Did you like it?" Gabe repeated.

"Yeah, I did. I . . . I've been kinda frustrated with temple prep, though."

"Really?" He stepped into her line of sight again. "Why?"

Alice took a deep breath. "Well . . . all right, I'll ask you this. Can you give me an example of a symbol used in the temple?"

"Sure."

Alice blinked. "You can?"

Three other people came to get programs. Alice handed them over without looking at them.

"Uh-huh. Sealing rooms usually have mirrors on opposite walls."

"They do?"

"Yeah, and the mirrors reflect each other over and over, so that if you look into one, it looks like you can see for eternity."

"So that's how they're symbolic?"

Gabe nodded. "Yeah, because marriage in the temple is for eternity. Also, if you look into one of the mirrors, or if you and your spouse look into one of the mirrors, you see yourselves reflected over and over. Sometimes a sealer will say something like, 'Look in this mirror and consider your ancestors, and look in the other and consider your descendants.'" He paused. "Both marriage and families stretch on into eternity. I mean, if you think about it, everything done in the temple lasts for eternity, as opposed to just for time."

"For time? Time is our mortal life, right?"

"Yeah. A marriage done just anywhere lasts for time, but the temple isn't for time only. It's not 'til death do you part."

Alice nodded. That much she'd known already.

It was near time for the meeting to start, so she put the rest of the programs down on the table, and she and Gabe went into the chapel together.

"Where's Spencer?" Gabe asked.

"At work." She sat down in the nearest empty seat and scooted over so Gabe could sit next to her.

He took the seat after a moment's hesitation. "Work, huh?"

"He works at the hospital. Illness doesn't observe the Sabbath, you know."

Gabe nodded.

Bishop Baker got up and began speaking.

"So," Gabe whispered, "when do you go through the temple?"

"Saturday. Ten o'clock session."

The organist began to play the opening hymn. Alice reached for a hymnbook, but the girl next to her grabbed it. She ended up having to share with Gabe. His singing voice was so quiet that she suspected he was only mouthing.

After the song was over and before the bishop began speaking again, Gabe said, "Can I come?"

"To what?"

"The temple session, on Saturday."

Alice shrugged but smiled politely. "I don't think the temple workers will stop you."

He smiled, and Alice noticed how his eyes caught the light just so when he looked at her. She looked away quickly.

20

The Night Before

Okay, Alice thought that afternoon after church, *I'm losing it.* She was in her room again, pacing. *Yes, Gabe Spinelli is cute. But he's a kid! Besides, I'm dating someone else.*

The apartment phone rang, and she went to the front room to answer it. Cynthia was home—Alice could tell from the shuffling sounds coming from her room—but she was keeping the door closed.

"Hello?" said Alice.

"Hey," came Spencer's voice. "So, Friday night, before you go to the temple, I say we have a little party."

"Okay."

"All right! So, your place? At, say, seven?"

"Sure . . ."

"What's wrong?"

Alice sighed. "My roommate and I had a little . . . talk."

"Did you to talk to her about the gospel?"

"Not really."

"Well," he said, "maybe you should. If she doesn't understand that, she can't understand you. Should we move the party somewhere else? I'd offer my place, but I don't have a roommate. We could do a double date here, I guess, but—"

"Let me ask Cynthia first."

"Just let me know. If I don't hear from you, I'll be at your place Friday. I'm seriously excited that you're getting your endowment!"

"Thanks," said Alice.

"Okay, see you then, and I'll bring food."

Wonderful, she thought as she put the phone down. *What am I supposed to tell Cynthia?* Doing a double date sounded awkward too, though. Even though the ward population had stabilized, Alice hadn't made any new friends. She knew everyone's name and felt comfortable sitting next to them, having casual conversations with them, and even calling them at home for church business, but her closest friend in the church was still Monica. And Gabe, maybe. If he counted as a friend.

In the end, Alice left Cynthia a note on the counter asking her to please be around on Friday because Spencer would be over. Cynthia responded with a note of her own saying that was fine, since she didn't have plans. Cynthia worked a long, hard week and was sitting on the couch in her sweatpants when Spencer arrived. When he knocked, she got up to answer the door.

"Hi!" Spencer said enthusiastically. He had another bag of Mexican food.

Cynthia turned around and rolled her eyes. Alice, who was sitting at the table reading her scriptures, was the only one who saw it. "Come in," Cynthia said with false cheerfulness. She went back to her room and shut the door.

Spencer, who still stood in the doorway, frowned.

"Don't mind her," said Alice. "She's just in a mood."

"Is this about you getting your endowment?" he asked.

"You know," said Alice, taking the bag from him, "I'm not even sure she knows about that. Come in."

The phone rang, and Alice looked over and saw that it wasn't in its cradle. A split second later, Cynthia emerged from her room with it and said, "It's your mom." She forced another smile at Spencer, handed the phone to Alice, then withdrew.

Alice tried to ignore her rudeness. "Hi, Mom," she said into the phone.

"Oh, honey, your father was here, and it was horrible."

"He was? Why?" Spencer was still standing, so she gestured for him to sit down at the table.

"He wanted the glass bowl that Aunt Sally gave us, but I don't know where it is. Do you know, honey?"

"I don't even know what bowl that is."

"Well, he thinks I gave it to you in order to hide it from him, and so he's on his way over to your place."

"What?" He was the last person she wanted there right now.

"Honey, I'm so sorry." Her mother burst into tears.

"No, no, it's okay, really. Mom, it's fine. I love you, and I'm sure it will all be fine."

"He says he wants everything that came from his side of the family. He even wants the bedroom set his parents gave us for our anniversary ten years ago."

"What does your lawyer say?"

"I haven't talked to her."

"You should if she's drafting documents for you."

"Do you think I'll have to give up the bedroom set?"

Alice shrugged. "I have no idea."

"Oh, Alice . . ."

"Do you need me to come over? No, wait, I can't until Dad gets here." *No way I'm leaving Cynthia to handle that alone,* she thought. *My dad going through her kitchen? That would be ugly.*

"Oh, no, I'm fine." But her mother sobbed as she said this.

"Mom, it'll be all right, really."

Spencer got up from the table and headed down the hall. *Yes, good,* she thought. *Go use the bathroom while I try to get this situation under control.*

"Mom," she said, "just relax, okay? It's just a bowl. If you want, I'll buy you another one."

There was the sound of a knock. Alice turned toward the front door but realized the sound had come from the other direction.

"Cynthia?" She heard Spencer's voice.

Uh-oh, thought Alice.

"Hmm?" came Cynthia's answer.

"Mom, I—I'll call you back. Love you. Bye!"

"Can I talk to you for a sec?" Spencer asked through the door. "I'm afraid I might have offended you somehow."

Cynthia opened her door. Her expression was polite, but Alice could see from the way she held herself that she was irritated. Alice hung up the phone and tried to catch Spencer's eye.

"You haven't offended me," said Cynthia. "I just think you and I have two very different views of the world."

Alice took a deep breath. Cynthia's no-lying policy made for some very awkward conversations sometimes.

"So, aren't you at all interested in the restored gospel of Jesus Christ?"

"Uh, Spencer," started Alice.

"No. I'm not. Go away now." Cynthia shut the door.

Spencer turned to Alice and raised an eyebrow. "Is she always like that?"

Cynthia opened the door again. "Was this your idea, Alice? Did you send him back here?"

"No," promised Alice. "Spencer, I appreciate what you're trying to do, but now's really not the best time to proselytize."

"So, you're not worried about your roommate's decisions? That she'll be denied the blessings of exaltation?"

"*Thanks,*" said Cynthia in a low voice. "Please leave."

"Cynth," tried Alice, "look—"

There was a knock on the front door. Alice ground her teeth. How was this for timing?

"Who's that?" asked Cynthia.

"My dad." Alice crossed the front room to answer the door, and, sure enough, it was her father. He looked exhausted, defeated. For a moment, he just stared at her. He still wore his suit from work. The sun was setting, so the light outside was dim. "Hi," said Alice, "I don't have the bowl. I have no idea what it looks like, but Mom never gave me a bowl of any kind."

Her father nodded and shrugged as if he wasn't even sure what she was taking about. Alice moved to look him in the eye, but he looked over her shoulder. "Hello," he said. There was a note of surprise in his voice.

She glanced back and saw that Spencer stood only a few feet behind her. "Oh," she said. "Spencer, this is my dad. Dad, Spencer. My boyfriend."

Her father's gaze darted to her face, his eyes widening slightly. After a moment's hesitation, Alice stepped back and let him enter the apartment. He reached out a hand to Spencer.

"Nice to meet you," he said as the two exchanged a handshake.

"Likewise," said Spencer. "Why don't you come on in and have a seat? I've been looking forward to meeting you."

Alice's father glanced back at her as if to say, *Why is he inviting me in? Isn't this your house?*

Dad, she thought, *don't. Don't start making judgments about him. I don't care what you think anymore.*

Still, her stomach churned when the two men seated themselves on the couch. She considered telling her father that he wasn't welcome and asking him to leave, but something—morbid curiosity, perhaps?—made her sit down on the chair and watch instead.

"So," said her father. "How long have you two been going out?"

"For quite a while," said Spencer.

At the same time, Alice said, "Almost four months."

Her father looked back and forth between them.

"Four months?" he asked.

Spencer nodded. "And I'm hoping to convince your daughter to marry me," he said.

"You are?"

Alice's father looked at her. She kept her expression blank.

"But I'd like to get your blessing first," Spencer added.

"My . . . blessing?"

"Yes, sir."

Alice looked down at her hands. She felt her father's gaze on her again, but she didn't return it.

"So I suppose it's my job to interrogate you now and see if I approve?" he said.

"Something like that." Spencer smiled.

"Be careful," said Alice. "He's a litigator."

Her father chuckled, which was always a bad sign right before he sized up one of her boyfriends.

"Ask away," said Spencer.

"What's Allie's middle name?"

Spencer looked surprised. "What?"

"Her middle name. What is it?"

"Dad," said Alice.

"Just let him answer."

"I . . ." Spencer shrugged.

"It's the same as her mother's name."

"Oh, okay."

"So what is it?" her father pressed.

"I'm sorry. I don't know."

"I see. When's her birthday?"

"It's . . . in the fall?"

"Try summer," replied her father.

"Doesn't matter. I haven't had one since we started going out," said Alice.

"Mmm," said her father. "How about her favorite color?"

"Dad, come on."

Her father looked back at her. "What? He said I could interrogate him."

"You're just asking him trivia. None of that matters."

Her father raised his eyebrow again. "Then how about this: Who is Brian McNeil?"

"Dad."

"Brian . . . who?" said Spencer. He turned to Alice with a look of confusion.

"My ex-boyfriend," she explained. "Emphasis on *ex*."

"She was with him for three years. Can you name Alice's siblings?"

"She doesn't talk about her siblings much."

"Because I don't have any," said Alice. "It was a trick question."

"Oh." Spencer nodded.

Alice's father shook his head slowly. "I take it you're a Mormon?"

"A member of The Church of Jesus Christ of Latter-day Saints, yes."

"Right, okay. How long has Allie been a member of your church?"

"A year. She goes through the temple tomorrow."

Her father glanced at her again. She looked away.

"Who baptized her?" he asked.

"Darren Jarmer. Another ex-boyfriend."

Alice felt her spirits lift a little. *He does know some of the answers,* she thought.

"Does she know her religion pretty well, would you say?"

"Pretty much, yeah."

"What's her favorite scripture?"

"Dad!"

"All right, fine. What's her favorite book of scripture? Bible? Book of Mormon? Uh . . . what are the others? Doctrine and Covenants, and that Pearl one. I forget."

Spencer shrugged. "I don't know."

"Why did she get baptized?"

"Because the Church is true?"

"That's your best answer, son?"

Spencer shifted in his seat.

"Dad, stop," said Alice.

"He said I could—"

"Question time is *over*." She glared at him.

Spencer started. "Alice, that's no way to—"

"It's all right," said her father. He got to his feet. "Allie, I'll call you about your mother and the property inventory later." To Spencer, he said, "Ask her to marry you at your own peril, son. You two have a nice night." He went over to the door and let himself out.

Alice rested her forehead on her hands.

"Alice," said Spencer. "You were pretty disrespectful to him."

"Sorry," she said in a dull tone of voice. "He seems to enjoy picking my life apart. It gets on my nerves."

"That's no way to talk about—"

"He's *my* father, Spencer. Please don't lecture me about how to treat him."

"What's gotten into you tonight?"

Alice took a deep breath. "I'm sorry," she repeated. She looked over at him. "I'm just under a lot of stress."

"Because?"

"Because I'm going through the temple tomorrow morning?"

Spencer's expression grew stern. "You don't want the blessings of the temple?"

"I do, which is why I'm going, but—"

"Your testimony isn't strong enough to carry you?"

Alice stared at him. "Excuse me? Speaking of being disrespectful."

"I'm just being honest."

"No, *I'm* being honest. My testimony's not perfect, but believe me, I've got one. I've thought about it long and hard and—"

"Having a strong testimony is as easy as—"

"It's *not* easy. Not for me. Not for anyone."

"Look, if you don't want to go to the temple—"

"I *do*."

"*Stop* interrupting me."

"Stop jumping to these conclusions. As my father's made abundantly clear to you, you don't know a whole lot about what's going on in my life."

Spencer got to his feet. "Why don't we just call it a night," he said. "I don't appreciate the way you're talking to me."

Alice bit back the impulse to respond in kind. "All right," she forced herself to say. "Good night. I'll see you—"

Spencer glared at her, strode over to the door, and let himself out.

"Tomorrow?" She shook her head and took a few deep breaths to calm herself.

The phone rang.

Alice trudged over to the counter and answered it. "Hello?"

"Allie? I saw that Spencer just left."

"Thanks to you, yeah."

"Hey, look I—"

"You're still *here?* At my building?"

"Yes. Listen, I came over tonight because your mother was screaming at me while I tried to do a property inventory—"

"Dad, don't insult Mom to me."

"I'm not insulting her; I'm trying to tell you what happened. Anyway, I was hoping you might reason with—"

"No. Not my divorce. Leave me out."

There was a pause. "I'm sorry about Spencer."

"It's . . . fine. Thanks for the apology. I'm fine."

"You want to talk? I can take you out for ice cream, maybe. Celebrate you getting your . . . endowment is it?"

Alice sighed. "No," she said, "I don't want to talk." Then she hung up the phone.

21

Endowment

After hanging up the phone, Alice went back to her room, shaken. For a moment all she could do was pace. Finally, she knelt down to pray. *Heavenly Father,* she thought, *I'm sorry. I should be telling my father that he's right, but I can't, because I can't bring myself to call him back. He's right about Spencer. Spencer doesn't know me well enough to know whether he likes me, let alone loves me. Which means that what happened the day of my baptism was what? A lie? A trick? A test? I don't see what I could have done differently. Spencer is the only guy who's been interested in me, unless you count Gabe, and . . .* She shook her head.

Tears came, which she wasn't proud of. She wiped her face with the back of her hand. *I can't marry Spencer,* she resolved. *I can't. I'm going to Phoenix, because that's what makes the most sense. That's what I've decided. I don't mean any disrespect.*

As she completed the thought, though, Alice felt dread. *I just told God that I reject His answer to my prayer,* she realized. *I don't think I'm supposed to do things like that.* The dread gave way to indignation. *But I can't marry Spencer,* she thought. *I can't! What self-respecting woman would?* Then the indignation faded and she felt . . .

Warmth, just the slightest touch of it, suffusing its way through her spirit. It eased her fears and laid her anxieties to rest. The sensation was like an ethereal blanket wrapped around her shoulders and a hand placed on her head, willing her to be at peace. Everything would be okay.

Alice exhaled. Her decision not to marry Spencer was acceptable. She didn't understand it, but she felt a peace she knew she had not imagined.

The sensation didn't diminish or waver. Alice knelt for a moment longer, then closed her prayer, got up, and lay down on her bed. As she did, she felt as if someone were laying a blanket over her, like her father had done when she was a child. Alice let herself relax.

* * *

There was a knock at her door. Alice opened her eyes and was surprised to see light streaming in through her window. She sat up and turned to squint at her clock. It was seven A.M. Alice had only meant to lie down for a few minutes, but a few minutes had clearly turned into all night.

"Alice?" came Cynthia's voice. "You want breakfast?"

Alice wasn't quite sure how to answer that.

"You've got that temple thing at eight thirty, right?" Cynthia opened the door and peered around it. "Do you need me to drive you?"

"What?"

"Eight thirty, right?"

"Cynth . . ." Alice's eyes began to sting, so she shut them.

Cynthia flew across the room and put her arms around Alice. "You all right?"

"I'm so sorry about—"

"Forget about it, okay? Now, you want cereal? Reheated burrito? What? Come on, it's *me*. Let me help you."

* * *

An hour and a half later, Cynthia dropped her off in the temple parking lot. "I'll be back at noon," she said.

Alice turned and looked at the imposing building. The parking lot was relatively empty, and she didn't see anyone else on the temple grounds. *Am I really ready for this?* she wondered. *This is the temple. It's serious. I need to feel completely prepared. Am I?*

Another car pulled up behind her, and Monica jumped out the passenger-side door. "Sorry I'm a little late," she said. She took Alice by the arm. "Shall we?"

Alice paused a moment longer, then nodded. *I may not understand everything that's happened lately,* she thought, *but I'm willing to keep trying.*

* * *

An hour later they sat in the temple's chapel, wearing white, waiting for the endowment session to start. Alice rubbed her arms, shifted her weight, and tried not to be nervous. The room was nearly empty. Organ music played softly, and temple workers, also wearing white, padded softly past.

"This is so weird," Monica remarked. "On a Saturday, they're usually pretty full."

Alice shrugged and looked at her watch. It was a quarter to ten, and there was no sign of Spencer. She wasn't sure whether or not to expect him.

A woman came into the chapel and sat behind them. A few seconds later a man came in and sat next to her. A temple worker went over to speak to them in hushed tones. Alice wiggled her toes in her white slippers and stared down at the floor.

"The construction is amazing," Monica remarked. "They're built to such high standards. I mean, just look at the finish work. Look at the trim even."

Alice feigned interest in the trim.

Sean and another man entered the chapel. Sean came to sit on the other side of Monica. "Hey, Alice," he said affably. Alice smiled at him, considered asking if he'd seen Spencer in the dressing room, then decided not to.

Two more women walked in. Alice looked down at her hands. She'd had her nails done that week, but the polish was already starting to chip.

"Huh," said Monica. "Look who's here."

Alice looked up. Gabe stood in the doorway, looking uneasy. He met Alice's gaze for a minute, then looked over the rows of empty seats.

Alice twisted all the way around in her seat to face him and flashed what she hoped was a friendly smile when he looked in her direction again. Hesitantly, he smiled back, then began walking toward them.

"At least someone else came," said Alice.

"So . . . did you know he was coming?" Monica asked.

"Yes. He asked me if that was all right."

Gabe came to sit in their row, but at the far end.

* * *

Two hours later, Alice stood at the edge of the parking lot watching Monica and Sean's gray car drive off. People were arriving in greater numbers, and Alice stood off to one side of the concrete walkway so that she wouldn't get in anyone's way. She glanced at her watch. It was five minutes until noon, and she really wished she'd brought her sunglasses. They were still where she'd last left them on her vanity.

She turned around and looked up at the temple again, shading her eyes as she did. She looked at the tall, square spire and the angel Moroni perched on top. Behind her was the sound of traffic, the thrum of engines, and the occasional beep on Santa Monica Boulevard.

"Hey, Alice."

Alice turned in the direction of the voice and saw Gabe walking toward her on the path. He had his motorcycle jacket on, his helmet under one arm, and a backpack slung over his shoulder. His hair had grown out over the past few months and had developed some curl. The way the light shone down on him, his skin seemed almost to glow. His smile seemed more open and friendly than usual.

"Hi," she said.

He came over to where she stood. "So, what did you think?"

"Well . . . I definitely need to go again. I get the general gist, but that's about all."

Gabe nodded. "Yeah, I had to go about six times before I really felt like I understood even the basics of it."

"Six times?"

"Yeah." He shrugged and smiled. "I was kinda young when I went. Nineteen."

Which was only two years ago, Alice reminded herself.

"When are you going again?" he asked.

Alice shrugged. "Soon," she said. "Since I'll need to stock up on garments . . ."

"Oh, yeah." Gabe chuckled.

Her cheeks began to feel very warm. *Alice,* she told herself, *you probably shouldn't be talking to guys about your garments. They are underwear, after all.*

But Gabe didn't seem to notice. "I usually go on Thursday night at six o'clock."

"Uh-huh," said Alice.

"If you ever come at that time, I'd like to hear what you think."

"About?"

"The endowment. It'd be nice to talk to you in the celestial room afterward."

"Oh, okay."

Gabe looked down. "Um . . . so . . . Where's Spencer? At work?"

"No. He and I had a fight last night."

"And he ditched your *endowment?*"

"Yes, apparently."

Gabe's eyes widened slightly. "So are you guys, like, broken up now?"

"Probably," said Alice. "I'll have to figure that out this afternoon." She glanced at her watch again. Cynthia was already a few minutes late.

"I'd offer you a ride," said Gabe, "but . . ." He hoisted his motorcycle helmet and smiled sheepishly.

"Thanks," said Alice.

"So . . . um . . . Sarah and Ely are going miniature golfing this week, and . . . uh . . . Ely actually won tickets for four. He asked me if I want to go. Would you be interested?"

Alice blinked. Had he just asked her out?

He met her gaze for a second, then looked down. His face flushed.

"Thanks . . ." said Alice, "but no. You're a great kid, Gabe, but—"

"Emphasis on *kid,*" he replied

You read my mind, thought Alice.

"Well, all right. I guess I'll see you tomorrow." He managed an awkward smile and turned away from her.

Cynthia pulled up in her Jetta just as Gabe set out across the parking lot. Alice was grateful for the chance to make a quick getaway.

A blast of cool, air-conditioned air hit her as she opened the door. She ducked in, pulled her skirt all the way inside, and shut the door.

Cynthia had obviously just gotten out of the shower. Her hair was still wet and smelled like conditioner. "Who's that?" she asked, pointing at Gabe's retreating figure.

"Gabe. Lorraine's son. Darren's old roommate."

"He's *cute.*"

Alice wrapped the seat belt around herself and fastened it with a click. "Yeah," she said, "he is."

22

Cynthia's Advice

There was a message from Spencer on their voice mail when they got home. "Hi, Alice? I'd really like to talk to you. I'm still mad about last night but . . . call me, okay?"

Cynthia rolled her eyes. Apparently she could hear the message even though she wasn't holding the phone.

Alice deleted it.

Her roommate came to sit on one of the bar stools. "Are we done with Spencer yet?" she asked.

Alice paused, then nodded.

"Okay, why the hesitation? That bothers me."

"It's . . ."

"Is this part of that personal thing that I 'wouldn't understand'?" She made air quotes as she spoke.

Alice looked over at her. Cynthia seemed more concerned than disgusted or suspicious. "I . . . if you want, I'll tell you," said Alice.

Cynthia nodded.

"Okay," said Alice, "come back to my room so I can get my journal." She led the way down the hall to her room. Going to her vanity, she pulled open the drawer and got out her journal. Cynthia flopped down on the bed. Alice sat in her chair, opened the journal, and said, "Hear me out, okay?"

"Sure."

"On the day I got baptized—Boy, is this going to sound dumb." She shook her head.

"Just tell me."

"I had this . . . spiritual experience." Alice related the story, even reading some passages out of her journal. Her roommate didn't take her eyes off Alice the entire time.

"All right," said Cynthia when Alice was done, "so you felt that you *would* be engaged, not that you might be or could be—"

"Nope, *would*," said Alice.

"So . . . if you're not engaged by then, that'll mean this couldn't have been a revelation, right?"

Alice shrugged, shut her journal, and put it down on her vanity. "I don't know what that'll mean, but I know what I felt, Cynth. Really. It'd be so easy to dismiss it as wishful thinking, but I can't. That'd be a lie."

Cynthia shook her head. "I do not envy you right now."

"Do you think I'm losing it?"

"Not . . . completely."

"Be honest."

Cynthia looked around the room. "You read a lot of scripture now, and you've been dating a loser, but it's not like you've started talking to animals and writing on the walls."

Alice chuckled.

Cynthia smiled back at her. "I'll keep an eye out for other symptoms."

"I appreciate that."

"But if you did have a revelation—"

Alice shrugged.

"No, hear me out," said Cynthia. "If God did tell you something, wouldn't He be working to make it happen?"

"I appreciate you humoring me, but you're an atheist."

"Well, yeah, but I get the *concept* of God. Maybe you need to stop worrying about all of this and let what happens happen. I mean, if God's so wonderful, why would He want you to date chauvinistic jerks? I'm not an *expert* on Christianity, but I think God's supposed to work all this out."

Alice shrugged. "I'm going to Phoenix. I've decided."

"Which is the sanest possible decision," said Cynthia. "I'll miss you, though."

"Yeah, I'll miss you too. Thank you for driving me today."

Cynthia held up her hand. "Don't get mushy."

"You're very forgiving."

"No, I'm not. I'm sorry I could never say anything nice about Spencer. I know it was rude of me, but—" She shrugged.

"Well, you were right."

"I know," said Cynthia. She clapped her hand over her mouth and shook her head. "I don't know how you live with me."

"I don't know how I'll live without you."

"You could have a whirlwind romance in the next week, get engaged, and then have a loooong engagement. You could stay living here, and we could stay roommates until I find someone, and—"

Alice laughed. "Well," she said, "I did turn down a date—"

"With?"

Alice shook her head. "It's too embarrassing. I completely shut him down this morning."

"This morning, huh? Let's see, how many guys did you talk to this morning?"

Alice looked away self-consciously.

"*He* likes you?"

"He thinks he does."

"And you? Do you like him?"

"He's twenty-one."

Cynthia raised both eyebrows. "You dodged my question."

"Shut up, okay?"

"Call him."

"No."

"Alice!"

"I'm having dinner with his mother tonight, and he doesn't even know."

"Okay . . . that's complicated." Cynthia sat up. "But he is really, *really* cute."

* * *

That evening Lorraine welcomed Alice and Monica into her condo with more hugs. "Hello, angels!" she said to them. "Come in, come in."

Gina peered around the corner. She had the phone pressed to her ear.

"Gina," said her mother when she turned around. "Who is that? We have guests."

Gina put her hand over the mouthpiece and said, "It's my friend Meghan."

"Oh." Lorraine nodded. "Well, is it important?"

"She's really upset. She's crying."

"Okay, but don't stay on too long. Come in, girls. Have a seat."

Gina went and sat down on the living room chair with the phone still pressed to her ear. She shot a furtive glance at Alice and bit her lip.

Alice suddenly had a feeling it wasn't Gina's teenage friend on the phone.

Monica followed Lorraine to the kitchen, speaking in rapid Spanish. Lorraine burst out laughing and made some reply.

Alice went to sit on the couch. Gina looked at her, then looked away.

"Yeah, no, I know," she said in a low voice. "What? Okay, I don't *know*—" she glanced at Alice again—"but I believe you. She's the most beautiful woman ever."

Alice felt her face grow hot.

"I don't know what you should do."

"Is he mad?" Alice asked.

Gina looked startled for a moment, then shook her head. "Well, maybe you should try again. I mean, you said she hadn't broken up with Spencer yet. Maybe if she does?" Gina looked over at Alice.

Alice looked down.

"Or maybe not. I don't know what you should do. I know, I know, she's the smartest most amazing person *ever*. But can't you go miniature golfing with Hannah or something? Oh . . . she's dating Ian? Um, well, what about that other girl who asked you out? Well, who cares if she's annoying? It's just one evening."

"Gina," her mother chided, "you're being rude."

"No, it's okay," said Alice. "If her friend needs her."

"Okay, look, I'll call you back later," said Gina. "Love you too." She hung up the phone.

"Are you mad at me?" Alice asked her.

The girl paused, then shook her head. She glanced sidelong at her mother. "Why don't you like him?" she whispered. "He's been interested in you *forever*. Why don't you give him a chance?"

* * *

Lorraine had Monica bless the food, then she picked up the bowl of salad and passed it over to Alice. "Eat, girls, eat," she admonished. They were all seated around the table. Gina was even more quiet and withdrawn than she had been the last time Alice had been over.

Alice obediently served herself some salad and let Lorraine cut her a large slice of lasagna. "Thanks for having us over," she said.

"Oh, don't be silly. Besides, after dinner I have some questions for you about 529s."

"All right," said Alice. "I'll see if I can help."

Lorraine smiled at her. "Always so nice. Now, tell me, have you seen my son lately?"

Alice resisted the urge to glance at Gina. "Yes," she said, "at the temple this morning."

"Oh yes? He came with you?"

"Not with us. He was there for the same session."

"Yeah," said Monica. "I didn't get a chance to talk to him much. Did you, Alice?"

"A little."

Gina continued to stare down at her plate.

"How is he?" Lorraine asked.

"I don't know," said Alice. "Fine, I guess."

"Does he have a girlfriend?"

"Not that I know of," said Alice. She took a hasty bite of food.

"He's very picky about girls," Lorraine said for the umpteenth time.

Gina nodded in agreement.

Alice took a drink of water, then asked, "He used to date Sarah Nagel, right?"

Everyone at the table turned to look at her.

"Really?" said Monica. Then she caught herself. "Oh, that's right. They're pretty good friends, aren't they?"

"Yes, she's a funny girl," said Lorraine.

"Yeah," Gina agreed, "and she's a total flirt. Except when she was dating Gabe. He got made fun of a lot for dating her."

"I can imagine," said Monica.

"Well," said Lorraine, "he liked her."

Gina nodded. "He said that they had great conversations. He thinks she's really smart."

Never noticed that, thought Alice. *Sarah was lucky—real lucky—to have someone like Gabe think that about her. No wonder she can't get over him.*

"So, Monica," Lorraine said. "Tell me more about what your husband is working on. It's a new computer program?"

"Right, for digital photography," said Monica.

Alice dove into her food and tried just to focus on that.

* * *

That night Alice called Spencer, got voice mail, and left a message. "Spencer, it's Alice. Look, I wish you had come to the temple but . . . Anyway, things just aren't working between us, so I'm breaking it off." She hung up. She'd never dumped someone by voice mail before. It seemed pretty harsh.

But she couldn't quite bring herself to feel guilty about it, not after the way he'd treated her the night before. She got ready for bed and went to kneel down for a prayer. Cynthia's suggestion that God might be working to bring to pass His revelation came to mind. She thought that over for several minutes, then decided that as long as she felt she had done all she could, she should feel at peace. God wouldn't ask for more than that.

Meanwhile, she thought about Gabe. She wasn't sure what to do. She did like him, she admitted. She had for some time, in fact.

23

Two Dates in One Week

The next morning in church, Gabe took his program without looking up and went straight into the chapel. Alice looked in after him. He sat down in the back, rested his elbows on his knees, and stared down at his feet. His hair looked slightly more tousled than usual, but otherwise his appearance was as neat as ever. There was a perfectly ironed crease running down the length of his trousers, and his shirt had been carefully pressed and not roughed up by any of his friends. After a moment, he unzipped his scripture case and pulled out his scriptures.

Alice realized she was staring and turned around. Spencer was approaching. His steps slowed, and he looked away. "I got your message," he said to her. "So, I guess that's that?"

"I'm sorry," said Alice.

Still not looking at her, he took his program and went into the chapel. His shoulders were slumped. *Ouch,* thought Alice, *I really hurt him, didn't I? I am definitely regretting the voice mail breakup now.* Even so, she didn't feel the slightest desire to patch things up.

Leslie and Sarah came around the corner. "You should definitely take Gabe," said Sarah. "Just call him."

"I can't call a guy," said Leslie.

"Oh, you can call Gabe," said Sarah. "He's totally fine with stuff like that."

Alice raised one eyebrow and handed them both programs.

She glanced at her watch, put the rest of the programs down on the table, and went in. As she walked past Gabe, she could feel his gaze on her. She sat down in an empty seat and turned to look back at him.

He quickly looked away.

* * *

"Alice!" Cynthia yelled as Alice came into the kitchen. "If you keep coming in here every two minutes, I'm going to throw this rolling pin at your head." She was rolling out dough for cookies on a counter liberally dusted with flour.

Alice went around and sat down on one of the bar stools. "Sorry," she said. "I was just going to refill my glass with water." She set her glass on a clear spot on the counter.

"Which you did five minutes ago, and ten minutes before that. Just take the pitcher in your room."

"Okay."

Cynthia set the rolling pin aside. "What is it?" she asked.

"Nothing."

"Liar."

Alice sighed. "Tell me again that it wouldn't be completely crazy to call Gabe?"

"It would, but I think you should do it anyway."

"I just want to apologize, you know?"

Cynthia rolled her eyes. "Suuure you do," she said. "Ask him out already! And then come in here and tell me everything." She grinned, coated the rolling pin with flour, and resumed rolling out dough.

Cynthia knew her far too well. Alice went back into her room, took her cell phone off its charger, and got her copy of the ward list out of the drawer of her vanity. According to the list, Ely and Gabe used only cell phones.

With a hand that was already starting to shake, she punched in Gabe's number and hit SEND. She shut her eyes tight and brought the phone to her ear.

"'Lo?" came his voice.

"Hi . . . Gabe?"

"Hey, Alice. What's up?" He sounded cheerful enough.

"Not much. You?"

"Not much. You coming to the temple on Thursday?"

"I plan to."

"Cool."

Silence. Alice bit her lip. "Um . . . Gabe?"

"Yeah?"

"Can I . . . I mean, I'll understand if you're uh . . . if you don't want . . ." Her voice trailed off.

"Want what?" he asked.

She took a deep breath and tried again. "Can I take back what I said yesterday?"

"Which part?"

"The part where I shot you down and called you a kid."

"Oh yeah."

"Gabe, I'm sorry. I'm not normally interested in guys your age."

"Yeah, I get that."

"But look, can I take you out for ice cream or something? After the temple on Thursday, maybe? Make it up to you?"

"Uh, okay."

Alice let herself relax. "Okay," she said.

"So . . . what happened with Spencer?"

"He was, you know, himself."

Gabe laughed. "He's not *that* bad."

"Suffice it to say, I'll never be the kind of woman he's looking for."

"I see."

"I feel bad about it."

"Sarah used to date him, back when he was in the ward before."

"She did?"

"For, like, two weeks. She said he was really into laying down rules about proper . . . I dunno . . . displays of affection."

"Which isn't entirely a bad thing."

"No, it's not, but hand holding was only allowed in public. He made this huge deal about chaperones. He lectured her for twenty minutes on it." He laughed. "It's hard to get to know someone when they look down on you, you know?"

"Valid point." *And I have just learned,* thought Alice, *that I am not as perceptive as Sarah Nagel. That stings.*

"You were with him a long time, though. I'd heard he was talking about getting engaged."

"I guess he was pretty serious about that, but long story short, it didn't happen. I'm back in the singles pool."

"Which is great."

"Glad you think so."

"Okay, so what scriptures are you going to read before going to the temple again?"

Alice got up from her chair and sprawled out on her bed. "I don't know," she said. "I should probably brush up on the Old Testament."

"I'm rereading Exodus. There's some really interesting stuff about the temple in there."

"Really?"

Half an hour later, Cynthia stuck her head in the door. Alice was still sprawled out on her bed with her scriptures open in front of her. "Huh, I never thought about how similar those verses are," she was saying to Gabe. "But now that you mention it, that's really interesting."

Cynthia rolled her eyes and withdrew.

* * *

Monica called that evening. "Hey, Alice?" she said. "Lorraine's wanting to know if we can go to her condo for dinner again the first weekend next month. Sounds like she'd kind of like to make it a monthly thing."

"I'm free the first weekend of May, I think," said Alice.

"Well, you sound happy."

"I just asked a guy out," she admitted. "I broke things off with Spencer."

"Who's the guy?"

"Oh . . . no one you'd know," she fibbed.

* * *

That Thursday night, Alice met Gabe outside the temple. Much to her amazement, she wasn't all that nervous. It was just Gabe, she thought, and Gabe was easy to talk to.

The session made a lot more sense to her this time, and afterwards they sat in the celestial room on one of the couches under the chandelier. Alice asked Gabe question after question. His usual answer was to shrug and say, "I don't know, but here's what I think." Then he'd always ask her what she thought. Alice finally had to stop asking questions before it got too late. "Okay," she said to him, "now that we've done our temple work for the week, shall we switch gears and go out?"

"Sounds good," he answered.

Alice drove them both to an ice cream parlor. Gabe seemed entirely at ease. It felt so good, thought Alice. She was so tired of awkward dates.

"So," he said when they'd found a place to sit at one of the plastic tables. "Do you want to go miniature golfing with us?"

"When is it?" she asked.

"It's tomorrow. I completely understand if you have other plans." He stared intently at his ice cream as he loaded his spoon with another bite.

"I don't have other plans."

"Okay, so is two dates in one week too much for you? Because, you know, in Mormon culture, two dates in one week means you're a couple."

Alice looked at him. She couldn't tell from his expression if he was being serious or not. "It does not," she said.

"Oh, yes it does. And if one of those dates is miniature golf? I mean . . . that's a serious date. LDS guys don't take just anyone miniature golfing." He gestured with his spoon.

"Are Sarah and Ely going to be a couple after tomorrow?"

Gabe shook his head. "It'll just be their first date."

"So what kind of Mormon girl goes miniature golfing on a first date?"

Gabe put the back of his wrist to his mouth and choked back a laugh. "Is that why you said no when I asked you before?"

"No. That had more to do with me graduating from high school while you were still in junior high."

He shrugged. "You've given this age gap a lot of thought, haven't you?"

"Does it bother you?"

"No." He ate another spoonful of ice cream. "Why should it?"

"Because admit it, it's weird."

"I really like you," he said, meeting her gaze.

Alice looked down. "Gabe, I'm leaving in July."

He didn't say anything, just kept looking at her.

"For my job. Just so you know."

He nodded, looked at his ice cream again, and said, "So do you want to come tomorrow?"

"I don't know. If I say yes, will you think I'm easy?"

"Yeah, but I won't tell anyone." He winked at her.

She laughed. "Fine. I'll go."

24

Out of Time

The next evening Alice felt self-conscious all over again. It was one thing to go out alone with Gabe and quite another to go out with other people. When she arrived at the miniature golf course, everyone was waiting for her in front of the building that housed the video arcade and pizza parlor.

Sarah was wearing a very cute skirt and blouse again and spent more time staring at Gabe than paying attention to Ely. Ely seemed relatively unfazed by this. Gabe looked attractive in a long-sleeved shirt with the sleeves pushed up to his elbows, and he was ignoring Sarah. He'd glance over at her and occasionally reply to her comments, but as soon as he sighted Alice, he turned his attention to her. "Hey, Alice," said Ely when she stepped up.

"Hi," said Alice.

Gabe just smiled at her.

As she looked around the group, Alice felt old. *Ten years ago I could have been your babysitter,* she thought. Sarah glared at her, but Alice didn't find it all that threatening. She merely looked back and smiled.

They braved the crowds in the arcade to get their colored golf balls, putters, and scorecards. Gabe stayed right beside Alice, even resting his hand on her arm when the crowds pressed in close.

Seeing this, Sarah latched onto Ely's arm as they made their way out to the course. Ely gave her an odd look but didn't push her away. Sarah turned around to glare at Alice.

"Ignore her," Gabe told Alice in a low voice. He leaned in close to speak to her. "I guess she's having issues with me dating someone else."

"Not exactly your ideal double date then," said Alice.

"She's fine." He rested his hand on her shoulder again as they reached the exit to the arcade, then kept it there as they stepped through into the cooler air outside. The noise of people talking, video game explosions, and quarters dropping into slots stopped abruptly when the door swung closed behind them.

The miniature golf course itself wasn't too crowded. An orange-and-yellow sign pointed to the first hole, which featured a large mechanical dinosaur painted purple and pink. The dinosaur's mouth opened and closed at random intervals, and in order to sink the ball, one had to putt it through the dinosaur's open mouth. As they stepped up to the little rubber tees, Alice's cell phone rang. She pulled it out of her pocket and saw that it was her boss, Gretchen. "Sorry," she said, "I'd better take this." She handed her putter to Gabe and walked back toward the arcade, flipping her phone open. "Hello?" she said.

"Alice, hi. Sorry to call you after hours, but I'm looking at an ad the company has placed for your position."

"The one in Phoenix?" She stepped off the path and ducked behind a hedge that was pruned into a sharp rectangle.

"Yes. I know this is a month early, but do you have any other offers? If I could get a firm answer from you, it would help me when I confront the higher ups about this."

"I think it's okay," said Alice. "I mean, they haven't made an offer to anyone else, right? They're just covering their bases in case I say no."

"They're offering to pay the person fifteen thousand more than they offered you."

"Oh."

"Which is unprofessional, if you ask me. Alice, I'm going to have to resort to begging here. I would really like you to take this offer, and if you can give me a firm answer now, I'll make sure you get the higher salary. Can you commit?"

No. The word was on the tip of her tongue, but it defied all logic. She wasn't going to make that kind of money anywhere else, the move date was ten weeks away, and Gretchen was begging. Alice shut her eyes and thought hard. *Did God tell me to wait on deciding about my job? I don't know; that's the problem.* The seconds were ticking, and Gretchen was waiting.

"Yes," said Alice. "I'll submit my acceptance letter on Monday."

"Great! Thank you, Alice. I'll let you go now."

Alice said good-bye and switched off her phone. For a moment all she could do was stare at it. It was done. She'd made her final decision. She wasn't engaged to anyone, and she was on a date with Gabe Spinelli of all people. *Please, Lord, tell me I didn't just blow it.* She folded the phone shut.

"So you're definitely leaving?"

Alice turned. Gabe stood about two paces away, his hands in his pockets.

"Yes," she said, "I am." She put her phone in her pocket.

"When?"

"I need to be there June twenty-eighth."

He nodded. "I'll miss you," he said.

"Well, I'll miss you too." *And your family,* she thought. *Not that I can tell you about that.*

He didn't say anything else for several seconds.

"Anyway . . ." she began.

He stepped forward and put his arms around her, pulling her close for a hug, an earnest, desperate hug. He didn't say anything, only stroked her hair and inhaled deeply, as if memorizing her scent. Alice resisted at first, then reasoned that it was just a hug. She rested her cheek against his chest and put her arms around his waist. She could pick up trace scents of leather—from his motorcycle jacket, no doubt—detergent, and soap. It felt good just to be held, if only for a few seconds. Then Alice let go and gently pressed him away. "I'm sorry," she said.

He reluctantly let go but kept his arm around her shoulders.

Alice said, "Don't you think it'd be a bad idea to get involved right now?"

"You're still around for ten weeks," he replied as they started walking back toward the others.

"Yes, but after that—"

"I really like you, okay?"

She shrugged. "Look, Gabe, I like you too, but I *am* leaving and not looking for a relationship right now. We're clear on that, right?"

Gabe nodded but didn't look at her. He didn't remove his arm either.

* * *

When Alice got home, she was so keyed up that for several minutes all she could do was pace the front room. Cynthia peered out of her room, saw this, and came out. "What is it?" she asked.

Alice told her about the phone call from Gretchen.

"So . . ." said Cynthia, "that's that then? You're definitely going?"

"Yes."

Cynthia kept staring at her.

Alice paused in her pacing and tried to calm herself.

"You okay?" said Cynthia.

"I'm fine. It's just kind of sudden, that's all."

Her roommate nodded.

Neither of them brought up the subject of the revelation.

* * *

The next Sunday in church, Gabe sat on the table next to where Alice stood passing out programs. "If I ask you in a really suave way," he said, "will you come to my place after church and read next week's Sunday School assignment with me?"

Alice laughed. "Sounds kind of high school."

"I know; that's why I need to be really suave, and you can come for lunch if you like."

She looked back over her shoulder at him. "I don't know," she said.

Gabe nodded and averted his gaze. "You don't want to get involved."

"I've got enough stress in my life right now." Out of the corner of her eye, she saw the missionaries approaching and turned back around to hand them programs.

"Sister O'Donnell," said Elder Bradshaw with a smile. He and his companion took the programs and went into the chapel.

A few seconds later, Sarah and Leslie came around the corner. "So I told Hannah," Sarah was saying, "and she got all weird about it."

At the sight of Alice, Sarah paused. She glanced at Gabe, then looked at Alice again and forced a smile. "Hi," she said.

"Hi," said Alice and handed her a program.

Sarah took it, then took Leslie by the arm, and they both went into the chapel.

Alice looked back at Gabe. "What was that about?" she asked.

He shrugged.

"Did you have a talk with her or something?"

"I was nice about it."

"What did you say to her?"

Gabe looked at his shoes.

Alice glanced at her watch and went over to the table he sat on. "Off," she told him. "This space is for the programs."

He hopped down. Alice laid out the programs and turned to head into the chapel. "Alice," said Gabe. He put his hand on her arm. "Please, why can't we spend time together before you leave?"

"Gabe—"

"*Please.*"

She looked up at him and immediately wished she hadn't. Why did he always have to be so good-looking? His green eyes were catching the light again in that way they often did, but there was no hint of a smile on his lips. He looked downright unhappy. *All because of me,* thought Alice. "Fine," she relented. "I suppose it would be nice to have someone to read with."

"And about lunch?"

"Yes, all right. Thanks."

He smiled. Alice looked away. He was way too attractive for his own good.

They went into the chapel together, and Alice found two empty seats near the back. Gabe shook his head and kept walking. Puzzled, Alice followed him until he found two empty seats near the front. He gestured for Alice to take one.

She did, and he sat next to her. "What was wrong with the other ones?" she asked.

"I wanted more people to see me doing this," he said. He stretched out his arm and laid it casually on the back of the pew behind Alice.

"Staking your claim in front of all the other guys?"

"Pretty much."

"Look . . ." Alice shook her head. "Don't get the wrong idea, okay?"

He looked chastened but didn't remove his arm.

Nearby, a dozen nineteen-year-old girls turned to glare at her.

* * *

Ely beat them to the apartment after church and was lounging on the couch when they arrived. When Gabe opened the front door, Ely sat up straight and said, "I thought of a new way to ask Leslie out." He caught sight of Alice then and hesitated.

"What was the old way?" she asked.

Gabe smirked at that and went into the kitchen. Alice looked around. She barely recognized the place, it was so clean. The living area was entirely devoid of junk. The floor was vacuumed, the coffee table was dusted, and, stranger still, the doors to both bedrooms stood wide open, revealing neatly made beds. There wasn't so much as a stray shoe on the floor or a jacket tossed casually somewhere. The place even smelled like ammonia cleaner.

Missions really do wonders, Alice thought. *I guess Darren had been home from his too long.*

Gabe put a pot on the stove and started the burner with the click-click-click of the gas lighter.

"What can I do?" Alice asked. "I warn you, I'm a disaster in the kitchen but . . . can I cut something up?"

"Sure," said Gabe. He got a fresh pineapple out of the fridge. "You can slice this."

Alice felt awkward. "I don't know how," she admitted.

"I can show you," he said without missing a beat.

While Alice wrestled with the pineapple, Ely stayed on the couch. "But what if Leslie's with someone else?" he said.

"Who else?" asked Gabe.

"I think she might be dating Chris."

"What?" said Alice. She looked up. "*Chris?* I thought he was engaged to Julie."

"Chris who?" Gabe asked.

"Chris Donaldson," said Ely. "I saw them talking in the parking lot."

"Oh," said Gabe, "big deal."

"I'm pretty sure he's engaged," said Alice. "Julie was flaunting the ring this week in Relief Society *again*."

Gabe glanced at her.

"Sorry," said Alice. "That probably sounded bitter. I didn't mean it that way. I just . . . I'm not good at that kind of girly stuff. You know, if you like Leslie, dating her best friend isn't exactly a good idea."

"We're just friends," said Ely.

"That's not the point."

Gabe brought a can over to the sink. Alice stepped back while he rinsed it under the tap and then went to jam it into the electric opener. He looked back at her, smiled, and gave her shoulder a squeeze.

This isn't exactly a good idea either, Alice thought. *Why couldn't I just say no to him?*

When the can opener stopped, Gabe tugged the can loose and poured its contents into the pot on the stove.

"You know what else?" Ely went on.

"Should I care?" Gabe answered.

Alice tossed the mangled pieces of pineapple skin into the garbage. "Do you always just lounge while Gabe cooks?" she asked. "You're just as bad as I am."

"Yup."

"He's got dish duty," Gabe explained.

"Yup. Okay, so I was talking to Leslie and she kept laughing for no apparent reason. She was totally giving me a complex."

"Does he always talk about the girls he likes?" Alice asked.

"Yes," said Gabe.

"*No,* I talk about myself too. But anyway, I'm definitely asking her out. Do you think she'd say yes?"

"I don't know," said Gabe. "Just ask her."

"Is Alice going to be around all afternoon?"

Gabe looked over at her. "I hope so," he said.

Alice laid the knife on the cutting board. Gabe, seeming to sense her unease, stepped over and put his hand on her shoulder again. He lowered his chin and looked her in the eye.

"All right, I'm leaving," Ely announced. He went back into his room and shut the door.

"I know you're moving soon," said Gabe. "You've said it ten times since this morning." With his finger, he brushed a stray lock of hair back from her forehead. "I'll be okay with it when it happens, I promise."

25

Outnumbered

The following morning, Alice typed up her acceptance letter for her Phoenix job and carried it to Gretchen's office. Gretchen accepted it with a brief but genuine smile. Alice turned around and went back to her office. *Done,* she thought. *No changing it now.*

* * *

That evening when Alice got home, she found Cynthia standing in front of the open refrigerator. "Gabe taught me how to chop stuff," Alice said. "Do you need me to chop vegetables?"

Cynthia looked up. "Gabe called a few minutes ago, and I invited him over for dinner."

"What?"

"He seems nice."

"Wait, he called and said what?"

"He's much nicer than Spencer."

"Cynth."

"What? He just wanted to talk to you, and I said you weren't home. He heard the sound of me putting pots on the stove, and he asked if I was cooking, and we got to talking about working as waiters and . . ." She shrugged. "So I told him he could come over and help us cook dinner."

"I'm trying to not spend too much time with him."

"Oh, and you're doing a really great job at that. You were over at his place for how long yesterday?"

"Just a couple of hours."

"Uh-huh. That's always what I do when I'm not interested in a guy."

"But—"

"You're leaving. I know. He knows. Everyone knows. But if you like him, just date him. I think you're being silly about this."

Alice dumped her purse on the couch and tried to think of a response.

Cynthia smirked at her. "He'll be by any minute."

* * *

When Gabe got there, he went straight to the kitchen. "Hey," he said to Cynthia, "I'm Gabe. Need help?"

Alice took his jacket and motorcycle helmet and hung them up while Cynthia replied, "Do you think you can train my roommate to boil water?"

"Cynth," said Alice, "you're making me look bad."

Gabe only laughed.

"And he doesn't care," said Cynthia. "I say you definitely date this one."

Alice's face flushed hot as Gabe quirked a smile at Cynthia.

* * *

Three nights later, Gabe was back again. Alice felt a little more in control because she'd invited him. Well, in truth, Cynthia had answered his phone call, and Alice had grabbed the phone before her roommate had the chance to invite him. This time he came bearing a paper sack with some fresh herbs. They looked like little plant clippings to Alice, but Cynthia was excited by them. "I haven't been able to find fresh basil at a decent price for weeks," she told Gabe.

"I know," he said. "I got this from work. It'll go bad soon, so they let us take it home."

Cynthia took the bag from Gabe. "Okay, Alice—"

"Don't say it," said Alice. "I get it. You like this one." To Gabe she said, "This is really low, bribing my roommate with cooking supplies."

Gabe blinked innocently as he rummaged through one of the drawers. That was when Alice knew that her roommate wasn't just kidding around. Cynthia never let anyone else have the run of her kitchen.

* * *

That next Friday, Alice came home from working late and found the blinds of the apartment still open. Given the lights were on inside, everyone in the apartment complex's courtyard could see Gabe and Cynthia sitting at the dining room table. He had his homework books spread out, and she had her laptop in front of her. Cynthia never left the blinds open. It prevented them from being alone together, Alice realized. It was simple and unobtrusive. On the counter, behind them, was a meringue pie.

Alice unlocked the door and stepped in.

". . . been working since you were eleven years old?" Cynthia was saying. "How is that legal?"

Gabe twisted around to smile at Alice before he replied. "I don't think it is. I just . . . we needed money, and my uncle paid me some and taught me how to keep a bank account and use a checkbook and all that."

"Oh," said Cynthia.

"I started helping my mom with that stuff, and by the time I was fourteen, I pretty much did all of it."

This, Alice knew, was putting it nicely. Lorraine had told her about the fights she'd had with her son, the way he'd demanded control of the money, and how she'd finally turned it all over to him because he really did know more than she did.

Cynthia knew most of this too, but her expression betrayed nothing. "So is this guy your boyfriend yet, Alice?" she asked. "I like him."

"Oh, do you now? You're so subtle about it. And *you*—" she pointed an accusing finger at Gabe "—have found my roommate's weakness for pastries, which is so not fair." She nodded in the direction of the pie.

Gabe smiled sheepishly and got to his feet.

Alice looked over the scene—Gabe's tentative stance, the dining room table covered with books and Cynthia's magazines, the spotless kitchen, and the clock that read 7:00 P.M. "Do you want to go out to eat?" she asked him. "I think Cynth deserves to be left all alone with a pie this evening."

"Hey," said Cynthia.

"Sure," said Gabe.

"Alice," Cynthia protested, "lock this thing up somewhere. You know I'm gonna eat the whole thing."

Alice only smirked at her as she took down Gabe's jacket and held it out to him. Then the two of them left, arm in arm, Cynthia still protesting in the background.

"So, are we together?" Gabe asked when they stepped outside.

"Looks like it," said Alice.

"Good, because I've been calling you my girlfriend since we went out for ice cream."

Alice gave him her best exasperated look, but he only smiled back at her.

* * *

That month, Alice and Monica's meal at Lorraine's was more awkward than ever. The first thing Lorraine asked when they stepped in the door was, "Have you seen Gabriel lately?"

Just last night at the movies, Alice thought. She shrugged noncommittally.

"How is he?"

"Um," Alice stammered. "I don't know."

It didn't help that Gina beamed at Alice whenever Lorraine had her back turned.

But Lorraine soon changed the subject to investments, and Alice sat at the counter and talked to Lorraine while she cooked. While they ate, Lorraine spent most of the time talking to Monica as Alice fought the immature urge to kick Gina under the table. The girl was positively smug.

"So girls," Lorraine said at the end of the evening. "My shift at work is changing, so I will not be able to do the first weekend in June. Will the twenty-fifth work for you?"

"Sure," said Monica.

"I'll make it work," said Alice. "I'm moving the twenty-sixth."

"You're moving?" cried Gina.

Lorraine also looked shocked.

So Gabe wasn't telling his sister everything. She nodded.

"But we'll miss you," said Lorraine.

"And I'll miss you too. You have to keep in touch, okay? Ask me money questions, keep me on my toes." She and Lorraine exchanged a hug before Alice and Monica stepped out the door.

* * *

A few weeks later, Alice came home to find Cynthia standing in the middle of the kitchen, looking haggard.

"Need me to help?" Alice asked.

Cynthia quirked an eyebrow at her and said, "Can you chop onions?"

"Mmm-hmm." Alice put her purse away in her room, washed her hands in the bathroom sink, then retrieved a knife and cutting board. Cynthia presented her with an onion. Alice cut into it and began peeling back the papery outer skin, her eyes watering in response to the pungent odor.

"Amazing," said Cynthia.

Alice looked up and saw that her roommate was watching her every move. "What?" she said. "It's not that hard."

"Two years of me trying to teach you says it is."

"So I'm slow." Alice cut the onion in half, set one half on the corner of the cutting board, and began chopping the other.

"I just never tried putting my arms around you when you got it wrong."

Alice scowled at her roommate.

Cynthia grinned back. "Things are going well with him, aren't they?"

"I guess."

"You guess?"

Alice put her hands over her face and shook her head. "He's so sweet to me. I've never had a guy be this nice, but I still don't know what'll happen—"

"When you leave next month. Yeah, yeah. Where is he tonight?"

"Working."

The phone rang, and Cynthia leaned across the counter to look at the caller ID. "Your dad," she said.

"Leave it then."

The phone rang three more times then went quiet. A few seconds later it rang again.

"I hate it when he does this," said Alice.

"What's his problem?" asked Cynthia.

The phone went silent, then a few seconds later began again. Alice reached over to the wall and unplugged the line.

In Alice's purse, her cell phone rang. She washed her hands, glanced at the display, saw it was her father, and turned it off. Half an hour after that, there was a knock on the door. "We're not here," said Alice. "No," she said when Cynthia began to cross the room. "Don't even look through the peephole. If it's my dad and he sees your shadow, he won't leave."

Cynthia returned to the kitchen. "You sure everything's all right?" she asked.

"I've got better things to think about."

The knocking finally stopped. Alice breathed a sigh of relief.

* * *

Alice's father tried to call five more times the next day while she was at the office. Alice hit IGNORE on her cell phone every time and told the receptionist out front to tell him she was out if he tried coming by. She worked in relative peace that afternoon, and there was a spring in her step as she headed out that evening.

She drove over to pick Gabe up from his apartment and found him more worn out than usual. "Work was really bad," he told her as they walked down the stairs from his apartment. "I had two sorority parties in my section, and they were trying to see who could be the most demanding."

"So would you rather not go to another restaurant tonight?" she asked him.

"Are you kidding? I learned all these new ways to annoy waiters."

Alice laughed. They got into her car and drove to Santa Monica, where they had dinner in one of the small cafés along Third Street. Halfway through the meal, Alice's cell phone rang. She looked down at it, where it rested at the top of her purse. "Mom" flashed on the display. "Sorry, this is my mother," she said to Gabe as she picked up the phone, flipped it open, and said, "Hi, Mom."

"Oh, Alice!"

"What's wrong?"

Gabe looked concerned.

"Hasn't your father told you?" said her mother.

"No. I haven't spoken to him in a while."

"The divorce settlement. He says I need to sign it or else he's going to get the court to impose a worse one on me."

"What?"

"The divorce settlement. Our lawyers drafted it last week, and your father demands that I sign it."

"What does your lawyer say?"

Gabe put his fork down.

"She wants me to sign it," said her mother.

"Okay."

"And I know it's the right thing to do. This one is very favorable to me. I get to keep the house and my car but . . ." Her mother began to sob. "When I sign it, I won't be married to your dad anymore."

"Mom . . ."

Her mother kept crying.

"How long do you have to decide?" Alice asked.

"Five hours."

"What?"

"The offer expires at midnight. Oh, Alice, what do I do?"

Gabe put his hand on Alice's arm. "What is it?" he mouthed.

Alice took the phone away from her ear. "My parents' divorce may be final tonight."

"Oh."

"Alice?" asked her mother.

Alice put the phone back to her ear. "Yeah, Mom?"

"What do I do, Alice?"

"Well . . ." She heaved a deep sigh. "Sign it, I guess."

"I thought you'd say that." Her mother really broke down then.

"Mom, what do you need? Should I come over?"

Gabe was still resting his hand on her arm.

"I don't know, I don't know," her mother moaned.

"I can be there in half an hour."

"Well . . ."

"Let's go," said Gabe. "You can drop me off at my place or I can come or whatever. It's your call."

Alice nodded. "Mom," she said, "I'm on my way."

* * *

Twenty minutes later, Alice pulled into her mother's driveway. Gabe had offered to come with her, so he still sat in the passenger seat. "I'll wait out here," he told her. "If you want me to come in or anything, call my cell. Otherwise, don't worry about me, okay?"

"Gabe, I really—"

"I'll be fine." He took her hand and gave it a squeeze.

Alice returned the gesture and got out. Her mother didn't answer when she rang the doorbell, so she unlocked the front door and let herself in. "Mom?" she called.

A sob let her know that her mother was in the kitchen. Alice found her mother seated at the counter, a document spread out in front of her.

"I can't do it," she told Alice.

"Oh, Mom." Alice went over to give her a hug.

"The court will just have to impose whatever it wants."

"Mom . . ." Alice realized that her throat was starting to constrict. "It has to end sometime, you know."

"I know."

Alice's cell phone rang. She fished it out of her purse and saw that it was Gabe. "Hello?" she said.

"Alice, a tall, older guy with brown hair just pulled up. He's got this blond woman in the car with him. They're getting out and heading toward the front door. Is it your dad?"

"Yes, and I forgot to lock the front door," said Alice. She darted to the entryway, but not before her father opened the door and stepped inside. The bluish light from the streetlamp outlined his silhouette.

Alice stopped in her tracks. "Did you skip class the day they covered restraining orders in law school?"

"Hello to you too."

"Alice?" came Gabe's voice over the phone. "Do you need me to come in?"

"No," Alice answered him.

"Are you sure?"

"Yes, it's fine."

"On the phone with someone?" her dad asked.

Alice shut her cell phone, then realized she'd just hung up on Gabe. "Dad . . ." She tried to collect her thoughts. "You can't just come waltzing in here."

"Suzie," said her father. He stepped aside to reveal the blond woman Gabe had told her about. She was about her father's height and age, with a willowy build. "This is my daughter, Alice."

"Hello, Alice!" she said with a cheerfulness that was entirely out of place. She stepped into the entryway, and the light illuminated her pale features.

"Look, Allie," her father said, "I just came by to see if your mother's signed the settlement."

"Mom has until midnight." Alice turned on her heel. "And I'm calling the police. You know you're not supposed to be here."

"Allie," he called after her.

Alice picked up her pace. She'd need to use her mom's landline so they could trace the call if necessary.

26

The Divorce

When Alice returned to the kitchen, her mother was on her feet.
"Is your father here?" she asked.

"He's not supposed to be," said Alice. She grabbed the phone off the wall and placed her cell on the counter.

"Annabeth," came her father's voice, "don't let her do that." Alice turned around. Her father was standing just inside the kitchen door. Suzie was next to him, staring at Alice's mother with a look of exasperation and disgust.

Alice began to dial, but her mother stepped over and took the phone out of her hands. "Mom!" said Alice.

"Honey, don't," her mother said. She hung the phone back up.

"Did you sign yet?" Alice's father asked.

"Oh, Harold . . ."

"Did you sign?"

Suzie flipped a strand of hair over her shoulder and said, "We agreed this would all be over by the end of today. That's a *good* offer." She pointed at the document laid out on the counter.

"Mother," said Alice, "they are not supposed to be here harassing you. There's a reason you got that restraining order."

Alice's cell phone rang, and her father snatched it up from the counter.

Alice held out her hand to him, demanding that he pass it over. "What are you doing?" she asked.

"Who's Gabe?" he asked, looking at the display.

"Just give me the phone."

Her father pushed a button and handed it back to her. "He can wait, whoever he is," he said.

Alice glanced at her phone, frowned, then turned to face her mother. "How often have these two been coming over? Be honest."

But her mother wasn't looking at her. "Harold," she said, "isn't there any chance we can—"

"No, Annabeth. We've had this conversation a thousand times. Just sign the settlement."

Alice's mother began to cry.

"Dad," said Alice, "enough, okay?"

The front door opened.

Alice's father whirled around. "Who's here?" he demanded.

"It's Gabe," said Alice. She crossed the room and brushed past her father. Gabe stood just inside the front door.

"You all right?" he asked her.

"Yes. Everything's fine."

"Allie, what's he doing here?" her father demanded.

"I called the police when you didn't answer your phone," Gabe said.

"What?" Alice's father roared. "What business is this of yours?"

Gabe ignored him. "You sure everything's all right?" he said to Alice.

"I asked you a question!" yelled Alice's father. "Allie? Who is this guy?"

"Everything's just *great*," said Alice. "Can't you tell? This is my family, by the way." She gestured back over her shoulder.

"Alice Annabeth O'Donnell," her father shouted, "I am talking to you!"

Gabe refocused his attention then. "Hi, my name's Gabe," he said.

Alice's father darted across the entryway and shook angrily as he demanded, "And what do you think you're doing here?"

"I brought him, Dad. Leave him alone."

"You!" Her father turned on her and grabbed her by the arm. "Allie, I've offered your mother a great settlement, far better than what she could win if a judge decides. But you know how she is. She's had that thing for days. You've got to get her to sign it. Don't you under-stand that?"

"I understand that if she doesn't, you won't like it."

"She *will* regret it if she doesn't," he said. "I think I've played nice long enough."

"And when I show the judge the police report that shows you were here in violation of the restraining order—"

"Are you paying attention to any of this? Allie, I have given your mother nearly everything in exchange for my freedom. If you want to rob me of what little I'll have left—"

"Not feeling pity here!"

Her father's grip tightened like a vise. He brought his face very close to hers. "All I want is to get married and move on."

"For how long?" She raised her voice. "Suzie, I should let you know that if you have any bad days or you ever make my dad less than happy, he's gone. That's his idea of commi—"

Alice winced as her father brought up his hand to slap her. The slap never came, though. Instead, Gabe stepped over, grabbed her father's wrist, and yanked him around so that the two men faced each other. Slowly, Alice's father let go of her. His face went pale.

"I called 911 a few minutes ago," Gabe said evenly. "So if you don't want to be here when the cops arrive, you'd best get gone." As if on cue, a siren began to wail in the distance.

Gabe let go of her father's wrist but maintained eye contact.

"Suzie, honey?" her father called. "We need to leave now."

Alice backed away. Gabe came around and put his hands on her shoulders. "You all right?" he whispered.

"Yes." Alice rubbed her arm. "I'm fine."

Suzie marched through the entryway, giving Alice and Gabe a venomous look as she did. Alice's father was holding open the front door for her.

"Annabeth!" he shouted. "Sign the document! Now! Tonight!" He followed Suzie out the door, leaving it wide open. They went straight to his car, got in, and drove off.

With a sigh of relief, Gabe pulled Alice close and gave her a hug.

"Thanks," she said, hugging him back. "I need to go check on my mom."

He followed her back into the kitchen, where they found Alice's mother signing the agreement. She propelled the ballpoint pen across the page with more force than necessary, nearly ripping the document.

"Mom," said Alice.

"I'm *done* with this. I hope he's happy. May he and Suzie have a *wonderful* marriage. I wish her all the joy *I've* had these last thirty years." The pen slipped out of her hands and clattered to the floor as she began to sob again.

The sirens drew up to the house, and the blue flashing lights flickered through the still-open front door, casting reflections on the oven, the window, and the mirror in the entryway.

"Mom," said Alice.

"Go home, honey. Just go."

"I can't leave you alone right now."

Gabe slipped out into the entryway, and Alice heard him say, "Back in the kitchen," to the police officers.

A moment later, a uniformed police officer stepped into the room. "What happened?" he asked.

"My father was here," said Alice, "in violation of a restraining order."

"I see. Well, ma'am," he addressed himself to Alice's mother, "we'll need to ask you some questions. You too," he told Alice.

* * *

Half an hour later, Alice and Gabe stood on the front lawn answering the last of the officer's queries. Then he let them go.

"I'll take you home," Alice told Gabe. "Then I need to come back here for the night."

"Alone?"

"Dad doesn't have the key," she told him. "I'll keep the door locked."

He still looked concerned.

"It'll be all right," she said.

"Okay," he said, but she could hear the hesitation in his voice. "I could call Ely and have him pick me up."

"No, Mom's asleep right now." Alice had persuaded her to take some sleeping pills before she tucked her into bed. "She'll be fine until I get back."

Gabe nodded and let Alice lead him back to her car.

"I am so sorry about this," she told him.

"It's not your fault." He got into the passenger seat and shut the door.

Alice did the same on the driver's side. "This has got to be your worst date ever," she said.

"No." Gabe chuckled. "You can't beat my senior prom. My date took off with another guy halfway through."

"Second worst, then." She started the engine and backed the car out of the driveway.

He reached over gave her shoulder a squeeze. "I'm just glad the cops came before anyone got hurt," he said.

"*I'm* glad my father didn't go after you." Alice shifted the car into drive. "You'd be the second boyfriend he's bullied in two months." She glanced at him out of the corner of her eye and saw that he was smiling at her, like he often did. "What?" she said.

He shrugged. "I just like it when you call me your boyfriend."

She reached over and rested a hand on his knee. He covered it with his own.

"Your dad tried to beat up Spencer?" he asked.

"No, not physically. He just asked him a bunch of questions and made him look stupid. But it made it clear to me that I shouldn't have been dating him."

"So he caused the breakup?"

"I guess you could say he helped me see the light."

"That must have been rough."

Alice glanced at him again. He was looking back at her. "Not really," she said. "I didn't have a deep emotional attachment to Spencer. That was one good thing about his rules, I guess—he kept me at arm's length."

Gabe tightened his grip on her hand, curling his fingers around hers. "Was it harder with Darren?"

"Well . . . yeah." Alice concentrated on navigating the freeway entrance ahead and didn't look at him. "Of course it was. Even just kissing someone changes things." She hazarded a glance over at him and saw that he was looking down. His thumb caressed the back of her hand.

"But Gabe," she told him. "It's not like I'm an innocent Molly."

His grip on her hand didn't lessen, and she could feel his gaze on her.

She took a deep breath. "Gabe, look, I . . . don't know how much Darren told you about my past. I haven't always kept the law of chastity, you know." Her face felt hot. "I was a different person before I was baptized."

Gabe continued to look at her for a moment. She couldn't read his expression from out of the corner of her eye. Finally he said, "Means you get what baptism's all about."

Alice stroked his knee with her thumb. "Very diplomatic."

"I'm not being diplomatic. I'm serious. Look, Darren used to make comments about you living with some guy before—"

"Which I did."

"But that was then."

Alice didn't know what to say next, so she just focused on driving. She felt tense and awkward. She wondered why she'd even brought it up.

They sped along the freeway. The traffic was light, and in less than fifteen minutes they were at his apartment. Alice shut off the engine and got out to walk him to the door, wondering what he could possibly be thinking.

Gabe stayed silent. He kept a hand on her shoulder but seemed distracted as they climbed the stairs. Alice's face still felt hot. The quad was very still; the lights were on in other apartments, but no shadows moved across any blinds.

Gabe's apartment was dark, though the porch light was on.

"So," Alice said, stopping in front of the door. She turned to face him. *Say something intelligent,* she ordered herself.

"So?" he replied.

"Thank you again, for . . . helping with . . . everything. My family and all that."

Gabe nodded and looked down. After a moment, he looked up, moved his hand to cradle her jaw, and stepped forward.

Before she could react, he was kissing her. A sensation like electricity coursed through her. Her knees felt like they would buckle. He broke off, kissed her again—a shorter kiss this time—and then he rested his forehead against hers. With his thumb, he caressed her cheek.

Alice let out her breath, opened her eyes, and smiled at him. He smiled back, then slipped his arms around her and pulled her closer to him. It felt so good to relax in his embrace, to soak in his warmth, to feel the soft fabric of his shirt against her cheek and listen to his heart racing.

Hers was doing the same. *Such bad timing,* she thought. *Why does this have to happen now?*

"Alice," he said, "I love you."

That made her start. The warm, secure feeling dissipated, and she let go of him and stepped back.

He stayed where he was, looked away from her, and put his hands in his pockets. "I . . ." He hung his head. "I guess I'll see you later." He got out his keys.

She couldn't think of a single thing to say as he unlocked his door and went inside. She couldn't even focus her thoughts until she forced herself to gather her wits. *This is all too weird,* she thought. *I need to get back to my mom. I just can't deal with this . . . situation.* She jogged down the stairs to her car, flipped open her cell phone, and called Cynthia.

When Cynthia heard about Alice's altercation with her parents, she said, "I'm coming too. I'll pack your stuff and my stuff, and we'll both spend the night. Give me the address."

"You don't—"

"What's the address?"

Alice gave it to her.

"All right, see you there in a little while. You got a specific outfit you want me to pack?"

"I just need my powder-blue suit and some nylons, I think. I've got everything else I need at Mom's house."

"Okay, got it. I'll see you soon." She hung up.

Alice restarted her car, backed out of Gabe's driveway, and headed for her mother's house. She still felt numb. *He thinks he's in love with me? He's out of his mind.*

The drive back was lonely, despite the lack of awkward tension and embarrassment. Her mother's house seemed emptier still when Alice arrived. She went upstairs to check on her mother, found her sleeping soundly, then went to the second bedroom and got a set of sheets out of the closet.

Cynthia arrived while Alice was making up one of the living room couches as a bed. "You sleep in the regular bed upstairs," Alice told her.

"It's your old bed," said Cynthia.

"It's my old house, so do what I say."

Cynthia rolled her eyes. "Here's your suit." She handed it to Alice. "You all right?" she asked.

"It's been a rough night."

"Yeah, I know. Is Gabe okay with everything?"

"He's fine," Alice said, though just a little too quickly.

"Alice, what happened?"

"I'll tell you later. Go ahead and use the bathroom first."

"All right." Cynthia kept glancing back over her shoulder as she headed up the stairs.

Alice hung her suit in the closet, then got a nightgown from her old dresser. She checked the front door again to make sure it was locked, then went to sit on the couch. She felt completely drained. *And what do I do about Gabe? I don't even know what to think.*

Cynthia shut the door to the bathroom upstairs and turned on the shower. Alice leaned over and snagged her purse from where she'd left it by the couch. She fished out her cell phone and stared at it.

She heard the shower door roll open and shut. Alice flipped open her cell phone, brought up Gabe's number, and sat for a moment with her thumb poised over the SEND button. What could she even say to him? He was just getting too attached. She took a deep breath, pressed the button, and put the phone against her ear.

"'Lo?" he answered.

"Did I wake you up?"

" . . . No."

"That's good. I . . ." She paused and chewed the inside of her cheek. "Um . . . Okay, look I . . ." *I what? Want him to leave me alone? Don't want to kiss him again?* "I forgot to tell you good night."

"Yeah?" She could hear a hint of a smile in his voice. "That's right, you did."

"So when will I see you again?"

"Whenever you want."

Now it was her turn to smile.

"Are you at your mom's?" he asked.

"Yes. Cynthia's here too."

"That's good. Will you do something for me?"

"Yes. What?"

"Keep your cell phone near you, and call me if anything happens."

"All right, but I'll be fine. You don't need to worry."

"Can't help it. Sorry."

"Call me tomorrow?" she asked.

"Okay."

"Okay, I'll talk to you then."

"I love you."

Alice bit her lip.

"Does it make you uncomfortable when I say that?"

"Yes," said Alice, "it does."

"Tough."

Alice fought the urge to grin. She shook her head. "Good night," she told him, keeping her voice as stern as she could.

"Night," he said with a hint of a chuckle.

Alice slowly closed her cell phone. Upstairs, Cynthia was getting out of the shower. Alice took off her shoes and lay down on the couch. After a few seconds, she gave in and let herself smile as she drifted off to sleep.

27

"I'd Stake My Reputation on That"

The next morning, Alice took one look at her mother and called in sick at work. She saw Cynthia off with a hug and a heartfelt thank-you, then spent most of the morning trying to get her mother to eat. She read over the settlement and called her mother's lawyer to let her know that it had been signed. She also explained about her father's late-night visit.

"Right," said the lawyer. "Put your mother on the phone."

Alice did, and her mother immediately burst into tears. Alice left the room. About five minutes later, her mother, still looking upset, but considerably more collected, found her and handed the phone back.

"I'll send a runner over to get the settlement," the lawyer said, "and we'll give it to the judge to sign today. It's your mother's call, and that's what she wants."

Alice thanked her and hung up, then put the document in an envelope and gave it to the young man in a polo who came by half an hour later. Her mother sat at the table in the kitchen, staring off into space.

"Mom," Alice said to her, "isn't there anything I can do? Is there somewhere you'd like to go?"

Her mother didn't answer.

Alice's cell phone rang, and she went to answer it. "Hello?"

"Hey." It was Gabe. "How's work?"

"I didn't go." She ducked into the other room. "My mom's a wreck."

"Oh. I'm sorry."

"I just don't know what to do."

"Any way I can help?"

"I don't think so. I'll call you later, all right?"

"All right. Love you."

Alice paused.

"Talk to you later," he said before the line cut out.

Alice went back into the kitchen.

"Who was that, honey?" her mother asked.

"Gabe. My . . . boyfriend."

Her mother sat up straighter. "What? Since when did—"

"Mom, don't even start," said Alice.

"It's just that—"

"Please. I really don't want to hear a lecture about how evil men are right now."

"All I want is to protect you. After what I've been through—"

"Well, I'm sorry things didn't work out in your marriage, Mom, but I'm not you, and Gabe is *not* Dad. Gabe really stuck his neck out for me last night, and I'm not going to stand here and listen to you insinuate that he's out to hurt me." Alice folded her arms across her chest and tried to rein in her temper.

Her mother looked taken aback. Then she slouched down and resumed staring off into space.

"Mom!" said Alice. "You cannot keep doing this." She began to pace. "What do you need? Another vacation? More yoga classes? Name it. You know I'll get it for you."

Her mother slouched still farther in her chair. "You can't buy off my problems," she said.

"I *know* that. But there's nothing else I can do. I mean, I'm here spending time with you today, and it's not making the slightest bit of difference, is it?"

Her mother glanced at her reproachfully, then looked away. After a long pause, she said, "I don't know. I don't know how you do it. Your father comes in and tries to push you around, and you're . . . immune! You just stand up to him and tell him to leave you be. I can't do that. I could never do that."

Alice stopped pacing. "I know this is really harsh, but you don't have to deal with that anymore."

Her mother nodded slowly. "I know."

"Does knowing that help at all?"

"I'm sorry, honey, but I'm still sad about losing him."

"It's okay," Alice said as she took a seat opposite her mother. "It's got to be devastating. I try to imagine, but I can't. Not really."

Her mother nodded again. "My life seems so empty now."

"Even after a year?"

"Yes, even after a year. I guess I should just get a job and get on with things, but—"

"Mom, I never told you to do that. I just want you to stop hurting and start healing. I'll support you no matter how long it takes."

"Honey, why did you side with me? You and your father were so close, and—"

"He broke his promise and really hurt you. It's that simple. And I love you. And in case you're wondering, I'll keep loving you, no matter how long this takes."

Her mother managed a watery smile. "Once you move to Phoenix, I won't see you very often."

"You want to come to Phoenix? Try starting over there?"

"I have no idea what I want. I guess that's the real problem, isn't it?"

Alice decided it was best not to answer.

Her mother looked over at her. "What would you do if you were me?"

"Inventory my assets, plan a budget, set some goals, and throw myself into getting things together. And read scriptures and pray." Alice shrugged. "It works for me."

"The first part makes sense. The second . . . I've never been interested in religion."

"Fair enough," said Alice. "Whenever you want to go over your accounts, we can do that together."

Her mother shuddered. "Being responsible for my own money's always frightened me."

"Mom, you need to know how to manage money or else you'll always be a slave to it."

Her mother took a deep breath. "All right. I should get started on that today, I guess."

* * *

That afternoon, her mother made them lunch and then sent Alice on her way. "Just call me later," she said. "Meanwhile, I know you've got work to do."

Alice intended to drive straight to the office but found herself driving to Gabe's place instead. She pulled up just as Ely did.

"Perfect!" he said when she got out of the car. He bounded up the stairs to the front door. Gabe's motorcycle was parked in the driveway, so Alice knew he was home.

"What's perfect?" she called up to Ely.

Ely opened the front door and announced, "I have accounting homework!"

Gabe's voice came from within. "Is Alice here or something?"

"Yup."

"Hi," Alice called out. She came up the stairs and stepped into the apartment. "I probably can't help him anyway. It's been years since I did the introductory classes."

Gabe was standing in the kitchen with a dish towel slung over his shoulder. He was dressed casually in a T-shirt and jeans and was scowling at Ely.

"What?" said Ely. He went into his room, dumped the contents of his backpack on the bed, and shut his door.

Alice smiled at Gabe.

"Hey." He looked somewhat surprised to see her. He wiped his hands on the dish towel, draped it over the sink, and came over to where she stood.

"Sorry to just drop in," she said.

"I don't mind. You all right?"

"Not really, no." On impulse, she stepped forward and hugged him.

He returned the embrace. "What happened?"

"Nothing, really." She let go. "I guess I'm just now feeling the fallout from the last twenty-four hours. Look, I'm sorry if—"

He shook his head, kept his arm around her shoulders, and led her over to the couch. Once they were both seated, he kissed her on the forehead and said, "It's all right."

She leaned against his shoulder and let herself relax.

With one hand he stroked her hair, and with the other he helped her settle in place against him. "I love you, you know," he said.

"So you keep telling me."

"Yeah, well, get used to it."

Alice heard Ely's door open. "Oh *man!*" he said. "Come on, guys; I still don't get double-entry bookkeeping, and I'm gonna *fail.*"

Gabe chuckled. Alice just shook her head.

* * *

She ended up staying at the apartment through the afternoon. While Ely and Gabe did homework, Alice paged through Gabe's copy of *Jesus the Christ*. Like the other book he'd loaned her, this one was all marked up, which had been no mean feat. The author, James E. Talmage, had put together extensive footnotes and citations already, and Alice read Gabe's additions with interest. Gabe sat next to her on the couch and, every now and then, he'd glance over at her and they'd exchange a smile.

At around four, she called her mother's house.

"Hello?" came her mother's voice on the other end of the line.

"Mom."

"Hi, Alice. How are you?"

"Fine. You?"

"Better. Thanks for checking up on me."

"Of course."

"I'm cleaning house right now. I'll call you if I need anything."

"All right." They both hung up.

Gabe looked up when Alice folded her phone shut.

"Everything seems to be under control," she told him.

"Good." He moved closer and put his arm around her shoulders. She leaned back against him and resumed reading. Four thirty came way too soon. He shut his book and got up from the couch.

Alice did the same and returned *Jesus the Christ* to the bookshelf in the corner.

Ely headed back to his room and shut the door.

Gabe disappeared into his own room and reemerged a couple of minutes later wearing his uniform for the restaurant and his motorcycle jacket.

"I'll call you when I get off work," he told her as he adjusted his collar.

Alice nodded. "Thanks for letting me come here."

He came over to her and gave her a hug. "I lo—"

"Gabe, look . . ."

He stopped midsentence, stroked her hair back from her face, then took her hand in his and kissed it, keeping his gaze locked with hers all the while. "I can be patient," he said.

* * *

The next day at work she found a folded piece of paper on her chair. It was Gretchen's handwriting. *Alice, please come see me when you get in.*

Hope this wasn't from yesterday, thought Alice. She headed for the stairs. Gretchen was talking to someone else in her office when she arrived—Rodney, Alice guessed by the sound of his voice. As she neared Gretchen's open door, she heard him saying, ". . . just think that perhaps you should reevaluate whether or not you want Alice O'Donnell for this position."

Alice stopped midstride, then stepped back so that she wouldn't be seen. *This doesn't sound good,* she thought.

"She's one of the best I've worked with," said Gretchen.

"She's twenty-six, practically fresh out of school."

Alice frowned.

"Rodney, where is this coming from? Alice has been a model employee ever since she got here."

"The COO had a lot of questions about promoting someone that young, and the salary you want us to pay her isn't reasonable."

Are they considering revoking their offer? Against her will, Alice's spirits began to lift.

"The salary goes with the position," said Gretchen. "If she can do the job just as well as an older person, she deserves to be compensated. Besides she's one of the best there is. I'd stake my reputation on that."

Oh, great. No pressure.

"I know that," said Rodney. "I went ahead and put in the request for the pay raise, but I just wanted to let you know I didn't think it was a very reasonable thing to do."

"If she'd been forty, Rodney, you wouldn't have thought twice about it."

"I just want to make my position on this clear."

"All right, you have."

"I'll see you at the meeting this afternoon."

Alice went to duck behind a filing cabinet as he came out and tried to look like she was just arriving when he walked past.

Gretchen was sitting at her desk, scowling at a document. Alice knocked on the open door.

"You wanted to see me?" she said.

Her boss looked up and smiled. "Yes, I did. Come in." She tossed the document she was looking at into her outbox.

Alice took a seat in one of Gretchen's chairs and waited for her to say more.

"I just wanted to let you know that I got you that higher salary," Gretchen said.

"Really?" asked Alice. She kept her voice neutral. "That's great."

"Will you have all of your projects here wrapped up by the twenty-third?"

Alice nodded. "Yes," she said. "I should be all ready to move then." Her stomach sank as she said it.

* * *

Four weeks later, Alice felt like she'd researched every housing option in Phoenix that was in her price range. She'd had a lot of long conversations with realtors and apartment managers. One night, after a particularly trying round of phone calls, she went out to the front room to find Gabe there, seated on one of the bar stools arguing with Cynthia about how to make marinara sauce. Cynthia was in the kitchen, brandishing a long-handled wooden spoon.

"I don't care if your name is Spinelli," she was saying. "I've put in *hours* of research. I've probably been making this sauce longer than you've been *alive*."

"Yeah, but I inherited a family recipe," Gabe replied, his eyes twinkling with amusement. "*Several* family recipes that have been used in gourmet restaurants on three continents."

Alice cleared her throat, and the two of them stopped bickering and looked at her. "Oh," she said, "don't let me interrupt."

"Nah, you know he's here to see you anyway," said Cynthia. "He's only picking on me to pass the time."

"I wasn't picking on her," said Gabe. "We were having a serious discussion about food."

"To which I can contribute nothing," said Alice. "And no—" She pointed at her roommate with mock severity—"do not ask me to judge between the two of you."

"Like I'd stand a chance against Gabe. You're way too in love with him to see straight," said Cynthia.

Alice flinched. Gabe glanced at Cynthia, then Alice, then looked away.

"Well," said Alice, trying to save face, "rest assured that I will let either of you feed me anytime."

Gabe managed a chuckle. Cynthia gave Alice an odd look, then put the spoon down and left.

Alice went over kiss Gabe on the cheek. He smiled at her, stroked her hair back from her face, and then stood up to give her a hug.

* * *

"You're killing him, you know that?" said Cynthia later that evening. She'd come into Alice's room without knocking and sat on her bed.

Alice was already in bed, reading, so she looked up with surprise and drew her feet under her so that they wouldn't be sat on. "What are you talking about?"

"He is so in love with you, and you're stiff-arming him."

"I am not. He's fine. Besides, we've only been dating for eight weeks."

"He's not fine. He's miserable. Every time he looks at you, he looks like his heart's going to break. And I don't care if it's only been a couple months; Alice, you guys have a real connection."

"He's only twenty-one and—"

"Don't say that. He is *not* a kid. He's young, but who cares? You do love him. I can tell."

"Cynth . . ."

"But if you don't tell him or show him, you'll lose him. Is that what you want?"

Alice closed her book. "I'm moving, and there's nothing I can do about that. I just don't want to hurt him any more than necessary. All right?"

"You'll regret it if you don't tell him. I guarantee it."

28

Moving Preparations

"So, about being apart," said Gabe over the phone.

"I know it's not ideal," said Alice. "And I understand if you don't want to do the long-distance thing."

"That's the fiftieth time you've said that."

"Well, I am moving the Monday after next and— "

"I know! You think I ever forget that?"

Alice shut her eyes. She stood on the balcony of the Phoenix apartment she would soon be moving into. It was a small place. After hours of research, she'd given most of her furniture to Cynthia. She realized she didn't want that much space if she was just going to be by herself.

"Alice . . . are we . . . look, I just gotta ask. We're staying together, right?"

"If that's what you want."

"*Yes,* it is! Do you? Isn't it what you want? Or are you fine to just end it when you move?"

"Gabe, come on. What is this? High school?"

"Excuse me for being younger than you. Like that'll ever change."

"I didn't mean—"

"You're fine with just ending things, aren't you?"

"No . . . no, come on. Look, if what you want is—"

"I want to be with you, all right? I *love* you. I really love you, and I don't want you to leave, and . . . I want to still be your boyfriend a week from now and a *month* from now, and I—call me immature—I want to know that that's what you want. To be with me. To keep being my girlfriend."

"Gabe . . ." Alice shifted her weight. "Of course it's what I want."

She heard a rustling sound, as if Gabe were shifting his phone from one ear to the other. "Really?" he asked, still sounding a little guarded.

She shut her eyes and remembered Cynthia's advice. *But I can't say I love him after dating him eight weeks. Only eight weeks!* "I'm . . . I really care about you," she said in a low voice.

"I'm gonna miss you."

"Same here."

"Are you coming by after you get in tonight?"

"It won't be until after ten."

"So are you coming by after you get in tonight?"

Alice let herself laugh. "Yeah. Provided Ely's okay with it." Ely had taken to sulking in his room whenever she came over. Things with Leslie had not worked out as he'd hoped. As Leslie and Sarah put it, they were "such good friends."

"Who cares about him? I love you," Gabe said.

"I'll see you later."

"Okay, later. Love you."

They hung up. Alice shut her eyes for a moment. The heat was making her sweat buckets. Her fingers left damp smudges on her phone as she folded it shut.

She dragged open the sliding glass door of the apartment and stepped back inside, the cold air making her shiver a little as she pushed the door shut again.

The apartment was very plain. The walls were white, the carpet peach, and the countertops in the corner kitchenette gray. *Cynthia would throw a fit,* thought Alice. *Or she will the first time she comes out to visit.*

Even though she'd looked the place over thoroughly, she found herself going over it again, opening random cupboards, staring dubiously at the stove. On her third circuit, she made herself stop.

She folded her arms across her chest, bowed her head, and realized she was on the verge of tears. *Get control,* she told herself. *Everything's fine. What's gotten into you?*

She pressed her hand to her forehead then went to a far corner of the room and got down on her knees. The memory of the warmth she'd felt during her revelation resurfaced, and she shook her head. It felt like eons had passed since she'd had that experience. She'd stopped writing in her old journal and had started a new one.

Lord, I don't know what to think anymore—ever since that revelation didn't come true. Or did I make the wrong choice? Am I not supposed to be here? I thought that you told me I'd be engaged by now.

Please, talk to me again. Tell me what I need to know. What did I do wrong? She forced herself to take a deep breath.

I'm still praying. I'm still trying to keep the faith. Talk to me. Please.

She continued to kneel until her knees grew sore. When she cracked an eyelid and looked down at her watch, she saw that fifteen minutes had gone by and she hadn't felt a thing. She sighed, closed her prayer, and got to her feet.

* * *

The following Thursday, Alice and Gabe went to the temple together as usual. They got out late in the evening, after the sun had set. The floodlights were on, illuminating the pale brown granite of the temple. The lawns had just been watered, so the smell of moisture and wet grass still hung in the air.

It was a quiet evening, but Gabe seemed to be positively bursting with excitement. Alice couldn't help but wonder what he was up to. They made it partway down the walk before he stopped, pivoted, and said, "Okay, I have *got* to tell you something."

"All right," said Alice, "what?"

He tried but failed to suppress a grin. "I talked to the admissions people at ASU!"

"Arizona State University?" Alice had heard of the school but knew nothing much about it.

"Yes. It's in Tempe, which is right next to Phoenix. I looked on a map. So—"

Alice put up a hand. "Gabe, you've got a full scholarship at *UCLA*."

"Yeah, well, I can work things out with ASU. I'm still poor as dirt so . . ." His grin faded. "You don't look happy."

Alice did her best to school her features. "ASU is probably a good school, I wouldn't know, but it's not UCLA. I'm a USC grad, and I'm still saying that."

He shrugged.

"I'm serious, Gabe."

"What, you don't want me to go?"

"No, I don't. I'm a numbers person, and I'm guessing UCLA is more competitive than ASU. The acceptance rate to med schools out of UCLA is probably higher. Now, if you know the numbers and can contradict me—"

"No, I didn't go looking up numbers," said Gabe. "Gimme a break, Alice."

"Well, you need to if you want to consider this."

"It's past the deadline for transfer apps! If I tell them I need to take another few weeks to compile research—"

"Then don't go. Transfer next year if it seems like a good idea."

"We'll have been apart for a year then."

"I know." She looked away from him. "I thought you said I didn't need to worry about you."

"You don't. This is *my* life we're talking about here. My decision."

"I know, I know," said Alice. "I just don't want you to do something that you may live to regret."

"And what I'm trying to tell you is that I care more about you than I care about all that." His voice took on a desperate edge. "If being with you requires a sacrifice, I'll make it. And it's not like I'm dropping out of school. It isn't *that* big of a deal, you know."

Alice shook her head. "Gabe, don't. Please." She put her hands on his shoulders and looked up at him. "I care about you so much. I'd never forgive myself if you did this and things didn't work out between us."

He raised his chin then. "Do you think that's likely?"

"I don't know. We've been together for nine weeks. That's barely enough time to . . ." She let her voice trail off.

He wouldn't look at her then. Alice could see that he was upset and scared.

"Look," she told him. "I'm serious when I say I care about you."

"Have you ever had a long-distance relationship work out?"

"Well, no."

He nodded as if to himself.

For lack of a better idea, Alice stood on tiptoe and kissed him. He kissed back, but Alice could tell that his heart wasn't in it. He was pulling away. *Which is just the way these things go sometimes,* she thought, *right? Let him do what he needs to do.* But her heart lurched as she thought this.

* * *

Over the next week, Alice berated herself for mishandling the situation. Gabe's gloomy, defeated air didn't lift the next morning or the morning after. His usual good cheer faded and was replaced with a quiet brooding that Alice hadn't seen in a long while. *This is how he was when I was dating Spencer,* she realized.

For her part, she wanted to keep telling him how much she cared about him, how unhappy she was that she was leaving. But his temperament made that difficult. His despair ran deep, she soon learned, and she could be nothing more than a spectator to it. Half the time he'd get upset when she told him she cared and would miss him, as if he feared that she was saying it just to lull him into a false sense of security before she took off and forgot all about him. Alice found this frustrating, but try as she might, she couldn't penetrate the emotional walls he set around himself.

As a consequence of all this, the next week flew by, and their time together dwindled until Alice was at the point of despair herself. On the following Thursday night, after they'd been to the temple, she went home, knelt down, and cried. Again, she poured out her frustrations to the Lord. *What am I supposed to do?* she demanded. *What am I supposed to tell him? That I promise everything will work out? Father, I just don't believe that anymore.* She put her head down on her arms while the tears kept coming.

The phone rang in the background, then stopped, and then there was a tap at her door. "Alice?" said Cynthia. "It's your mom."

Alice got up, opened the door just wide enough for Cynthia to pass the phone through, and said, "Hello?" Cynthia gave her a worried look. Alice shook her head as if to say that it wasn't anything serious.

"Are you all right?" her mother asked.

"Yes. What do you need, Mom?"

"It's not important. What's wrong? Did something happen with Gabe?"

"Sort of."

"Talk to me."

Alice frowned. She had never in her life talked to her mother about her personal affairs. Her dad had always been the one who was there for her when times got difficult, but her father had stopped calling as soon as the divorce was final.

"He didn't break up with you, did he?"

"No, Mom."

"Honey, what is it?"

"He's just . . . we're both having a hard time with me leaving."

"I hope things'll be all right."

Alice wiped her eyes with a tissue. "You're not going to warn me away from falling in love with him?"

"No. I think we've all heard enough of my bitter divorcée lecture."

Alice didn't know what to say then.

"I know I'm not much help with this kind of thing," her mother went on.

"I'll be all right."

"I know you will, honey."

Alice tried to think of a response. "Um . . ." she said.

Her mother burst out laughing. "I really am bad at this, aren't I? Well, what can I say? You always do seem to figure these things out."

Alice joined her mother in laughing. It felt good to bond at last.

* * *

The next day at work was so hectic that Alice wasn't able to finish all her projects, let alone pack up her office. That meant she had to go back to the office on Saturday. Fortunately, Gabe was also working that day. She would've been furious if she'd had to miss any more time with him.

She spent the morning finishing up her work, then ate her lunch and began packing up her office. She made it through most of her drawers before she came across a stack of pictures. The one on top was of her and Gabe. Someone had snapped it at a ward activity; it was just the two of them walking up to the rest of the group. Alice was in the middle of saying something, and Gabe was looking over at her. His hands were in his pockets, and his entire attention was on her. He had that half smile he often got when they were having a good conversation.

Alice sat down in her chair. *Why,* she thought, *didn't I get involved with him sooner?* She touched his image with the tip of her finger. *We could have had months together. All that time since Darren left I could have spent with Gabe.* She shut her eyes. *Father,* she thought, *I am so confused that I can barely think straight. I think I need a miracle of some kind right now.*

"Alice?" It was Gretchen's voice.

Alice's eyes snapped open.

Her boss was standing in her doorway. She was wearing jeans, and her hair was down and fell in ringlets. The casual look surprised Alice.

"Hi, Gretchen." Alice sat up straight and put the pictures back in her drawer.

"I hoped I'd find you here," said Gretchen. She was clearly upset about something herself, and, much to Alice's surprise, she closed the door behind her after she stepped in. "I need to talk to you," she said.

Alice nodded. "All right."

Her boss stayed on her feet a moment longer, then went to sit in the chair opposite Alice. "You remember Alan Waters from the Waters Firm?" she said.

"Yes . . . I think so."

"I'm going to work for him, and . . . I'd like you to consider coming with me. It'd mean staying in LA but—"

"What?"

"Or they have an opening up in the Bay Area. I can ask them if they'd consider you for that."

"But I've already accepted the offer in Phoenix."

"You have, but I made it clear that your acceptance was conditional, and . . . this company is not paying you the higher salary."

"They're not?"

Gretchen shook her head. "I asked Rodney about it yesterday, and when he told me the raise had been denied, that was it. I am fed up with these people. Look, I don't know if I can get you as much of a raise as—"

"I'd love to stay in LA," Alice blurted.

"You would?" Gretchen sat up straighter. "I might be able to get you a better salary up in the Bay Area."

"Well—"

"Look, I'll understand if you have second thoughts. Let me know your final decision Monday morning. You know my cell number." Gretchen gave her a hopeful smile.

Alice nodded.

"Great. Call me if you have any questions, all right?" Gretchen got up and left.

Alice stared after her, her heart soaring. Had her prayer just been answered, or was it just a coincidence? She massaged her temples in consternation. She wanted to be happy, but it almost seemed too good to be true.

29

The Proposal

Gabe worked late that evening, but Alice drove over to his place just after ten and was glad to see his motorcycle parked out front. She ran up the stairs and knocked on the door. Ely answered it and gave her a mournful look before stepping back to let Gabe past. Alice was puzzled. Gabe came to the door and leaned against the doorframe. He wouldn't look her in the eye.

"Gabe?" she said.

"I went ahead and filled out an application for financial aid today for ASU," he replied. "Had an interesting little talk with my mom about our finances."

"Oh." Alice shut her eyes for a moment. "I should have told you about that."

Gabe blinked. "Pardon?"

"She didn't mention me?"

He stood up all the way. "What are you talking about?"

Alice sighed. "I've been helping her with things ever since she got that inheritance."

"What inheritance?" he asked, his voice raised.

"Gabe, calm down, please."

"Calm down? Alice, I was about to tell you that my mother has decided that she wants to control the money again, which means there's no way I can go to ASU. Did *you* tell her to do that?"

Alice schooled her features and chose her words carefully. "Your mother called me last fall after she got an inheritance from your uncle. She told me she didn't want you to have to spend any more time managing the finances—"

"Oh, *great,* Alice, so you *are* the reason. How much did she inherit?"

"Maybe you should talk to your mom about this."

Gabe stepped all the way out the door and pulled it shut behind him. Alice took two steps back.

"I don't talk to my mother if I can avoid it. We don't get along."

"If you'd only—"

"She blew all of the family savings within months of my dad's death, did you know that?"

Alice nodded. "Yes. I did."

"Yeah? Well then she went to the bishop for welfare money, and when he didn't give it to her, she left the Church. Did you know *that?*"

"That's not exactly what happened."

"Oh, she changed a few details there, did she?"

"I don't think so."

"Alice!" Gabe took a deep breath and began to pace. "Ever since I was eleven years old, *eleven* years old, I have been working to keep my family's finances together."

"I know."

"And it'll be up to me to get another job to work off all of the new debts she's gotten herself into—with your help."

"What new debts?"

"Oh, she's got them. Believe me, I know."

"You do not. I helped her invest the inheritance."

"And was the swank new apartment part of that investment strategy?"

Alice shook her head. "It's a condo. She owns it."

"*What?* How much did she inherit?"

"Gabe, please. Talk to her."

"I can't believe this! You've been working with my mother, *behind my back?*"

"I didn't mean—"

"I suppose she's told you all kinds of awful things about me."

"No, she hasn't. She loves you. She'd do anything to be able to talk to you again."

Gabe was holding his head in his hands.

"Gabe?"

"I can't believe this. I can *not* believe this." He was getting more upset.

"Look," said Alice. "I love your mom. She's a wonderful person."

That extinguished his temper. He looked up at her, his eyes wide, and then his shoulders slumped. "You know, maybe it's a good thing you're leaving Monday."

"Gabe, wait a minute—"

The apartment door opened, and Ely peered out wearing a bathrobe. "Guys," he said, "it's almost eleven."

"Sorry," said Alice.

"Yeah, sorry," said Gabe.

"Gabe," Alice tried again. "Please. I don't want to fight with you."

"Well, next time you're offered a chance to screw up my life, don't, okay?" He went into his apartment and slammed the door.

* * *

The next morning Alice woke up miserable. *It'll be all right,* she kept telling herself. *Gabe will figure out that his life isn't ruined, and everything will be fine. He didn't mean what he said last night about wanting me to leave. He's young, remember? He can be emotional sometimes.* These thoughts didn't put her at ease, though. She sat up in bed and looked around her room.

Pray, she prompted herself. She got out of bed and knelt down, but she couldn't think of anything to say. After a couple of minutes, she got up and retrieved her old journal from her drawer. She didn't open it. Instead, she stared at it for a moment, then put it down on her vanity. *What am I doing?* she wondered.

The sound of cabinets banging shut in the kitchen let her know that Cynthia was awake. When Alice went out to join her, her roommate turned, took one look at her, and said, "What happened?"

Alice leaned against the counter. "Fight with Gabe. Another one."

"How bad?"

"I don't know."

Cynthia nodded. "Well, maybe with you leaving—"

"About that. What exactly are your plans for where you're going to live after tomorrow?"

Cynthia raised an eyebrow. "Why?"

"Because I'll probably stay. Gretchen left the company and offered to take me with her to her new job."

"Seriously?"

Alice nodded.

"That is so great! We can stay here. I was planning to move into a single unit that the landlord said would open up next month, but let's stay here."

Alice grinned and hugged her roommate.

* * *

As she passed out programs in the foyer later that morning, she was so distracted she couldn't even think straight. *He'll be by any minute,* she kept telling herself. She barely noticed any of the other people who walked past her. *Gabe,* she thought, *please don't stay mad.* She'd tried calling his cell phone twice that morning only to find he hadn't turned it on yet.

Out of the corner of her eye, she saw another person, too tall to be Gabe, come around the corner. He stopped right in front of her. Alice held out a program.

"A-Alice?"

She looked up and started. "Darren?" It was none other. He wore a black suit, blue shirt, and yellow tie that made him look every bit the successful lawyer. He stared at her with obvious unease.

"So, you're here," he said.

Alice raised an eyebrow. "Uh-huh. Want a program?" She waved the one she still held out to him.

He glanced down at it then back up at her.

An awkward silence stretched between them. Finally, Alice put the program back into the stack she was holding and shifted her weight from one foot to the other. "What, Darren?" she asked.

"I . . . sorry, I didn't expect to find you standing here in the foyer. I wasn't even sure you'd be in the ward anymore."

"Were you looking for me specifically?"

He nodded. "Actually, I was."

"Why?"

"Because I owe you an apology."

"Pardon?"

Darren looked self-consciously over his shoulder.

Alice turned and put the programs down on the table. Then she took Darren by the elbow and drew him aside. "What's going on?" she asked him.

"Alice, I'm sorry about how I treated you last fall."

"It's fine. I'm over it."

"Okay, great." He pursed his lips. "I'm not."

"So what do you want me to do about it? Tell you you're forgiven? You're forgiven. Feel better."

"You're still coming to church, I see."

"Well, yes."

"I'm so glad."

Alice rolled her eyes. "You think our breakup would affect that?"

Darren looked sheepish.

"Oh, get *over* yourself," said Alice.

He chuckled. "Fair point." He glanced at his watch, and Alice, seeing this, did the same. It was almost time for sacrament meeting to start.

"I need to find someone," she told him. She brushed past him and went into the chapel. There was no sign of Gabe. Ely sat a few rows in, next to his "good friend" Leslie. Alice went over to him and asked, "Did Gabe come with you?"

Ely looked up at her and shook his head. "He was eating breakfast when I left."

"So is he here yet?"

"I don't know." Ely shrugged. "Look . . . can you please leave me out of this?"

"Sure, sorry." Alice straightened and panned her gaze around the room. *I guess he could be in the balcony,* she thought. She turned around and saw that Darren, who had made his way to a seat in one of the middle pews, was beckoning to her. Alice couldn't think of a polite way to refuse, so she went over and sat next to him, but they didn't exchange so much as a glance as the bishop got up and called the meeting to order.

* * *

After sacrament meeting was over, Alice got up to leave, and Darren put his hand on her arm to stop her. She looked at him as if to say, *What is it now?*

"I've got to go, but I'll be in town for a few days," he said. "Can we—" he shrugged awkwardly—"get together sometime and catch up?"

She shrugged in return. "My phone number's the same as it was before." She began to turn away, but he stopped her again and held his arms out to her. After a moment's deliberation, she gave him a quick hug and turned around to leave.

When she did, her gaze fell on Gabe, who was sitting in the back row. He looked positively disheveled for Gabe—his hair was tousled, his shirt had a few wrinkles in it, and he had dark circles under his eyes. For a split second he looked her in the eye, then looked away.

"Gabe!" Darren called out. "Just the man I want to see! 'Scuse me, Alice." He pushed his way past her and strode up the aisle toward his old roommate.

Gabe made his way to the end of the pew to meet up with Darren. Alice, for her part, tried to follow Darren up the aisle, but it was hard to pick her way through the crowd while everyone in the chapel tried to exit at once. She lost sight of both Gabe and Darren in the press of people, and when she made it to the doorway, they were both gone.

He'll be in Sunday School, she told herself. She went straight there, but Gabe didn't show up before class started. Alice looked around several times during class but saw no sign of him. Between Sunday School and Relief Society, she did a quick circuit of the building. No Gabe. After Relief Society she did another circuit, then went out to the parking lot. Gabe's motorcycle wasn't there.

Alice pulled out her cell phone and called his. The call went straight to voice mail. "Hi, it's Alice," she said. "Please talk to me, okay? There's something I wanted to tell you last night. Call me on my cell." She snapped her phone shut with one hand and moved to drop it back into her purse, but it buzzed before she did so.

The number on the display wasn't one she recognized. She flipped the phone open again and said, "Hello?"

"Alice?" It was Darren.

"Yes?" she asked.

"Where are you?"

"At church." *Where else would I be?*

"I'm driving toward you. Walk out to meet me?"

Why? Alice wanted to ask, but she suppressed the urge to be blunt. "Something the matter?" she said.

"Please. Walk toward the temple. I'll be there in a few minutes."

Alice frowned with irritation. "Fine," she told him. "See you in a sec." She snapped the phone shut, dropped it in her purse, and set out toward the temple. *This is just what I need,* she thought, *a long walk in heels, in the sun. If I were a real Angelino, I'd drive.* But she just couldn't bring herself to do that. She marched past the parked cars, past the gate to the parking lot, past the visitors' center, and on toward the temple, which loomed ahead.

Darren's red sedan pulled up and parked in a space several yards ahead of her. Darren jumped out. Alice didn't vary her speed, so he jogged over to meet her.

"Walk with me?" he said, taking her by the arm.

"What is this?"

"Please?"

It wasn't as if she had much of a choice. He all but dragged her out onto the temple lawn, where the soft ground was easier on her feet. The heels of her pumps sank into the soil, though, and as the grass was still wet, Alice did her best to walk on her toes.

When they reached a shady spot, Darren let go, and Alice pivoted around to face him. "What's going on?" she asked.

"I had a talk with my old roommate."

"Gabe?"

"That's the guy. To, you know, catch up on what's going on in the ward."

Alice nodded.

"So . . ." Darren took a deep breath. "Alice, the last few months have been awful. It's been hard for me to live with myself. Everything you said to me the night we broke up was true, and I knew it. I am so sorry."

"And I forgive you."

"Right. Which I can't believe, but . . . thanks."

Alice nodded impatiently.

"Anyway," said Darren. "I want to make it all up to you."

Alice raised both eyebrows.

"If you'll let me." Darren reached into his pocket and pulled something out. He kept it concealed in his hand so Alice couldn't see what it was. It wasn't until he got down on one knee that she realized what was happening.

"Uh—" she started.

"Will you marry me?" He pulled open the ring box he was holding and held it out to her. Inside was a beautiful, very expensive-looking diamond ring.

For a moment, she couldn't reply. When she recovered her wits, she asked, "Are you out of your mind?"

His smile faltered. "I figured it might come as a surprise."

"Darren!" Alice pressed her fingers to her forehead. "I haven't seen you in months, and now you want me to marry you? Normal people don't do this. Is this a Mormon thing? Proposing to people that you aren't even dating?"

"Well . . ."

"And you talked to Gabe about this?"

"Yes."

"About whether I was seeing anyone?"

"Right."

"And what did he say? Just go ahead and propose?"

Darren gave her an odd look. "Well, at first he acted all strange, like he didn't want to tell me if you were involved with anyone. Then I told him what I planned, and he said that if I came all this way to apologize, maybe I was the best man for you."

Alice shook her head. "He's my boyfriend. You just asked my *boyfriend* if you could propose to me."

Darren's hand holding the ring box faltered. "You're dating *Gabe?*"

"I can't believe you asked him that."

"Gabe. My old roommate. Gabe."

"Yes, Darren. Gabe is my boyfriend."

"I see. But he said something about you moving tomorrow."

"Well, it turns out I'm not. Long story." She waved her hand as if to brush that aside. "But suffice it to say, no, I can't get engaged to you. I forgive you, and I wish you all the best. I'm *not* marrying you. Will you stand up already?"

He got slowly to his feet. "I don't understand. Why didn't Gabe tell me?"

"I don't know." *That's a good question,* she thought. *Maybe he was intimidated or . . . maybe he's ready to end it?*

Darren shook his head and looked down at the ring.

"You actually bought a diamond before coming down here?" asked Alice. "I assumed you'd be married to someone else by now."

"No. I couldn't possibly—Alice, I know this is completely inappropriate, but I'm still in love with you. And I want a shot at redemption here, a chance to undo all of the cruel things I said and did to you."

"Consider that done. I'm okay."

He shook his head again. "That's not enough. I prayed before I came down here. I spent an entire night praying and begging the Lord for guidance, and He answered me. Do you understand what I'm trying to say? I know the Lord approves of me doing this, I *know* it. Have you ever had an experience like that?"

Alice froze. The words from her prayer on the night of her baptism came to her mind: *Lord, will I be engaged before I have to make a final decision about my job? And will I know that he's the right man for me?*

The pieces began to fall into place. *I make my final decision tomorrow,* she realized. *I haven't made it yet. The time limit, or whatever, on my revelation isn't up. And someone's just proposed to me. Not just someone. Darren. The man I was thinking about when I said the prayer. Furthermore, one of those job offers would put me right by him.*

She felt sick.

"Alice?" Darren lowered his head and looked her in the eye.

"What? Sorry."

"My cell phone number." He held out a white business card to her.

Alice took it and stared at it.

"Please, think it over," said Darren. He placed the ring box on her palm and folded her fingers over it. It seemed to weigh a thousand pounds.

She took a deep breath and looked up at him. "I guess I can do that."

"Good. Thanks."

She nodded and put the ring and the card in her purse. "I need some time alone now," she said as she turned and marched off.

30

For Eternity

Alice held the ring box in her hand as she walked into the apartment. She stared down at it, went right past Cynthia, who sat at the table reading a book, and marched straight to her room. In the background, she was dimly aware of the sound of Cynthia shutting the front door. *Oh,* thought Alice, *I should have done that.*

"Alice?" her roommate called out.

Alice sat down at her vanity, picked up her journal, and flipped to her baptism-day entry.

"Alice?"

She felt too scattered to actually read it, so she just stared at it and held the ring box out in front of her. There was a tap on her door, then it swung inward and Cynthia peered in. Alice looked up at her. Cynthia looked at the diamond ring, the open journal, and then back at Alice. "So . . . how was church?" she asked. "Anything much happen?"

"Very funny."

Cynthia stepped all the way into the room. "Is that from Gabe?"

"No. Darren."

That clearly took her by surprise. "*Darren?* When did he—"

"Showed up this morning at church."

"And proposed to you?"

"Yeah."

"Oh, that's not right. He's messed up. And *why* did you take the ring?"

"I didn't say yes."

"What did Gabe say?"

"Gabe won't talk to me. He won't answer his phone, and I don't know where he is, and—"

"Did you try calling his mom or his sister?"

Alice put the ring box down. "No, I didn't."

She dug her phone out of her purse and dialed Lorraine's number. As she did, Cynthia reached over her shoulder, flipped her journal shut, and swiped it.

"Hey!" said Alice.

"You are *not* going to go by this, Alice. If you're even *thinking* of getting engaged to Darren while you're in love with Gabe, you're one step away from talking to animals and writing on the walls."

"Hello?" came Gina's voice from the cell phone.

Alice hastily pressed it to her ear. "Hi, Gina?"

"Oh, hi, Alice."

"Do you have any idea where your brother is?"

There was a pause. "He's here."

"He is?"

"Yeah, but he's talking to Mom in Spanish. I can't understand a word."

"Oh. Well . . . can I talk to him, please?"

"So Darren came back and proposed to you?" Gina sounded upset.

"Gabe told you about that, huh?"

"Yes. Did you say yes?"

"No."

"You said no?"

"Please. I need to talk to Gabe."

"I'll tell him to call you. He's busy right now."

Alice clenched her jaw. *Just put him on the phone!* she wanted to scream, but she took a deep breath and said, "Okay, thank you. Wait! Does your mom know about me and Gabe?"

"I dunno. I gotta go. Bye." Gina hung up.

Alice slowly put her phone down and realized that Cynthia had left the room. "Cynth," she called out, "what did you do with my journal?"

"I burned it!" her roommate replied from the front room.

"Very funny." Alice went out to the front room and found Cynthia sitting on the couch, an open book in her hands.

"You're not reading it," Cynthia said.

"Come on. Don't you think this coincidence is a little odd?"

"Yes, it is." Cynthia looked up. "Which is exactly why I'm not giving your journal back."

"But—"

"Forget it."

Alice rolled her eyes. "Would *you* be able to forget it?"

The landline rang. Alice glared at Cynthia once more before going to pick it up. It was Monica.

"Alice," she said. "I'm going to be late this evening. Sean twisted his ankle, maybe broke it. I don't know. We're waiting in the emergency room right now."

"Late for?"

"Dinner. At Lorraine's. Remember?"

"Oh, that's *right*." Alice pressed the heel of her hand to her forehead.

"You okay?"

"No, not really."

"What's wrong?"

Alice glanced over at Cynthia, who was still reading her book. "I'll ask you this," she said to Monica. "You believe in revelation, right?"

"Ask her if she can talk to squirrels," said Cynthia.

Alice turned her back on her.

"Yes, I do," said Monica.

"Okay, so say you had one that said you'd be engaged before a certain something would happen, and the day before that something would happen, someone proposes to you. And the day before *that*, you get a job offer in the city he lives in. Is that a sign you should say yes?"

"Definitely. Who proposed?"

"I'm going to hide all of the pens next," said Cynthia. "No writing on the walls. I worked hard on them."

Alice put her hand over her ear. "Darren proposed," she told Monica. "But I'm dating someone else."

"Oh," said Monica. "Look, Alice, there's a reason a lot of people your age aren't married."

"Oh, *thanks*."

"I don't mean to offend you. It's just that the Lord obviously wants to help you out, so He's made the choice easy."

"What is she saying?" Cynthia demanded.

"And if I say no, I defy the Lord?" asked Alice.

"Hang up the phone, Alice," said Cynthia.

"Well," said Monica, "yes. Anyway, let me know if I can help with the wedding, and tell Lorraine tonight that I'll get there when I can, or I'll call. I also left a message with Gina. I've got to get back to Sean."

"Okay."

Cynthia took the phone out of Alice's hand and pushed the button to hang it up.

"Cynth!" said Alice.

"You are *not* going to get engaged to Darren. Gabe would be *devastated*."

Alice put both hands over her face. "Cynth," she said. "Gabe won't talk to me."

"Because he cares about you! If he didn't, he wouldn't bother to avoid you. You have got to try to work things out with him. You know he loves you."

"And I love him." Alice lowered her hands and folded her arms across her chest.

Cynthia put the phone back in its cradle. "Right. And you've told him that?" she asked.

"No."

"Why not?"

"Because I'm stupid! I don't know. Because I don't see how it's possible, given we've only dated ten weeks. And because he's young and I don't want to lock him into a serious relationship. But if I lose him . . ." She shook her head. "No wonder I'm losing my mind."

"No," said Cynthia, "you aren't. I just want to make sure you don't. No getting engaged to Darren."

"Because no sane person would?"

"You aren't even *dating* him. You're with Gabe."

"Okay, I get that you prefer Gabe."

"Of course I do! He's *amazing*."

"Having you say that about my boyfriend is kind of weird."

Cynthia nodded, paused, then said, "I'd never try to steal a guy from you, Alice, because I care about you. But yeah, I'm a little jealous. Any woman would be."

Alice looked at her roommate appraisingly. *That was honest,* she thought. "You think he'll call?"

"Or come over. Give it an hour or two. Meanwhile, I'm feeding you lunch."

* * *

Alice spent the next four hours sitting on the floor of her room. She'd tried to pray, but her thoughts were too tangled and random. She tried calling Gabe's phone twice. The first time it went straight to voice mail. The second time it rang several times then went to voice mail. *He's screening me,* she thought. In the end, she stared off into space, tried not to think about Darren, and tried not to despair.

At a quarter to five, there was a knock on the front door.

Alice got up, wiped her eyes, and went out to answer it. It was Gabe. He had his motorcycle jacket slung over his shoulder, and his eyes looked slightly red. "Hi," he said. He didn't look her in the eye.

"Hi." Relief flooded through her.

"Can we talk?" he asked. "There're some things I need to say."

"Of course." She stepped back and let him in.

Gabe went over to the couch and sat down, draping his jacket over the couch arm. Alice sat next to him. She could see that he was upset, so she kept a respectful distance, even though she wanted more than anything to put her arms around him, to have him hold her and tell her everything was okay between them, that he still loved her.

He didn't look at her as he started to speak. "Alice," he said, "I understand if you want to marry Darren."

"What?" Alice's eyes widened.

"He called me a few hours ago and told me what happened and how he prayed all night before coming down here."

"Gabe—"

He put up his hand. "This is hard enough, okay? Just let me finish."

"Are you breaking things off?"

He stared off into space, then changed the subject. "Look, about my mom. Turns out she just got a promotion and a raise. I saw all of her accounts this afternoon—her *real* accounts—and I still can't believe it.

You really did . . . I mean . . . you . . ." He sighed in frustration and shook his head. "Our financial problems are *gone*. I didn't think that was possible, and I can't ever repay you for that."

Alice shook her head and opened her mouth to tell him he didn't owe her anything.

He talked over her again. "Mom acted like the last ten years didn't matter, just like you said she would. She gave me this big hug and told me how happy she was to see me, and we had a really good conversation. Anyway, back to Darren—"

"Can I talk now?"

"Let me *finish*, all right?"

"Gabe—"

"Please!" He looked over at her. She saw desperation and sadness in his expression.

She bit her lip.

"I assume you didn't say no to Darren," Gabe continued, "because you're thinking it over, like he said. And I assume you didn't say yes, because things aren't settled between us."

"And you're going to settle them?"

"Yeah."

"But—"

He looked her in the eye. "He's a good man, Alice, a really good man. Your relationship with him was what brought you into the Church in the first place. I know he wasn't always the ideal boyfriend. I know way more about that than either of you wanted me to know." He looked at the wall for a moment. "But he does deserve a second chance. When I was talking to him this morning, I could just see it. It was like he was full of light. I knew he'd become a better person and that he still loves you.

"Meanwhile, you and I have only been together two months. And it's been amazing but . . . He showed me the diamond this morning. I don't have anything like that to offer you."

"Gabe . . ." Alice didn't know how to finish that thought. *So I really am supposed to marry Darren? What is this, Lord, some kind of sick joke?* She shut her eyes.

Gabe sighed and got up. Alice began to get up too, but he put his hand on her shoulder and gave her a look that told her to stay put. "I'm not finished," he said.

She sat back down, tears stinging her eyes.

He got down on one knee.

Alice's heart skipped a beat. She watched numbly as he pulled a worn ring box out of his jacket pocket and opened it. Inside was a plain gold band. "This was my mother's," he explained. "She gave it to me after I told her what happened today. She had to sell her diamond ten years ago, you know, so this is all we've got."

Alice's throat was so tight she couldn't respond. She blinked, and a tear slid down her cheek.

"I love you," he said. "And I think you're amazing. And do you know what I've wanted more than anything since the moment I fell in love with you? Do you even know when that was?"

Alice shook her head.

"December fourth of last year."

Whatever Alice had been expecting, it wasn't *that*. She gave him an odd look, and he chuckled. His cheeks flushed a little.

"The day after you broke up with Darren. Remember? You came walking into church all confident, and you stared him down."

She opened her mouth to contradict him. She hadn't "stared him down," but Gabe kept on talking.

"I'd already thought you were gorgeous," he said, "but when I saw *that,* I wanted to be with you more than anything. I mean, I know that was kind of a dumb thing to want.

"But I watched you every Sunday. You kept coming, and you sat by yourself for months, and I . . . I wanted to sit next to you, but I couldn't bring myself to do it. So I just stared at you and prayed about you.

"And then, that time you came with us to do baptisms? I was so in awe of you."

In awe? She hadn't done anything awe-inspiring that she could think of.

"You were reading the scriptures, and I could tell you were really thinking about things. Spencer came over to hit on you, and you ignored him. When I saw you on a date with him, I was so jealous, I didn't know what to do. I couldn't stop wishing that you were with me instead—I couldn't. Believe me, I tried.

"And then when you went to receive your endowment and Spencer ditched you? You went through alone. I can't even imagine doing that. I had four cousins and five classmates with me when I did mine, and I was still scared to death. You just seemed so calm."

She tried to catch his eye, but he was looking off into space. "Gabe—" she whispered.

"I never expected you to go out with me, you know? When you called me back and asked me out—I was in shock, seriously. But you let me keep coming over. You called me your boyfriend . . . and that one night we had our first kiss . . ." He sighed shakily and looked up at her. "I *love* you, Alice. That was one of the most amazing nights of my *life*. I've loved you since before I even really knew you, and now that I do know you . . . I don't know what I'll do without you." He shut his eyes and seemed to collect himself.

"I mean—I'll be all right," he continued. "I just . . . Since the moment I fell in love with you, I've wanted to be with you, just to have even *one* date with you. I didn't think that prayer would actually get answered, but it has." He looked down at the ring and held it out to her. "And I know I'm not the guy you want to marry, but . . . I do want to marry you. I would have proposed on the first date if I thought I had a chance. I don't *want* to stop loving you, ever. I'd do anything to be with you for eternity." He held her gaze for a moment longer, then looked away. "And I . . . I just wanted you to know that."

Alice looked down at the gold band he held. *Ten weeks, Alice*, she reminded herself. *You've only been with this guy ten weeks.*

"I . . ." she began. Her throat was still tight, so it came out as a whisper. She cleared it and tried again. "I do love you, you know."

He froze, then looked up. "You do?"

She nodded. "And I'm sorry I never told you before. I've been pretty stupid about all that, but . . . my answer's yes. Of course I want to marry you."

He blinked and stared.

Alice broke down. "I am so sorry," she said. "Here you've been so devoted and done so much for me, and I've been pushing you away. I am *so* lucky you had the courage to come here today and say all of this. *You're* amazing. And Gabe, I don't want to stop loving you either."

"You're . . . you're serious?"

"Would I *joke* about this?"

"I . . . sorry, I'm just having a hard time believing it." He got up and sat next to her, slipping his arms around her waist.

She leaned against him and hugged him back. "I love you," she repeated.

"Love you too."

She looked up. He was grinning a broad, half-disbelieving grin, and she found herself laughing and grinning right back. The gnawing stress that had plagued her for the last ten weeks began to ease. Things were going to be all right after all. She stroked his chest with her fingers.

Gabe let her go, took the ring out of its box, and held it out to her. She smiled and held out her left hand. He slipped the ring on her finger, then leaned forward and kissed her.

When he pulled away, she said, "So . . . when you told your mom about us, what did she say?"

"That she already knew. Gina was telling her all along, little brat. I *told* her to keep it to herself."

"Oh . . ."

"You're still coming to dinner, right? Mom said that if you said yes, I could come too."

"What? I mean, yes, I'm going, but—"

"We know which one of us she likes best, huh?" He laughed.

Alice just grinned.

"When I told her I wanted to propose, she went and got the ring and begged me to go through with it. She even started planning the reception. Seriously."

"Wait a minute!" shouted Cynthia.

Alice jumped and twisted around in her seat. Her roommate was standing at the end of the hallway, hands on her hips. "*I* get to do the reception," she declared.

"How long have you been listening?" Alice asked her.

"Pretty much the whole time. But I do get to do the reception, right? Come *on*."

"Maybe."

"Alice!"

"Give me my journal back."

"You're sitting on it. It's under the couch cushion."

"Your journal?" said Gabe.

Alice nodded. "I think I should show you something." *And then,* she thought, *I think I owe Someone a long prayer of gratitude.*

Epilogue

You are such a Molly, Alice thought to herself as she adjusted her veil in the brides' room of the temple. *You just got married to a guy you've been with for five months. Before you know it, you'll be driving a minivan and baking casseroles.*

She looked at her reflection. *You're going to have to stop grinning at some point, you know. You've been at it for days. Your face is hurting; give it a rest!*

The temple workers had been surprised when she'd asked to be by herself in the brides' room. She guessed most brides had attendants. She swapped her soft slippers for satin pumps, took one more look in the mirror, and headed out.

Gabe was in the waiting area talking to Ely, Monica, and Sean. Ely saw her first and nudged his roommate—former roommate.

Gabe came over and took both her hands in his. "So, how are you, Sister Spinelli?"

Alice squeezed his hands, then let go so that she could give him a hug.

"There is a huge crowd waiting outside," Monica told her.

"What, for us?" said Alice.

"Yes, silly. I think most of your ward showed up."

Alice turned to Gabe, who shrugged. "Sarah said something about us being the center of all the ward gossip," he said.

"Which I'm sure had nothing to do with her spreading it."

Gabe shrugged again and laughed.

* * *

Alice's mother, Lorraine, and Gina stood at the front of the crowd. When Alice and Gabe stepped out of the temple and into the late afternoon sun, everyone burst into applause. Everyone, that is, who didn't have a camera. More than two dozen were being aimed at them from every direction. Alice tolerated it as best she could, but she was grateful when the flashbulbs stopped popping and she could hug her mother and Lorraine.

"Hey, what about me?" said Gabe to his mother when she hugged Alice a second time.

Lorraine laughed and reached up to pat him on the cheek. "Such a good boy," she said, "bringing Alice into the family."

Alice's mother chuckled. "Have I told you how much I like this woman?"

Gabe rolled his eyes. "I can't exactly argue, can I? Wait, Mom, come back here." He gave Lorraine a hug.

"Where's Cynthia?" Alice asked.

"Over at the church," said Gina, "making sure everything's *perfect.*"

Around them, the crowd began to disperse as people began walking toward the meetinghouse for the reception. Through the dissipating throng, Alice saw her father's black sports car pull up.

Her mother noticed it too and gave Alice an uneasy look. Alice gave her another hug, said, "Love you, Mom," then marched on ahead as best she could in heels to meet her father. Gabe and the rest of the party followed behind at a more leisurely pace.

Alice's father was alone. He got out of the driver's side and flashed her a smile. Alice picked up her pace still more. "You came!" she said.

"Of course I did. But it looks like I'm late."

Alice shook her head. "We're doing the ring ceremony over in the church. You're right on time."

Her father looked over her shoulder and seemed ill at ease. Alice turned around and saw that Gabe was just a few paces away. Gabe was pleasant enough, though. He came over, smiled, and held out his hand. "Glad you could come."

Her father nodded in return and shook his hand. Alice's mother, Lorraine, and Gina brought up the tail end of the party. Her mother refused to even look at her father, but the others all said hello and kept walking toward the meetinghouse. Lorraine put her arm around

Alice's mother and laughed at something she said. Gabe went over and threw his arm around his sister, then leaned against her, pushing her off course until she laughed and pushed back.

"Hey," he said, as they zigzagged along, "no picking on me. It's my wedding day. You have to be nice."

"Then stop picking on *me*."

Alice and her father remained behind. "So, how have you been?" she asked.

"Do you really want to know?"

"Will it make my life more complicated?"

He shrugged.

"Look, Dad—"

He held up his hand. "Let's save the awkward conversations for another time, all right?"

"I've missed you."

"Likewise, kiddo. But you've done all right for yourself." He nodded in the direction of Gabe's retreating figure.

"Very diplomatic."

"When have you ever known me to be diplomatic?"

Alice laughed. "Well, I dunno, we haven't talked in a while."

"You sure you want me to come—"

"Yeah."

He looked at her a moment longer, then held out his arm to her.

Alice took it, and together they walked across the parking lot toward the church.

About the Author

Photo by Mary J. Mann

E. M. Tippetts lives in New Mexico, which is where she grew up. A former attorney, she did her undergraduate degree in philosophy, politics, and economics at Oxford University and her law degree at UCLA. She practiced real estate law and estate planning, with a specialty in literary estate planning, but she has always wanted to be a writer and used to get up at 5 A.M. to write before going to work. She joined the Church as an adult shortly before meeting her husband, Trevor.